T0153905

BLACK
WIDOWER

Patricia Moyes

FELONY & MAYHEM PRESS • NEW YORK

All the characters and events portrayed in this work are fictitious.

BLACK WIDOWER

A Felony & Mayhem mystery

PRINTING HISTORY

First UK edition (Collins): 1975
First US edition (Holt, Rinehart & Winston): 1975
Felony & Mayhem edition: 2018

ISBN: 978-1-63194-155-9

Manufactured in the United States of America

Library of Congress Cataloging-in-Publication Data

Names: Moyes, Patricia, author.
Title: Black widower / Patricia Moyes.
Description: Felony & Mayhem edition. | New York : Felony & Mayhem
Press, 2018.
Identifiers: LCCN 2018033129| ISBN 9781631941559 (trade pbk.) | ISBN
9781631941771 (ebook)
Subjects: LCSH: Domestic fiction.
Classification: LCC PR6063.O9 B5 2018 | DDC 823/.914--dc23
LC record available at https://lccn.loc.gov/2018033129

BLACK WIDOWER

This book is for Tony and Betty and Horatio,
who look after our special island for us.

AUTHOR'S NOTE

Any book set in such a real-life location as Washington, D.C., is bound to be, to a certain extent, a mixture of fact and fiction: consequently, I would like to make it clear which is which.

All the characters in this book—American, British, and Tampican—are purely fictitious, and bear no resemblance whatsoever to any real persons, living or dead. I stress this in particular in the case of the diplomats, politicians, doctors, policemen, and other public figures portrayed.

There are no such streets in Georgetown as Oxford Gardens and Exeter Place, and Maycroft House is imaginary—but anybody who knows the area will recognize all three as being typical. Chevy Chase is real, but if it has an Episcopal Ladies' Club, I have not been able to trace it. The Georgetown Garden Tour, however, is a delightful reality, and my good friends at 3320 Dent Place (whose garden has indeed been featured on the tour) have kindly given me permission to use their address.

The islands of Tampica and St. Mark's are entirely fictional, and so is Pirate's Cave Hotel—although it does more or less resemble several superb Caribbean resort establishments which I know. On the other hand, Antigua, St. Thomas, and St. John's are all real places.

A word of caution. Please don't try to book yourself on a direct flight between Dulles International Airport and Antigua, as described in the book. You have to change at Puerto Rico.

Finally, my most sincere thanks to Dr. Pierre Dorolle and his colleagues at the World Health Organization in Geneva, who once again spared their precious time to set me right on medical details.

P.M.

The icon above says you're holding a copy of a book in the Felony & Mayhem "Vintage" category. These books were originally published prior to about 1965, and feature the kind of twisty, ingenious puzzles beloved by fans of Agatha Christie and John Dickson Carr. If you enjoy this book, you may well like other "Vintage" titles from Felony & Mayhem Press.

———◆◆◆———

BLACK WIDOWER

CHAPTER ONE

THE INVITATION CARDS were very impressive.
Under a complicated gold-embossed coat of arms, the die-
stamped legend, in flowing italic type face, read:

His Excellency the Tampican Ambassador
and Lady Ironmonger
request the pleasure of your company
at a Reception

on Thursday, April 14th

Cocktails 6-8 p.m.   *The Embassy of Tampica*
R.S.V.P.   *3119 Oxford Gardens, N.W.*
                                      Washington, D.C. 20007

The impression of quiet dignity was only marred by the fact
that the words "To say Hullo!" had been written across the top
of the card, in a childishly looped hand, by a purple ball-point

pen. This addition had been Mavis Ironmonger's own idea, and Michael Holder-Watts, Counsellor to the Embassy, was currently remonstrating with her about it.

"You're just an old stuffy-pants, Mike," protested Lady Ironmonger. "I think it's nice. A sort of homey touch." She leant back in her armchair and gave him a long, slow look from her violet eyes.

"My dear Mavis," said Michael, "for heaven's sake get it into your thick head that Eddie isn't just a bright, young Tampican lawyer any more. He's an ambassador, and you're his lady wife—and you'd better start behaving like it."

"But Mike," Mavis pointed out, "when Tim and Elvira Beckett gave their farewell party in Tampica, Tim himself wrote 'To say good-bye' on all the cards. And he was a governor-general, which is much higher up than an ambassador."

"That was quite different. The Becketts had been in Tampica for years, and they were inviting personal friends."

"Very, very good friends," agreed Mavis Ironmonger, in a soft, husky voice.

"To some of whom," Michael added tartly, "Elvira for one was undoubtedly delighted to say good-bye."

"Oh, Mike, don't tell me you're *jealous*." The violet eyes opened wide. "There never was anything between me and Tim. Well, only the tiniest little twinkle."

"Your tiny little twinkles have led to plenty of trouble in the past. I just hope you'll start behaving yourself now."

"Oh, *Mike. How* can you say that? You know you don't mean it."

"Mavis, once and for all…"

"Of course I'll behave myself in public. But in private, Mike darling…"

Half an hour later, retying his Old School Tie in front of an ornate gilt-framed mirror, Michael Holder-Watts said, "Well, if you absolutely insist, for God's sake spell 'Hello' with an *e*, not a *u*."

"Why?"

"Because that's the way the word is pronounced."

"I always say 'Hullo.'"

"I stand corrected. It's the way the word *should* be pronounced, by anybody who speaks the Queen's English."

"Oh, Mike, you are *beastly* to me..."

The next day, the invitation cards—purple ink and all—began dropping through the letter-boxes of Washington, and ended up on the desks or breakfast tables of diplomats, statesmen, politicians, social celebrities and other notables. They produced a mixed bag of reactions.

"Tampica?" remarked an antipodean ambassador to his secretary. "Where the hell is Tampica?"

"It's that Caribbean island that became independent a few weeks ago, sir. You know how they always rush to open up an embassy here. Shall I accept for you and Mrs. Braithwaite?"

"In the Commonwealth, are they?"

"Oh, yes, sir."

"Oh, very well. Needn't stay more than a few minutes. Got to show the flag."

"Tampica?" said a prominent New England senator to his wife. "You really ought to know, my dear. She's a very new country, but already she's making a brave stand against the United States government that will certainly embarrass the White House. A question of the U.S. naval base. Certainly we'll go."

"Well, well, well," said Prudence Barrington, adjusting her reading glasses and holding the invitation at arm's length.

"Just fancy that. Eddie Ironmonger. Why, I remember him at Sunday School. Such an attractive child, with those bright eyes and white teeth lighting up his chubby, little black face. And now to think he's His Excellency the Ambassador! What a surprise!"

"The surprising thing," replied her husband, "is that he's only an ambassador, and not prime minister. It's a disgrace." The Right Reverend Matthew Barrington, Anglican Bishop Emeritus of Tampica, cleared his throat angrily and took a gulp of coffee.

"Whatever do you mean, Matthew? Surely it's a great honor for any man to be his country's ambassador to the United States?"

"For most men, yes, I agree. But Eddie Ironmonger is by head and shoulders the most outstanding figure Tampica has produced—and she needs her best men now, at this moment in history. Goodness me, I've followed Eddie's career all the way from that waterfront slum, through schools and scholarships—First Class Honors at Oxford—Gray's Inn—absolutely brilliant. Alpha plus."

"Then why...?" Prudence Barrington's kindly, rather vague face looked troubled. "Oh, you mean because of Mavis? Well, just because she's an English girl—"

"English hussy," corrected Matthew, always a stickler for the *mot juste*. "Miss Luscious Lollipop of nineteen-sixty-two. And that's the whole trouble. Now, don't misunderstand me—" The Bishop held up an admonitory hand, although his wife had shown no sign of wishing to interrupt. "I would never reproach anybody for humble origins, and I am aware that many charming and...em...virtuous girls may enter beauty contests, and even occasionally win them. But I fear that Mavis Watkins was not one of them. Her behavior at the time, and ever since...well, as you know, everybody tried to warn Eddie, but he was young and impressionable and in a strange country..."

"But we'll go to the reception, won't we, Matthew?"

"We will. Indeed we will. Poor Eddie. He will need all the friends he can muster..." Matthew Barrington sighed deeply, and began buttering a third slice of toast.

"Normally," confided Mrs. Otis P. Schipmaker II to her friend and neighbor Mrs. Margaret Colville, "Otis and I never go to parties at these jumped-up little embassies—but this is a *must.*"

"Is it? Why?"

"Because of *her*, of course. *Everybody's* talking about her. I wouldn't miss it for the world. Otis didn't want to accept, but I just insisted. Will you and John be there?"

Margaret smiled. "Not invited," she said. "Not important enough. Anyway, John will be in New York then, for the conference."

"Oh, honey, what a shame. You *should* be there—*she's* English, you know. Oh, well, we'll meet again for coffee and I'll tell you *all about it.*"

"...not really an embassy at all," said Magnolia Belmont to her husband. "Just a house in Georgetown...embassy and residence all rolled into one. Why, the whole itty-bitty island of Tampica isn't any bigger than my sister Melinda's estate in Texas. Me, I just do love these quaint, simple, primitive folks, but I reckon we'll pass this one up, honey? Anyways, don't we go to Florida that week?"

Senator George Belmont studied the invitation card. Then he said, "No, baby. This one we accept."

"But George—"

"I know how y'all feel, honey, but we have to make sacrifices. This is a question of the U.S. naval base."

"I don't care about your silly old naval base. Little me wants to go to Florida." Magnolia was pouting in true southern style.

Her husband was conciliatory. "I'm sorry, sweetheart. It's not just as simple as the naval base, see? These darned nigg— black people—are getting too damn cocky, and you know how soft the White House is...somebody's got to stand up and be counted...somebody's got to represent the silent majority, and anyhow I'm on that committee..."

Magnolia smiled at her husband. A proud smile. "I'm sorry, honey. I didn't realize it was like that. Certainly we'll go."

❀ ❀ ❀

"...Uncle Tom of the worst sort!" declaimed Franklin D. Martin to an enrapt audience in a rickety church hall in North East Washington. "Traitor to his own people! Sir Edward Ironmonger..." He swept a mock bow. "Accepting phony titles from Whitey! Well, man, he shouldn't have been dumb enough to come to Washington, D.C. Shall we show him, or shall we show him?"

"Right on!" chanted his listeners.

"Outside the embassy, April fourteen, six-fifteen! Who'll be there?"

"We'll be there!" screamed the audience.

"Who'll carry banners?"

A handful of people jumped up, waving their arms. "Right on!" shouted the rest.

Franklin D. Martin became business-like. "Banner-carriers give their names to the committee before leaving the hall," he said. "The committee is me. The rest of you, assemble April fourteen six o'clock outside the Georgetown Pig Station in Volta Place, for a protest march on the Tampican Embassy."

"You gonna get Pig permission?" called an unbelieving voice from the hall.

"Man, you'll see what we gonna get," replied Franklin D., ominously.

One way or the other, the invitations caused quite a stir.

Thirty-one-nineteen Oxford Gardens was not a large house by Georgetown standards, but it was a very pretty one. For those who know Georgetown only as a vaguely remembered name from American political novels, a little history is perhaps in order.

Long before Washington, D.C., was established as the capital of the uneasily-united states of America, tobacco merchants from Virginia had been bringing their precious cargoes of dried leaves up the Potomac River to the port of Georgetown, there to be transferred to larger vessels for shipment all over the world. High above the port, the Rock of Dumbarton rose, a wedge-shaped height towering between the Potomac River on the south, and the stream known as Rock Creek on the east.

Soon, the rich merchants began to build great, beautiful houses for themselves on Dumbarton Rock—pleasantly cool in the hot, humid summer weather; close to the nerve-center of the port; isolated in shady green gardens. In the year 1750, Georgetown was established as a city and its boundaries marked by engraved stones; it remained a favorite residential area, even when the silting-up of the Potomac drastically curtailed the tobacco trade in the port at the foot of the hill. Consequently, it came as no great surprise when George Washington, who knew and loved Georgetown, decided to found his national capital city on the far side of Rock Creek in 1791. It was a pleasant site, on the river, strategically poised between North and South. Nevertheless, Georgetowners tend to remember that their city preceded the nation's capital by some forty years.

Today, after various changes in fortune, Georgetown is again a quiet, pleasant residential area. Some of the great mansions still remain, set in acres of show-piece gardens. At the other end of the scale, little wooden frame houses originally constructed as slave-quarters change hands at vastly inflated prices. In between, solidly successful businessmen have continued over the years to build themselves modest but comfortable houses, each with its plot of garden, and these are the most sought-after dwellings in Washington.

The government of Tampica, marshaling the meager resources available to it, had considered the possibility of renting an expensive downtown office suite as an embassy, and purchasing a mediocre suburban house as the ambassador's residence. Fortunately, Edward Ironmonger—who had great good taste and had lived in Chelsea for some years—was able to convince his countrymen that 3119 Oxford Gardens, a red-brick house built at the turn of the nineteenth century in the heart of Georgetown, would serve both purposes and be a better long-term investment.

Consequently the house had been purchased, and now the green and purple flag of Tampica flew proudly outside its yellow front door. Inside, while Sir Edward and Lady Ironmonger were at the White House presenting their credentials, a somewhat grim conference was taking place in the Ambassador's study on the ground floor. The conferees were Counsellor Michael Holder-Watts and First Secretary Winston Horatio Nelson.

The two men could hardly have presented a greater contrast. Holder-Watts, fair and willowy and full of the charm that only an expensive British education can bestow, was one of the few Foreign Service officials who had elected to take Tampican nationality with the self-professed object of guiding her representatives through the first, thorny steps of the diplomatic jungle. His veneer of delightful, Wodehousian vagueness and social polish gave no hint of the incisive judgment and steel-trap ruthlessness under the surface. And at the moment, Michael Holder-Watts was very worried.

Winston Horatio Nelson had been born a few years later than Edward Ironmonger, in the same waterfront slum on Tampica Harbour. According to family legend, his great-great-great-great-grandfather had been a sailor in Nelson's ship, H.M.S. Boreas, which had put into Tampica briefly while on patrol in the West Indies in the 1780s. This accounted for Winston's slightly lighter coloring as compared to Eddie, for example, and also for his name—for the local ladies, unable to differentiate between one British sailor and another, had apparently dubbed them all Horatio Nelson. Ever since, the eldest son of the family had been christened Horatio, and the family's Anglomania had led them to add the name Winston in the case of the baby born during the Second World War.

In spite of all this, Winston Horatio Nelson—known to his friends as Winnie—had grown up to be a fanatical fighter for independence. He had not—as he was the first to admit—the mental ability of his neighbor and hero, Eddie Ironmonger. He had won no scholarships to Oxford nor First Class Honors. However, with the help of his good friends Bishop and Mrs. Barrington, he made full use of the educational facilities which Tampica had to offer, completed his schooling in Antigua, and returned to throw himself with vigor into the life of a civil servant on the up-grade. He also recognized brilliance when he saw it, and thus had attached himself firmly to the coattails of Edward Ironmonger, which was why he now found himself as First Secretary of Tampica's Embassy, sitting in a study in Georgetown and discussing with Michael Holder-Watts how to avert disaster at the Embassy's first official reception. The object of their concern was, of course, Mavis Ironmonger.

"If we can just get through this first evening without a frightful scandal," Michael was saying, "things won't be so bad. All the local ghouls seem to have heard about her reputation, and they're turning up in their hordes, rubbing their hands in anticipation. If only she can behave herself this once—"

"You are optimistic, Michael, as usual," said Winnie. "I foresee very little hope."

"Well, I've done what I can. I've given orders that she's to be served nothing but tomato juice, and she's promised—for what it's worth—just to stand quietly in the receiving line, shaking hands and keeping her mouth shut. Meanwhile, it's up to you and me to keep a sharp eye on her all evening."

"Up until seven o'clock, I shall be pleased to help you."
Winnie's slightly precise English always gave Holder-Watts the
impression that he was speaking an acquired language, rather
than his mother tongue. "However, Bishop Barrington has
kindly invited me to take dinner at his house. I have a rendezvous with him and Mrs. Barrington at seven o'clock, and I will
drive them home. They have no car, I understand."

Michael frowned. "That's a nuisance. Can't you get out of
it?"

"I fear not. I owe a great deal to the Bishop, and it is many
years since we met. I would not care to appear rude."

"Does Eddie know you'll be leaving the reception early?"

"Of course. Naturally, I asked his permission. He is quite
agreeable."

"In that case, I suppose there's nothing I can do about
it." Michael's handsome face clearly showed his displeasure.
Normally, he made a good job of disguising his dislike of, and
contempt for, Winston Horatio Nelson, but this sort of thing
really riled him. These people, he reflected, had no sense of
the proper way things should be done. Nelson's duty obviously
lay in staying at the Embassy throughout the reception—but
no. For some devious reason of his own, he had arranged to
swan off to dinner halfway through the function. Michael
could not imagine offhand what personal favor or advantage
Nelson hoped to gain from the elderly, retired Bishop and
his wife, but he was sure there was something, real or imaginary. And Eddie, of course, condoned such behavior. For all
his brilliance, he was only a Tampican, after all. Otherwise,
how could he ever have made the monumental blunder of
marrying Mavis?

Michael said, "It's all very annoying. I shall have to enlist
Eleanor, and you know how she feels about Mavis."

"With good reason, I believe," Winnie remarked icily.
Michael Holder-Watts affected him in much the same way as
squeaky chalk drawn slowly across a blackboard. The arrogance
of the man! Everybody knew he was sleeping with Mavis, but

far from being ashamed of the fact he appeared to think he could get away with enjoying her favors while at the same time holding her in public contempt. No...Winnie was honest, and he rephrased his thought...he *did* get away with it. All Winnie's sympathy was with Eleanor Holder-Watts.

As a matter of fact, Mavis Ironmonger's amorous adventures were so numerous, so casual and so indiscreet that the wives of most of the men involved merely shrugged their shoulders and laughed, reckoning Lady Ironmonger to be no more than a natural hazard encountered by every personable man who visited Tampica. Eleanor Holder-Watts, however, had reacted more drastically.

She came from an English middle-class family—pillars of respectability with none of the moral elasticity of the aristocracy. The actual fact of Michael's infidelity mattered much less to her than the assault on her dignity. She behaved toward Mavis Ironmonger with icy correctness and was laughed at for her pains, not only by Mavis, but also by Michael, the more sophisticated Europeans in the Caribbean, and even by Eddie Ironmonger himself. Within the present Embassy, Winston Horatio Nelson was the only person who felt true sympathy for her, and—even had she known about it—she would have rejected it as coming from an inferior. Eleanor's life in Washington was not proving easy.

"Oh, well," Michael remarked, "I expect she'll enjoy being appointed as watch-bitch over H.E. It'll reinforce her illusion of moral superiority."

This was too much for Winnie. "I trust you are not implying," he said, "that Mrs. Holder-Watts is *not* morally superior to Lady Ironmonger?"

"I've never really thought about it, old boy," said Michael, infuriatingly. "Anyhow, this is the plan of campaign. At the first sign of trouble, one of us moves in and gently but firmly removes Mavis from the scene of action. Takes her up to her room, and locks her in if necessary. If she's been at the booze and is obviously sloshed, the story is that she is ill and being treated by some sort of rare drug, which renders even the smallest drink lethal—and that she was given a Bloody Mary by mistake. Remember, get her out of the way as quickly and quietly as possible, and then make sure you spin the tale to anyone who was involved. There'll be about three hundred people all told, so with any luck a lot of them won't see—whatever there may be to see." He stood up. "I'm not looking forward to it, but I don't see what more we can do."

CHAPTER TWO

THURSDAY, APRIL FOURTEENTH, turned out to be one of those spring days when Washington really excels herself. For once, the Japanese ornamental cherry trees around the Tidal Basin had burst into a glorious profusion of pink blossom exactly on time, delighting the crowds of sightseers on the Mall. In the cool, sparkling sunshine, the Lincoln and Jefferson Memorials had never looked more elegantly Grecian, the Washington Monument more monumental or the White House whiter. The Stars and Stripes fluttered proudly from Ministries and Departments, and the Capitol fittingly crowned the scene, like a gigantic wedding cake.

Up the hill in Georgetown, the tree-lined, cobbled streets, with their traditional red-brick pavements, were also coming to life. Gardens were waking after the hibernation of the cruel months, and decking themselves with hyacinths, tulips, and daffodils. On Wisconsin Avenue, the great shopping street that bisects the area from north to south, pavement-squatting hippies in outrageously colorful outfits were the unmistakable harbingers of spring.

The trendy boutiques festooned their windows in a riot of way-out fashions, and even the owners of dark little antique shops got busy with feather dusters. The Georgetown Coffee Shop produced a windowful of growing herbs for sale. The French Market did a roaring trade in enormous lunchtime sandwiches, and put up endearing notices in inaccurate English begging their patrons not to eat them in the car park. White-painted garden furniture was hauled out from garages and basements, scrubbed, and set up in a thousand patios. Summertime lanterns and bright umbrellas blossomed in back yards, while in grander gardens porcelain elephants and jaguars took up their summer stations.

It was the time of the year when Margaret Colville always decided that the high cost of living in Georgetown was well worth it. She and her husband had been renting a house there for four years—ever since John had been lured away from the London School of Economics to work at the World Bank. In London, they had lived in Chelsea—so, to them, Georgetown was like coming home. Margaret knew that most of John's colleagues considered that they must be crazy to squander so much money in rent, but she would not have traded their tiny frame house and square of sunny back garden for a modern split-level rambler in any smart suburban development. Especially in the spring.

The latest excitement, of course, had been the setting-up of the Tampican Embassy in Oxford Gardens, just around the corner. Plenty of diplomats had their private homes in the area, but this was the first actual embassy to break away from the Massachusetts Avenue–Kalorama Triangle quarter and move into Georgetown. Naturally, it caused comment, curiosity and speculation.

As Michael Holder-Watts had remarked, gossip runs like a brush fire in a city the size of Washington, more especially in that small section of it which revolves on the diplomatic carousel. Under British rule, Tampica had been a holiday play-ground for wealthy sun-seekers from both sides of the Atlantic, and word had quickly spread about Mavis Ironmonger's reputation. Bishop Matthew Barrington had not been exagger-ating when he declared that—unencumbered by Mavis—Sir Edward would almost certainly have been elected the first prime minister of independent Tampica.

As it was, shortly before independence he had been knighted by a grateful British sovereign for services to the law in Tampica: an elderly and less able colleague had been elected prime minister, and Eddie and Mavis had been sent off to Washington to see whether Lady Ironmonger could pull herself together and learn to behave decently in time for the next Tampican general election—which, rumor had it, would be very soon, if all went well. Sir Samuel Drake-Frobisher was known to have accepted the premiership reluctantly, and was only too eager to retire and hand over party leadership to Edward Ironmonger.

Most of this information, spiced with racy episodes from Mavis Ironmonger's past, had filtered through even to the Colvilles, and although Margaret was no gossip, she had her natural share of human curiosity and looked forward to catching a glimpse of the notorious lady. However, apart from the comings and goings of a few dark-skinned girls whom she took to be secretaries and domestic staff, Margaret had been unlucky.

One day, it is true, on her way back from the supermarket with her arms full of groceries, she had caught sight of a chauffeur-driven limousine moving away from the Embassy. In the back, elegant and relaxed in a coat of dark, supple sables, sat a blonde woman of such astonishing beauty and obvious breeding that she quite took Margaret's breath away. Cool as an ice princess, not a hair out of place, her long fingers pale against the pigskin upholstery of the car, a single string of perfectly matched pearls at her throat, she epitomized aristo-cratic, understated excellence. It never even crossed Margaret's mind that this could be the sluttish Mavis Ironmonger. She remembered that the Counsellor at the Embassy was an ex-British Foreign Service diplomat named Holder-Watts and jumped to the conclusion that the fair-haired beauty must be his wife, Eleanor. But Margaret was wrong. It was Mavis.

Tout Washington tends to arrive late at diplomatic cocktail parties, and to leave early. However, the Tampican reception had attracted such an unusual response that cars were piling up in Oxford Gardens well before six o'clock, keeping the local police busy and causing late-comers without chauffeurs to park several blocks away. In fact, many of the guests had already arrived by the time that Franklin D. Martin led his colorful, chanting parade of protesters from Volta Place across Wisconsin Avenue and into Oxford Gardens. There were the usual banners demanding "Kill the Pigs" and "Legalize Pot," but also a selection more appropriate to the occasion, reading "Uncle Eddie Go Home," "Death to the White Bitch," and even—rather obscurely—"Tampica for the Tampicans."

It was all very friendly and good-humored. The police kept a path free so that invited guests could reach the Embassy door. The demonstrators chanted a few slogans, waved their banners, and then began to sit down in rows on the pavement, smoking and chewing. Most of the guests were perfectly accustomed to making their way into the White House through ranks of political demonstrators, and would have felt the occasion to be slightly lacking in style if none had been there. As with wire-tapping and bugging, the inconvenience of stepping over demonstrators is outweighed by the fact that their presence proves one to be *somebody*, doing something worthy of other people's anger or curiosity. As Michael Holder-Watts remarked to his wife, the demonstration was just what was needed to make the evening go with a swing. Eleanor was not amused.

Inside the Embassy, everything was going suspiciously well. Lady Ironmonger, taken by surprise by the early arrival of so many guests, had been a few minutes late taking her place in the receiving line, but now the wheels of diplomatic hospitality were turning smoothly.

Sir Edward, handsome and beautifully tailored, was greeting his guests with exactly the right blend of dignity and affability, finding an appropriate remark to accompany each handshake, and keeping the line moving while appearing to have plenty of time for a personal word with each visitor. At his side, Mavis had never looked more chillingly beautiful. She wore a simple dress of very dark green wild silk with diamonds at her throat, and her ash-pale hair was drawn back into a chignon which accentuated the Garbo-like perfection of her features. To each guest, she proffered a tapering, lily-white hand, and most of the time—under Michael's watchful eye—she kept her mouth shut. Even her occasional murmured remarks—"Pleased to meet you I'm sure" and "Ever so nice to have you"—had the beguiling innocence of Eliza Doolittle's New Small Talk.

Every so often, while her husband chatted with a new arrival, she would refresh herself from a small glass of tomato juice. Michael noticed with satisfaction that several of Washington's most avid sensation-mongers were beginning to look decidedly glum. *The Washington Post*'s photographer caught her at a most opportune moment, shaking hands regally with the wife of the French Ambassador. Yes, it was all going beautifully.

By half-past six, all the guests had arrived and most of the demonstrators had gone home. The few who remained, including Franklin D. Martin himself, were lounging on the sidewalk, banners at the droop, chatting idly among themselves. Sir Edward and Lady Ironmonger had shaken some three hundred hands, and were now free to circulate among their guests. Eddie, with unerring instinct, made his way toward the New England senator whom he knew shared the Tampican government's view on the matter of the naval base. He intended to spend a minimum of time cementing this ally's support, before addressing himself to charming the opposition in the form of George and Magnolia Belmont.

Michael Holder-Watts, keeping a strict but unobtrusive eye on Mavis, saw that she was conducting an apparently decorous conversation with the Otis Schipmakers. A few minutes later, he saw that Winston Nelson had joined the group and was obviously detaching Mavis from the wealthy young couple (Otis Schipmaker's father had founded the Schipmaker chain of supermarkets). Michael suppressed a ripple of annoyance. He appreciated Nelson's motive, but how like the man to be so ham-fisted! Here was the first grain of fuel for gossip. He could just hear Virginia Schipmaker: "My dear, little men from the Embassy positively *surrounding* her, not allowing her to speak to *anyone…*"

However, to Michael's relief, Winston—apparently reassured—moved away from Mavis and smoothly took over the New England senator, leaving Eddie free to concentrate on the Belmonts. Michael mentally nodded his approval. Winnie could be quite intelligent at times.

Meanwhile, he saw the Schipmakers move to the other side of the room to talk to the Dutch Ambassador, while Mavis got into conversation with Prudence and Matthew Barrington. This was not so good. Michael knew the Bishop's opinion of Lady Ironmonger, and Prudence was well known for her innocent lack of tact. Unobtrusively, he moved over to where his wife, Eleanor, was gallantly trying to find common conversational ground with a Nigerian lady in superbly flamboyant national costume.

Turning on a little burst of charm, like a jet from a warm tap, Michael inserted himself into the conversation between the two women, and then said to his wife, "Have you had a word with Matthew and Prudence Barrington yet, darling?"

Eleanor followed his glance and took his meaning. "Oh, how nice, I didn't realize they were here. I must go and talk to them."

"Why don't you show them the garden?" Michael suggested. "I know they have to leave early, and Prudence has always been interested in flowers."

Eleanor smiled at her husband, proud and happy to be performing a really useful function, and went off to detach Mavis from the Barringtons.

Michael said, "That was a delightful party you gave last week, Mrs. Ngomo. I had never tasted Nigerian food before…" Out of the corner of his eye, he saw Eleanor steering the Bishop and his wife toward the hallway which led to the gardens. Another possible danger-point successfully navigated. "I hear your son is doing famously at Harvard. Wish I could say as much for my boy. Takes after me, I'm afraid." In fact, Jonathan Holder-Watts was currently covering himself with academic honors at Cambridge University, but England was a long way away, and Mrs. Ngomo was not to know. Jonathan, as shrewd as his father and destined for the Foreign Service, would certainly not have objected to being thus thrown to the wolves in the cause of diplomacy.

Mrs. Ngomo, undoubtedly pleased and flattered, made a gracious remark and turned away to greet a friend. Michael continued his peregrinations, always finding the right word, remembering family details, raising pleased smiles. Some minutes later, he became aware of Winston Horatio Nelson at his elbow. Winnie said, quietly, "All going well, I think, Michael?"

"So far, so good."

"I shall have to leave you soon. I am meeting the Barringtons at seven in the small library."

"Are you?" Michael consulted his watch. "That's a moot point. It's two minutes to seven now. Eleanor is currently showing the Barringtons around the garden, and the sooner they are out of here, the happier I shall be."

"Then I will go." Winnie flashed a brilliant smile, which failed to conceal his dislike, and disappeared through the door leading to the hallway, leaving the conversational buzz of the reception behind him.

The small library was empty when Winnie Nelson got there. It was a pretty, well-proportioned room at the front of the house, furnished with English eighteenth-century pieces, most of which Edward Ironmonger had picked up on his last visit to the U.K. The glass-fronted bookcase contained Eddie's own precious library of leatherbound English classics, and the rose-strewn carpet was handworked in *grand point*.

Winnie looked around him, and gave an angry little sigh. He knew that it was Eddie's favorite room, and he could not help feeling that it was a betrayal of Tampica. Eddie knew how Winnie felt—he would laugh, his wonderfully warm laugh, and slap Winnie on the back and tell him that if he'd been up to Oxford, he'd understand. The fact remained that Winnie had not, and did not.

However, he did not have long to indulge in the luxury of irritation, before the door opened and Prudence Barrington peeped in, tentatively at first, then with a big happy smile.

"Ah, so this *is* the right place. Hello, Winnie dear, you're looking very well. Come on in, Matthew, Winnie's here. So very sorry we're late, dear...we were looking at the garden, and there are some very interesting specimens...I'm afraid we lingered far too long..."

Winnie smiled back. Prudence might be a little ridiculous, but it was impossible to dislike her. Besides, he had known her all his life.

"But you are not late, Mrs. Barrington...see..." Winnie gestured toward the austerely elegant black marble clock on the mantelpiece, which had just begun to strike seven in a thin, severe chime.

"How very nice to see you, Winston. Are you enjoying Washington? Eddie seems to be settling in well, and even his wife appears to be...that is, one must not be uncharitable, of course..." The Bishop's voice trailed away unhappily.

Prudence said briskly, "She is a very beautiful girl. She and Eddie should do well here."

"I feel sure," said Winnie, in his careful English, "that Lady Ironmonger is most sensible to the responsibilities of her new position."

"Exactly," murmured Matthew. "Just what I meant..."

"And now, perhaps, we should be on our way," Winnie added. "We must not keep your excellent dinner waiting. My car is outside. If you are ready...?"

"Oh," said Prudence. "My coat..."

"It will be in the cloakroom, Mrs. Barrington...just across the hall...after you, sir."

The black policeman on duty outside the Embassy recognized Winnie, and gave him a smile and a friendly salute as he came out with the Barringtons. One or two of the protesters shouted ruderies about "Uncle Toms" and "Pigs" as Nelson and his white friends picked their way through the supine bodies on the pavement, but any small amount of steam which had ever propelled the demonstration had run out. A minute later, Winnie was behind the wheel of his gleaming silver Chevrolet, heading northward for Chevy Chase and trying to make some sense of Matthew's extremely confused directions as to the best route.

In the reception room at the Embassy, Michael Holder-Watts watched with impatient irritation as Winnie Nelson disappeared in the direction of the small library. Then he continued his progress among the guests. He was apparently relaxed and certainly charming, giving each visitor no more than half-a-minute of his time, and yet leaving each feeling subtly flattered and self-important. Within a few minutes, he had located and spoken with the most important of the visitors, and he allowed himself to glance in the direction of Lady Ironmonger.

All seemed to be well. Mavis was standing very straight, ice-cold and elegant as a snow princess, keeping her mouth shut. A Third Secretary bustled up with a swarthy, handsome gentleman in tow. Michael heard an indistinct murmur. "Lady Ironmonger...don't think you have met...Attaché... Israeli Embassy...may I present Mr. Finkelstein?"

Mavis, swaying just slightly, turned to the newcomer. She extended a drooping, lily-like hand, and at the same moment burst into song. To the tune of *The More We Are Together*, Her Excellency the Tampican Ambassadress bawled, at the top of her voice—

"Balls to Mr. Finkelstein, Finkelstein, Finkelstein
Balls to Mr. Finkelstein, silly old—"

"Oh, Christ," said Michael Holder-Watts.

One stride brought him to Lady Ironmonger's side. She gave him a ravishing smile, hiccoughed, and launched into the verse.

"Fuck Mr. Finkelstein—"

Michael somehow got her into a sort of judo-hold, pinning her arms behind her back, and twisted her body so that the unseemly words of the song disappeared into the lapel of his impeccably cut suit. He looked round desperately for help. Winnie, blast his eyes, must be well on the way to Chevy Chase with the Bishop. Eddie, on the far side of the room, was charming Senator Belmont and seemed unaware that anything was wrong—which was just as well. Otis Schipmaker, on the other hand, was standing alone, watching the scene with goggling fascination. The Third Secretary had turned purple and Mr. Finkelstein green, between them giving a tolerable impersonation of the new Tampican flag, and both were temporarily bereft of speech.

It was with the emotion of a drowning sailor who spots a lifeboat that Michael saw his wife come back into the room. She hurried over, and Michael practically threw Mavis into her arms, hissing, "Get her to her room and lock her in!"

Mavis showed signs of resistance, but Eleanor Holder-Watts was tall and wiry and stronger than she looked. She led the Ambassadress away, as Michael enveloped Mr. Finkelstein in a vast diplomatic handshake, which involved placing his other arm around the Israeli's shoulder and maneuvering him into the crowd and away from the scene of the crime.

"Poor Lady Ironmonger…victim of a rare allergy…being treated with one of these fancy new drugs…some idiot of a waiter…smallest amount of alcohol absolutely fatal…afraid she'll have to miss the rest of the reception…so brave… doesn't like it talked about…people don't realize what she goes through…"

The honeyed words poured out. They could not, of course, efface the blatant fact of Mavis Ironmonger's inexcusable behavior, but at least they gave Mr. Finkelstein time to recover, and provided a face-saver. Michael knew Finkelstein and respected him as both brilliant and charming. He also knew that he had suffered under Hitler in Germany, and he wondered how much a man could forgive. Brutality is sometimes easier to endure than ridicule.

Mr. Finkelstein squared his shoulders with a little shudder—a movement which served the double purpose of straightening his jacket and disengaging Michael's arm. He said, very quietly, "I am extremely sorry for Lady Ironmonger. Also for Sir Edward. May I ask you to present my respects and say my farewells? I fear I have another appointment and must leave now."

"My dear fellow…of course…so kind of you to find time to drop in…" Michael watched the strong, sturdy backview disappearing into the crowd of guests. "Dangerous," he thought to himself. "Very dangerous."

Meanwhile, there were other cracks to be papered over. Thanks to Eleanor the incident had been managed swiftly and efficiently, and Michael did not think that more than a handful of people had been aware of it. Of the foreign diplomats who had been in the vicinity, mercifully few spoke English with any real fluency. They might report that Lady Ironmonger had appeared to be intoxicated, and had been quietly removed from the reception, but with any luck they would remain unaware of the enormity of her offense.

As for Mrs. Ngomo, although English was her second language, Michael was reasonably sure that she was too well-brought-up to understand Mavis's obscenities. In any case, she had moved away and was now engaged in an animated discussion of pre-school education in Washington with the wife of the Indian Cultural Attaché. Michael mentally ticked her off as safe, and started looking for Virginia Schipmaker.

He soon spotted her, on the far side of the room, talking to Magnolia Belmont. Gossip had already informed him that Virginia and Magnolia hated each other with the peculiar intensity of two southern belles who had adopted different politics and life-styles—for although the Schipmakers and the Belmonts were both Democrats, they were as far apart politically as the Kennedys and the Wallaces. It was also rumored that Otis Schipmaker had his eye on George Belmont's senatorial seat. Michael felt reasonably sure that the close-knit bitchiness of the present conversation could have prevented either Virginia or Magnolia from noticing anything else that was going on. He breathed a small sigh of relief and moved to where Otis Schipmaker was presenting a square-cut back-view to the room, apparently engrossed in one of Sir Edward's Currier and Ives prints.

Michael laid a hand on Schipmaker's arm, saying quietly, "Nice to see you again, Otis. Let me get you a drink."

Otis Schipmaker turned slowly to face him. He had gone very pale, but his voice was light, almost amused, as he said, "Good grief. Michael Holder-Watts. What on earth are you doing here?"

"I work here. Hadn't you heard?"

"Heard what?"

"My new job. Counsellor to His Excellency Sir Edward Ironmonger, Ambassador of Tampica." Michael gave a little stiff mock bow.

Otis said, "But you're British—"

"No longer. Tampican. We were all given the option, on Independence Day. I thought it might be…amusing."

There was a pause. Then Schipmaker said, "I presume you also act as Counsellor to Lady Ironmonger."

"You presume correctly. Lady Ironmonger has always liked to be surrounded by close friends—as you doubtless remember."

Otis said, "See here, Michael. It was a long time ago—"

"And in another country. And besides...how's Virginia?"

Schipmaker's lips clamped into a hard line. "She's fine. And I hope that Lady Ironmonger is feeling better by now."

Michael looked at him steadily. "So do I. She's not at all well, I'm afraid, and some of the drugs they give her have unfortunate side effects. She has gone to lie down."

"It must make life difficult for Sir Edward," remarked Schipmaker, musingly.

"Life can be made difficult for lots of people, Otis," said Michael, brightly.

"Is that a threat?"

"Certainly not. What an idea. Just a random remark."

Under his breath, and masked by a social smile, Schipmaker said, "You're just the same little shit you always were, aren't you, Holder-Watts?"

Michael smiled broadly. "So delightful to come across old friends. I'll go and see about that drink..."

He moved away among the guests. A smiling word with Mrs. Ngomo...a reassuring pat on the arm for Dorabella Hamilton, the Ambassador's secretary, who looked shaken and in need of a morale boost...a friendly chat with the British Ambassador, who was an old acquaintance...the reception was in gear again, and running smoothly. In fact, it manifested that sure sign of a successful party—reluctance of the guests to go home. Eight o'clock came and went, and still the room was crowded. By quarter-past, however, people were thinning out, and Sir Edward was kept busy shaking hands in farewell. Despite the success of the evening, he looked strained and worried, and, catching Michael's eye, motioned imperceptibly that he required his presence.

Michael was at the Ambassador's side in a moment. Quietly, Eddie said, "Where the hell is Mavis?"—and then, to a parting guest, "Good-bye, Senator. So very glad you could come..."

Equally quietly, Michael said, "Upstairs. Resting. Not well."

"So very nice to have met you, Mrs. Braithwaite..." Sir Edward shook another hand, and added, *sotto voce*, to Michael, "What does that mean?"

"Drunk," said Michael.

"Go and get her and bring her down," muttered Sir Edward. "Must say her good-byes."

Michael glanced at his watch. Twenty-five past eight. He supposed Mavis might have sobered up. "O.K. If you think it's wise."

"Just do as I say... Good-bye, Mrs. Belmont...yes, it is a pretty house, isn't it?"

Michael made his way through the remaining guests and climbed the stairs to the first floor.

CHAPTER THREE

THE BARRINGTONS' HOUSE turned out to be a neat, white-painted rambler in a tree-shaded road just over the district line in Maryland. The half-acre of garden was pleasantly informal but obviously tended with loving care. Apart from the presence of some exotic specimens like tulip trees and magnolias, it might have been on the outskirts of a southern English town instead of in a Washington suburb—as Prudence Barrington remarked as she got out of Nelson's car at the front door.

"I am surprised that you are not homesick for the Old Country," said Winnie. "I find America very interesting, but I cannot imagine myself retiring anywhere except Tampica."

"Well, it's different for us, dear," said Prudence comfortably. She unlocked the front door. "Come on in." She opened a door leading off the hall, stuck her head round it, and said, "We're back, Muriel. Supper in half-an-hour, please." Then she led the way into the drawing-room, which was pleasantly and unfashionably furnished. "Come along in, Winnie, and have a drink. Yes, as I was saying, it's different for us. You remember the twins, don't you? Yes, of course you do. You all used to play together when you were little. Well, they're both married now."

Prudence gestured toward the slightly battered grand piano. On it stood two large, silver-framed wedding photographs. The two brides appeared to be identical, so that a casual observer might have suspected one girl of committing bigamy. Winnie, however, knew better. He studied the two pictures for a moment, and then indicated the one in which the bridegroom wore the uniform of the United States Navy.

"That's Janet, isn't it?" he said. "Her face was always a little more rounded than Jean's, and her hairline a little lower."

"Well," said Prudence admiringly, "you certainly have sharp eyes and a good memory, Winnie. Of course, you always had. Yes, that's Jan. She married Sam Bradley—he was a lieutenant at the naval base on Tampica."

"Now, now, watch your tongue, Prudence," remarked Matthew, who was busying himself at the drinks cupboard. "The whole subject of the naval base is a very sore one as far as Winston is concerned. He probably regards Jan as some sort of Mrs. Quisling. Sherry, Winston?"

"Oh, don't be silly, Matthew. Personally I was very glad to have the base on the island. It gave the girls a chance to meet some really nice young men, and their parties were great fun. Anyhow, Sam is stationed at Annapolis now—he's an instructor at the Naval Academy."

"Thank you, sir." Winnie took the glass from Matthew, with a slightly conspiratorial smile, and went on diplomatically, "Anyhow, I can see from the photograph that Jean married a civilian."

"Yes." Prudence's kindly face stiffened into an expression of faint disapproval. "Also an American. A tourist. In trade, if you understand what I mean."

"I am quite sure," said Matthew, "that Winston has no idea of what you mean. You really are a dreadful snob, my dear." To Winnie, he added, "The expression 'in trade' belongs to Victorian England. It indicates that a man makes his living by buying and selling, which was not considered a fit occupation for a gentleman at that time. It was perfectly acceptable, of course, to earn one's living by killing people, whether on land or sea, or—curiously enough—by ministering to them in the flesh as a doctor, or spiritually as a parson. Politicians were tolerated so long as they had an independent source of income. Best of all was to live on inherited wealth and do nothing. But, of course, you know all this."

"Things have changed since those days," Winnie said.

"Things have, but people like Prudence haven't," said Matthew, not unkindly. "In fact, I find it rather charming that she should patronize Jean's husband, who happens to be one of the richest men in the United States, just because his family made its money in the supermarket business and Homer chose to go into the firm. You've been here long enough to have heard of Schipmaker Maximarkets, I suppose?"

There was a moment of silence. Winnie's eyes went to the second photograph, flickering over the features of the civilian bridegroom. Then he said, "Yes, I can see a resemblance now. Otis Schipmaker and his wife are prominent in Washington society. They were at the reception this evening."

"Were they?" said Prudence. Winnie thought her voice sounded unusually cool. "I didn't see them. Otis is Homer's younger brother, of course. The whole family spent several holidays in Tampica—that would have been during the time that you were away at school. In fact, Otis was there when…that is, when Jean and Homer…"

Matthew said, "Jean and Homer spend most of their time on their farm in Virginia, about an hour's drive from Washington. They're not great socialites like Otis and Ginny."

"So you see," Prudence chimed in rather hastily, "both the girls have settled down in this part of the world, and that's why Matthew and I decided to retire here. After all, this is where our family is. Would it bore you to see some snapshots of our grandchildren?"

"Of course not, Mrs. Barrington," said Winnie gallantly.

The evening passed quietly and pleasantly. Muriel—a stout, smiling Tampican woman—served a simple but delicious dinner. Matthew opened a bottle of Beaujolais with a certain amount of ceremony. Winnie was pressed to give a complete account of all that had happened since the Barringtons left Tampica eight years ago. Reminiscences were exchanged of the old days at Tampica Harbour. Eddie Ironmonger was discussed at length—memories of his boyhood interspersed with predictions for his future. Nobody mentioned Mavis.

It was after dinner, as they sat over coffee, that Prudence suddenly exclaimed, "Oh! The news!" She turned to Winnie, a little apologetically. "I'm not really a television addict, but I do like to watch the ten o'clock news program, and now I'm afraid we may have missed it. If you don't mind...?"

"Of course, Mrs. Barrington. I shall be very interested to see it myself."

As Prudence fiddled with the switches on the antiquated black-and-white set, Matthew looked at his watch and remarked, "Don't worry, my dear. You should catch it all right."

But as the picture flickered onto the screen and the sound surged up, the announcer was saying, "...and finally, the sports report from Harry Duckett. Harry...?" The camera moved to a fresh-faced young man, who sat against the backdrop of a montage of sporting events. He began, "Good evening. In the match between Georgetown University and..."

"There you are! I knew it!" Prudence's voice drowned the telecaster's, in gloomy triumph.

"...and the Baltimore Orioles blanked the Milwaukee Brewers five to nothing, giving the Birds their fifth straight win of the season..." He hesitated, apparently receiving a sign from somewhere off-screen, then added, "I think George has another item for us...George?..."

The camera returned to the original newscaster, whose features were now adjusted into the stern lines of one about to announce solemn tidings.

"Here is a late news item which has just been handed to me. It has just been announced that Lady Ironmonger, wife of the newly appointed Tampican Ambassador, Sir Edward Ironmonger, was found dead in her room at the Tampican Embassy here in Washington this evening, following a reception attended by many diplomats and eminent Washingtonians. The cause of death has not yet been determined. I'll repeat that. Lady Ironmonger, wife of the newly appointed..."

Winston Horatio Nelson was on his feet, and Prudence Barrington instinctively grasped his hand.

"I must go back at once," Winnie said.

"Oh, my dear. Oh, I am so sorry..." It was not clear to whom Prudence was speaking. Then, as if coming out of a dream, she dropped Winnie's hand, and said, "Yes. Yes, of course you must go. Tell Eddie that if there's anything we can..."

"Anything at all..." echoed Matthew.

"I'll tell him," said Winnie, and ran out to the car.

Winnie was relieved to see that the Embassy looked very much as usual, at least from the outside. It was dark—curtains and blinds had been carefully drawn—but a glimmer of light from inside indicated that it was not deserted. A discreetly prowling police car and a strange limousine with a sticker indicating that the owner was a doctor were the only signs that anything was wrong. The demonstrators had long since dispersed, and the ten o'clock news announcement had not as yet attracted any gawkers. Winnie parked his car and let himself in through the front door, using his own key.

The large drawing-room where the reception had been held was dark, but a light shone from under the door of the small library, and Winnie caught the sound of voices. He opened the door and went in.

An agonized conference seemed to be taking place. Eddie Ironmonger was there, his handsome black face set in lines which were not only tragic, but—as Winnie instantly recognized—stubborn. One look at his old friend was enough to tell him that Eddie was taking some sort of stand which was unpopular with his advisers, and that nothing would budge him.

Michael Holder-Watts looked more angry than upset, whereas Eleanor had obviously been weeping, and still dabbed at her eyes every so often with an inadequate wisp of handkerchief. The party was completed by Dorabella Hamilton—the good-looking, Junoesque Tampican girl who was Sir Edward's private secretary—and a middle-aged white American with a small goatee and rimless glasses, whom Winnie took to be the doctor.

Dead silence greeted Winnie's entrance, punctuated only by a choked sob from Eleanor. He said, "I saw the television news. I came at once."

"Very decent of you," said Michael bitingly. "It might have been better if you had stayed here in the first place."

"Shut up, Michael," said Sir Edward sharply. Then, to Winnie, "So it's been announced. What did they say?"

"Just that Lady Ironmonger had been found dead, following a reception here."

"Nothing more?"

"Nothing."

"Good." Michael seemed about to speak, but Eddie silenced him with a gesture. He went on. "The fact of the matter, Winnie, is that Mavis committed suicide. What led her to do so, I will leave up to you to guess." He turned slowly and deliberately, and stared at Michael and Eleanor. Winnie thought he had never seen such loathing in a man's eyes.

The doctor, who had been polishing his glasses, said, "Sir Edward, I hesitate to contradict you, but once again I must point out—"

Eddie swung round to face him. "You have examined my wife's body," he said. "Tell this gentleman your conclusions."

"I was summoned by telephone to the Embassy at 8:45 P.M.," he said, precisely. "I was taken upstairs to Lady

Ironmonger's room. She was lying on the bed, and I was able to establish at once that she was dead."

"And the cause of death?" Eddie prompted, sharply.

"The cause of death," said the doctor, snappily, "cannot be positively ascertained without an autopsy." He cleared his throat and glared at Sir Edward.

Eddie controlled himself with a visible effort. In his best courtroom manner, he said, "Let me put it this way, Doctor. Is it possible that anybody could have survived a bullet wound in the right temple, such as you found on my wife's body?"

Infuriatingly, the doctor said, "Lady Ironmonger had sustained a wound in her right temple, apparently caused by a bullet fired at close range. You notice I say 'apparently.' Without an autopsy—"

"And could she have survived it?"

"It is unlikely, but nothing is impossible, Sir Edward." The doctor stood up. "I will not have words put into my mouth. Lady Ironmonger is dead. That is all I am prepared to certify unless and until I am permitted to remove the body to proper premises and perform an autopsy."

So that's it, Winnie thought. He went over to the Ambassador and put his arm round his friend's shoulders. "What can I say, Eddie?"

Sir Edward raised his left hand and clasped it over Winnie's. Quite irrelevantly, it occurred to Eleanor Holder-Watts that the two hands—the velvet-black covering the coffee-brown—were very beautiful. She started to cry again.

Eddie said, "Don't try to say anything, Winnie. Just get that man out of here. And come to my study, please." His hand tightened over Winnie's for a moment, and then he turned and strode out of the room.

The silence that followed his exit was pierced by a silvery chime from the clock on the mantelpiece. The doctor glanced at his watch, as if for reassurance, nodded to himself, and said, "Eleven o'clock. Well, it seems that Sir Edward is adamant, and of course this is Tampican territory. There is nothing more that I can do. There is nothing more that I *will* do while I am denied the proper facilities. Good night, ladies and gentlemen."

He followed Sir Edward out of the room. A moment later, the front door slammed, and there was the sound of a car starting up and driving away.

"I'd better go to the study," Winnie said. Nobody answered him.

The Ambassador's study, which was situated at the back of the house, was lit only by a single desk lamp which threw a small, intense circle of white light onto a document which lay on the dark green leather blotter. Sir Edward himself was sitting at the desk, in the shadows outside the ring of light. His elbows were on the desk, his forehead supported in one hand.

Winnie closed the door softly behind him, and said, "He's gone, Eddie."

Without lifting his head, Sir Edward said softly, "Set it down...that one may smile and smile, and be a villain..."

Winnie stopped dead. Then he said, as lightly as he could, "Don't tell me you are casting yourself as Othello, Eddie?"

The Ambassador lifted his head, and looked at Nelson. "The quotation," he said, "is from *Hamlet*. Never mind. It was estimable to recognize it as Shakespeare—for a Tampican." They both smiled at that. It was a childhood joke, something impossible to share outside the small circle of people who had experienced at first hand both the humiliation and the pride. "Come and sit down, Winnie. Give me your advice."

Winnie sat down. He said, "That's clearly impossible, and would be a waste of time. You have decided what to do."

There was a long pause. Then Eddie said, "It is more complicated than you perhaps realize. Mavis shot herself with my revolver. She must have taken it from my desk, earlier on. That may or may not be significant. You remember, some of us were discussing only the other day whether or not it would be more sensible to keep the gun in our bedroom rather than here in the study. Mavis may have moved it just for that simple reason, and then...anyhow, she was lying on her bed with this…this wound in her head. Please understand, Winnie, I am not being emotional about this. At least, I am trying to be objective."

"An apparent suicide," said Winnie carefully, "normally requires a post-mortem examination and an inquest, in order to—"

Ignoring him, Sir Edward went on, "Michael found her. Another fact which may be interesting. The last guests were just leaving. He waited until they had gone, and then told me. It was only then that I discovered the truth."

"The truth?"

"That Mavis had been guilty of some sort of silly indiscretion at the reception. Whereupon Michael and Eleanor had seen fit to…to manhandle her up to our bedroom and lock her in, leaving the key outside. It was over an hour later, when I noticed that she wasn't at the reception and asked Michael about her, that it occurred to him to go and see if she was all right. He found her dead. That is his story. We shall see."

There was a pause. Then Winnie said, "You still haven't told me what you propose to do. Obviously, you are unwilling to involve the United States—"

"I refuse," said Eddie quietly, "to have any American doctors or policemen interfering in Tampican affairs."

"And yet you called the doctor?"

"Of course. Her death had to be certified." Sir Edward paused, then added, "When I think that we might have found her in time…"

Winnie said, "The doctor did not consider that her death was instantaneous, then?"

"You heard what he said. He is not prepared to give any opinion, other than that she is dead, without an autopsy."

Rather uneasily, Winston said, "It is usual in such cases, Eddie."

"I know it is usual. The matter is being attended to."

"What do you mean?"

"Dorabella is already in touch with Tampica by telephone. I have to speak to Sam personally. I am sending for Doctor Duncan."

"Will he…" Winnie hesitated. "…will he get here in time?"

"In time for what?"

"I have always understood that the sooner the autopsy is performed, the better," said Winnie, unhappily.

"My dear Winnie, what do you expect the doctor to find? The autopsy is a mere formality. Poor Mavis killed herself. I do not intend to subject her body to the barbarities of strangers. Would you?"

Winnie was saved from replying by the ringing of the telephone, followed by a single sharp buzzing note. He threw an interrogative look at the Ambassador, who nodded. Winnie picked up the receiver.

"Nelson here."

"Winnie?" Dorabella's voice was calm, as usual. "Please tell Sir Edward that the Prime Minister is on the line."

Winston put his hand over the mouthpiece, and said, "Dorabella's got Sir Samuel for you. Says he's on the line, in person."

For a tiny moment, Ironmonger almost smiled. He appreciated efficiency, and his personal secretary had certainly shown it. Then he picked up the desk telephone—at the same time indicating to Nelson that he should continue to listen on the other extension.

"Ironmonger speaking."

Faintly, crackling with static electricity and annoyance, the voice of Sir Samuel Drake-Frobisher came across the ocean from Tampica. "Eddie? What on earth do you want at this time of night? I'm in the middle of an important dinner party. If Dorabella hadn't—"

"Did she tell you, Sam?"

"Tell me what?"

"That Mavis is dead."

For a moment, the line went so silent that Sir Edward added, urgently, "Can you hear me, Sam? Are you still there?"

"I heard you. I am very sorry, Eddie. Please accept my sympathy." The Prime Minister's voice had become stiff and formal. Even across two thousand miles of telephone line, Winnie could sense that Sir Samuel was controlling considerable anger. He would never, of course, say anything to wound an old friend in his bereavement, but it was clear that he did not consider Mavis's demise a fit subject for a late-night personal telephone call.

Ironmonger said, "I want a lot more than your sympathy, Sam. I want you to get hold of Doc Duncan, put him on your private yacht and send him to Antigua at once. He should be able to catch the night flight at 4:30 A.M. and be here by breakfast time."

There was a little pause, and then Sir Samuel said, "I understood that Mavis was already dead?"

"She is."

"Then what can Doctor Duncan—?"

"Sam," said Ironmonger, "there are...unusual circumstances. The American doctor wishes to remove Mavis to a hospital and perform an autopsy. As a result, there might well be a police inquiry and even court proceedings. In the United States."

"Good God. We can't have that."

"Exactly. I thought you would see my point, Sam. I'm sure you agree that the best thing is for Doc Duncan to come here, make his examination, and return tomorrow by air to Tampica with Mavis's body. He can perform the autopsy there if he considers it necessary. Of course, his findings will have to be made public. But whatever happens, it will happen within Tampican jurisdiction."

The Prime Minister said, "You are quite right, Eddie. I congratulate you on your clear thinking at such a tragic moment. I'll make it my business to see that Duncan is on that aircraft. I'm sorry, Eddie. Really sorry. I heard you were both doing so well in Washington."

"It is unfortunate," said Sir Edward, with no emotion that Winnie could distinguish in his voice. "However, it has happened and must be dealt with as quickly and wisely as possible. Thank you, Sam. Good night." He rang off and turned to Winnie. "Now please ask Dorabella to come. There are things to be arranged...the airline...undertakers..."

"Perhaps I could—?"

"No, thank you, Winnie. I would prefer Dorabella to handle this."

"Very well." Feeling snubbed, Winnie made his way back to the small library, pausing at Dorabella's small office to deliver his message.

Michael and Eleanor were sitting, one each side of the fireplace, not speaking. Winnie said, "And now, Michael, perhaps you'll tell me what actually occurred at the reception. I gather our fears were realized."

Michael smiled, a tired smile. "The understatement of the century," he said. "If it hadn't been unspeakable, it would have been terribly funny." He proceeded to relate the circumstances of Lady Ironmonger's introduction to the Israeli diplomat, illustrating the anecdote where appropriate with bursts of song. Eleanor removed her handkerchief from her red-rimmed eyes and let out a sudden, high-pitched giggle. It sounded more shocking than Mavis's honest obscenities.

"So you see, Winnie," Michael concluded, "there was really nothing for it but to remove the lady as quickly and quietly as possible. You had left by that time, of course"—there was a light but bitter irony in his voice—"and so I had to rely on Eleanor. It was she who got Mavis upstairs."

Winnie Nelson was looking puzzled. "I don't understand," he said. "Why should Lady Ironmonger single out Mr. Finkelstein for her attack? As I understand it, she had never even met him—and our country is on excellent terms with Israel."

Wearily, Michael said, "She didn't single him out, Winnie. She was as tight as an owl, and it was his bad luck to be called Finkelstein."

"I still do not see—"

"Then I'll explain. Mavis Watkins—in the interval between graduating from a cheap school of modeling and her election as Miss Luscious Lollipop—worked as a mannequin in a wholesale dress establishment in Poland Street."

"Poland Street?"

"Or thereabouts. It is," Michael explained, "an area of London which is thickly populated by the cheaper end of the garment trade, which is almost entirely in Jewish hands. The life of a model girl there is a million miles away from the glamour of couture shows and fashion magazines. It's an ill-paid and exhausting life, working long hours in stuffy, cramped quarters, struggling endlessly in and out of nasty cheap clothes and parading them to bored provincial buyers. Of course, some firms treat their girls very well, but others don't. Like all oppressed minorities, the girls let off steam by thumbing their noses at the bosses, in one way or another. The mythical Mr. Finkelstein is, to them, the epitome of all money-grubbing, slave-driving, bottom-pinching garment manufacturers—and the song you have just heard is a dressing-room favourite."

"You are very well-informed," said Winnie, stiffly.

With no trace of embarrassment, Michael said, "Oh, Mavis told me all about it. She often used to sing that song— when we were alone, of course. You might almost say it was her signature tune. So, of course, when she was actually introduced to a Mr. Finkelstein in person—"

Changing the subject, Winnie said, "You say that she was drunk. I thought she had promised to stick to tomato juice."

"So did I," said Michael grimly. "The waiters all swear blind that they served her nothing else, but she might easily have got around one of them, and now, of course, he'll never admit it. No, I don't know how she managed it, but she must have been drinking almost neat vodka, to get into the state she did in such a short time. Eleanor says she could hardly stand by the time she got to her room."

"It was horrible, Mr. Nelson," said Eleanor. "Disgusting. She kept on singing all the way up the stairs—dreadful, vulgar songs, you never heard such words. I thought we'd never get to the bedroom. Then she just flopped down on her bed and seemed to be sound asleep. I thought it was the best thing she could do. I simply came away as fast as I could. I locked the door behind me and left the key in it, as Michael told me to."

"Eleanor did splendidly," said Michael, defensively. "Of course, Eddie's breathing fire and brimstone at both of us now, but that's only to be expected. When he comes to his senses, he'll have to agree that we did the only possible thing." He paused, and then added, "Funny. You know, I think he was really fond of her, in spite of everything."

"She was his wife," said Winnie, coldly. This remark brought no response, so he added, "Well, go on. What happened next?"

"Nothing, really," said Michael. "Eleanor and I went around the room trying to smooth things over with anyone who might have noticed the incident. Mr. Finkelstein left in a huff, and I can't say I blame him. The evening limped toward its longed-for close. Around half-past eight, when Eddie was making his polite farewells, he asked me where Mavis was. I told him. He insisted she must come down and make a final appearance. I couldn't really argue with him. I went upstairs, unlocked the door—and found her dead."

"And the gun—what do you think about the gun?" Winnie demanded.

It was Eleanor who answered, in a flood of near hysteria. "That's the awful part, Mr. Nelson! It seems almost as though she did it on purpose...planned it just to embarrass us and make us look ridiculous...I don't know how she could do such a thing!"

"What do you mean, Mrs. Holder-Watts?"

"Shut up, Eleanor," said Michael, easily. "The point is this, Winnie. She shot herself with Eddie's gun."

"So I understood. But—"

"He kept it in his desk drawer, as I expect you know. Well, after Mavis had been found, and everybody was running round like beheaded chickens, Dorabella calmly remarked that she had noticed early this afternoon that the gun was missing from the drawer. Dorabella didn't worry because she remembered the conversation we had the other day—you were there, I think—about it being more sensible to keep the gun in the bedroom in case of intruders, so she just concluded that either Eddie or Mavis had moved it. But now, both she and Eleanor seem to think that Mavis planned her suicide deliberately, took the gun, and then got good and stinking to cock a final snook at the diplomatic world before she went. It's pure guesswork, of course, but Eleanor feels rather strongly about it."

"It was a...a *dreadful* thing to do," said Eleanor tearfully. "Mean and spiteful and cruel and unpatriotic and..." She searched for the ultimate word. "...and *common!*"

"Mavis *was* common, darling," said Michael. "We all knew that."

"I'll never forgive her," sobbed Eleanor. "Sir Edward may be only a Tampican, but at least he's a *gentleman!*" And, having packed the maximum possible snobbery, bigotry and lack of tact into one short sentence, she ran out of the room, her handkerchief to her eyes.

A heavy silence followed her departure. Then Michael yawned, stretched and said, "I imagine Eleanor has gone home." The Holder-Wattses had rented a little Victorian house on the next street. "I may as well join her. There seems nothing to be done here."

"Nevertheless, I will remain," said Winnie. "It is true that Eddie appears to have no need of my services, but I feel it my duty to stay."

Michael had risen and walked to the door. He said, "Pity you didn't feel that way earlier this evening."

Winnie said, "So you insinuated before. I fail to see how my presence could have improved matters."

"Do you? Well, in that case, better not try to puzzle it out. It might keep you awake at nights." Michael opened the door.

"One thing does puzzle me, Michael. How did the newsmen get hold of the story so quickly?"

"Oh, that was Eddie's idea. As soon as the doctor had confirmed that Mavis was dead, he got Dorabella to ring the U.P.I. and give them a short statement."

"My goodness me." Winnie spoke with a sort of affectionate, amused admiration. "I don't believe I would ever have thought about that at such a moment."

"Many people wouldn't, dear boy," said Michael lightly. "But Eddie is exceptional, as we know. That's why he is an ambassador and we are not. Eddie is very, very careful. Good night."

Winston sat quite still. He heard the front door close behind Michael, and then the house was silent, apart from the faint tapping of Dorabella's typewriter in the Ambassador's study.

CHAPTER FOUR

THE SHRILLING OF the front doorbell woke Winnie from his uneasy cat nap on the library sofa. He scrambled to his feet and glanced at his watch. Ten past three. Doctor Duncan would not even have taken off from Antigua. He hurried out into the hallway, and had the front door open before Dorabella appeared, tired but businesslike, from the back of the house.

An impeccable, middle-aged gentleman in a dark suit stood on the doorstep. Gravely, and in hushed tones, he said, "My name is Rollins. Rollins Funeral Services. May I come in?"

Dorabella laid a hand on Winnie's arm, and gently but firmly pushed him aside. She said, "Please do, Mr. Rollins. It was kind of you to come so promptly, and in person. I explained to you on the telephone what is necessary."

"Yes, indeed, madam." He turned to Winnie and bowed. "Please accept my deepest sympathy, Sir Edward."

Winnie was wide awake by then. He said, "No, no, Mr. Rollins. You are mistaken. May I present myself...? Winston H. Nelson, First Secretary."

"Ah, yes…most understandable…" murmured Mr. Rollins, somewhat obscurely. Then, to Dorabella, "And now, if I might see Lady Ironmonger, I can make the necessary…em…"

Dorabella said, "I'll take you up." Winnie noticed that, for the first time, she seemed nervous and ill at ease. Her hand, in which she held a key, was not quite steady.

Winnie said, "I'll go up with Mr. Rollins, Dorabella."

"Sir Edward asked me to—"

"I expect he didn't know I was still here." Winnie held out his hand for the key. "Come on, Dorabella. You've been through enough for one night. Let me take over."

She gave him a tiny smile. "All right. Thank you, Winnie." She handed him the key. "Nothing is to be touched unless it is absolutely necessary. Mr. Rollins will be taking measurements for the coffin."

She turned, and almost ran back toward the study.

"This way, if you please, Mr. Rollins." Winnie preceded the undertaker upstairs, their footsteps inaudible on the deep pile of the golden carpet. Irrelevantly, Winnie remembered that the stair carpet had been the subject of a lively disagreement between Eddie and Mavis. Eddie had picked pale gold, to complement the deeper sheen of the old waxed wooden stairs and banisters. Mavis had wanted dark red. Eddie had dismissed red as vulgar. Mavis had retorted that pale gold would get filthy in no time, with all the people using the staircase. Eddie, of course, had won. Now, as he climbed the stairs ahead of Mr. Rollins, Winnie saw for the first time that the carpet was already showing signs of grubbiness. He felt an unexpected stab of sympathy for Mavis Ironmonger.

"Here we are," he said. He unlocked the door of the Ironmongers' bedroom and stood back to let Mr. Rollins in.

What was left of Mavis Ironmonger was lying on one of the twin beds—a long, slender outline covered by a white sheet. The room reflected most precisely the differences of taste and character of the Ironmongers. The lime-green carpet and matching slub-silk curtains had of course been chosen by

Eddie, so had the beautiful antique English walnut furniture. Mavis's touch was proclaimed by a collection of Disney-like animals in glass, china and wood on the table by her bed; by the frilly pink skirt which made a mockery of the Queen Anne dressing-table; by the serried ranks of scent and cosmetic bottles glimpsed through the open door of her adjoining bathroom (Sir Edward's bathroom, leading off his dressing-room, was almost Spartan in its simplicity). Over Mavis's bed hung a painting (an expensive original) of a saucer-eyed comic strip child clutching a puppy, and on the bed she kept a big, lifelike angora cat, made of white rabbit fur, which acted as a cover for the wisp of transparent froth which she called her nightdress.

Now, however, the cat lay askew on the floor beside the bed, with pink nylon spewing from its interior, like intestines. Beside it, also on the floor, was a Smith and Wesson lightweight revolver, which, if it were not Eddie Ironmonger's, was certainly its twin.

Winnie was somewhat surprised to see that the revolver had been carefully outlined in soft white chalk, which made a blurred, powdery design on the soft pile of the carpet. The nightdress case had been similarly treated, and two other chalk marks were so positioned that Winnie took them to mark the spots where Mavis's right hand and foot had been touching the floor when she was found. Eddie, as Michael had remarked, was certainly careful.

Working with a solemn reverence which thinly masked highly professional speed, Mr. Rollins gently removed the sheet from Mavis's body. Predictably, death became her magnificently. She lay, like the Lady of Shalott, serene and remotely beautiful in her dark silk dress, with her fair hair tumbling from under the white silk scarf which the doctor had placed, loosely, to cover the wound in her head. Never again would vulgarity, drunkenness, or obscenity stain her flawless features. From now on she would exist as an exquisite silver-framed photograph on Sir Edward's desk. As such, she would probably help his career considerably. After all, to be a handsome widower mourning a lovely young wife never did anybody's charisma any harm.

Mr. Rollins had taken a notebook from his breast pocket and was making discreet, valedictory jottings, casting a practiced eye over Mavis in the same way that Winnie, as a boy, had seen old boatbuilders in Tampica Harbour size up planks for a hull, or canvas for a sail. The true expert has no need of a measuring tape.

Mr. Rollins worked fast. He was just making his final entry in the notebook when the door opened and Sir Edward Ironmonger walked in. He did not even glance at Mr. Rollins, but went straight to Winnie, and said softly, but with fury, "Please leave this room at once."

It was like a slap in the face. Winnie did not trust himself to say anything, for fear of desecrating the death chamber. Expressionless, he walked out of the room, down the stairs and through the front door into the brisk, clear, Georgetown night.

His car was still parked outside the Embassy, and he got into it and revved up the engine with unnecessary vigor. Then he drove off down the deserted, lamplit street. A few minutes later, he was inside the comfortable bachelor apartment which he had rented in a modern block near the Washington Circle. He had intended to go to bed and try to snatch some sleep from the remnants of the night, but instead he found himself pouring out a generous measure of scotch and sitting down gloomily in a large armchair to drink it. It was not more than ten minutes before the telephone rang.

Wearily, Winnie stretched out his arm and picked it up. "Nelson."

"Winnie? This is Eddie."

Winnie said nothing.

"Winnie, I'm calling to apologize. And to explain, if I can. I'm sorry I said what I did."

Stiffly, Winnie said, "It is I who must apologize. Your orders were disobeyed."

"Let me explain, Winnie. It is true, I told Dorabella that nobody but she, myself and the undertaker should go into that room until Doctor Duncan arrived. I was angry and upset when I learnt you were up there. I admit it."

"You had every justification. You are His Excellency the Ambassador, after all."

"For God's sake, Winnie. Just listen, will you? Why do you think I issued those orders?"

"It is hardly for me to surmise."

"Come off it, Winnie. I've got enough to worry about, without you—"

"I'm sorry."

"Above all, don't apologize. Can you come back to the Embassy right away? Dorabella's out on her feet, and I'm sending her home. Now, don't start getting prickly again. She's done the donkey-work, and the difficult part is about to begin. That's why I need you."

"The difficult part?"

"Another statement to the press. I don't want to talk about it on the phone. Please come, Winnie."

"I'll be right over."

Four-thirty A.M. As Winnie parked his car, he saw a little knot of people assembled outside the door of the Embassy. He supposed that one or two of them must have been there when he left—he simply had not noticed. The curt announcement on the ten-o'clock-news bulletin had obviously been enough to cause the stationing of a look-out in the vicinity of Oxford Gardens. Later on, the comings and goings had alerted news-sensitive antennae. The ghouls were gathering, and Winnie could not hope to escape them as he walked from his car to the front door.

"Mr. Nelson!" Somebody was bright enough to know his name. The others took it up.

"A statement please, Mr. Nelson!"

"What was the cause of Lady Ironmonger's death?"

"Was it during or after the reception?"

"What's the medical report?"

"No comment," muttered Winnie, fumbling for his key.

"When did you last see Lady Ironmonger alive?"

"Will there be an autopsy, Mr. Nelson?"

"Have the police been called in?"

The key slid into the lock, and turned. Winnie said, "A further statement will be issued in due course. Thank you, gentlemen. Good night."

He opened the door just far enough, slid inside, and banged it behind him. Eddie Ironmonger stepped out of the shadows into the lighted hallway. He said, "Press?"

"I'm afraid so."

"It was only to be expected. That is why we have to make another statement before Duncan arrives."

"I don't see that it's any journalist's goddam business," said Winnie crossly.

Eddie laid a hand on his arm. "That's what I have to explain to you, Winnie. Come into the study."

As soon as he entered the study, Winnie was aware of the heavy smell of cigar smoke in the air. Typical of Eddie, he thought. Good cigars were the Ambassador's one great luxury, but Dorabella was a nonsmoker, and even under the stress of this evening's tragedy, Eddie had not lit up until his secretary had gone home. Not for the first time, Nelson speculated on his chief's extraordinary attention to detail. Was it self-discipline, good organization or just habit? He did not know.

He said, "I thought everything was explained by now."

"Not by a long chalk, Winnie. It is bad enough to have to contemplate the fact that Mavis killed herself. But the truth may be even worse."

Winnie felt a cold breath of fear, like an icy draught on his back. "You're not suggesting she was murdered?"

"I'm not suggesting anything at the moment. I'm just saying that we must be very careful." There was something uncanny to Winston in this echo of Michael Holder-Watts's words. "By forbidding you to go into that room, Winnie, I was trying to protect you. Don't you see that? If...if the worst should happen...it is very important that those who are patently innocent should do nothing to compromise themselves. You were not even in the Embassy when Mavis...created that scene. You were driving Bishop and Mrs. Barrington home—nobody could want more trustworthy witnesses. I want to keep you entirely—untainted. You see, the rest of us are in a different position."

"What do you mean?"

Patiently, Eddie Ironmonger said, "Eleanor was in the bedroom—she took Mavis up there. Michael was there—he found her body. Naturally he called me—and later it was also necessary for Dorabella to go into the room. That makes four people, not including the doctor and the undertaker. Four was already too many. Now it is five."

"I'm sorry."

"I've asked you before not to apologize." For the first time, Sir Edward's smooth façade seemed on the point of cracking; then he squared his powerful shoulders, and said evenly, "It is just in case of any unpleasant possibilities that I intend to draft another statement to the press. We are keeping this a strictly Tampican matter, but not only must everything be completely aboveboard—it must be seen to be so. Do you have a pen? Write this down and see how it looks."

He paced up and down beside his desk. "A doctor has been summoned from Tampica to establish the exact cause of death of Lady Ironmonger, wife of etc. It can be stated that apparently Lady Ironmonger did not die of natural causes, but no more positive announcement can be made until the medical reports have been received. Lady Ironmonger's body will be flown home to Tampica this morning...no, change that...will this morning be flown home to Tampica, where an autopsy will be performed if doctors consider it necessary. Their findings will be made public, and another statement issued in due course." He paced the length of the room again. "No, delete the last bit about a further statement. Unnecessary. Their findings will be made public. Full stop. Funeral arrangements will be announced later. Read that back, would you, Winnie?"

Winnie did so. Ironmonger nodded. "That should do. We can't stop the gossip, so I intend to forestall it as far as possible. Telephone that through to U.P.I., if you will, and then go home and get some rest. Tell the carrion crows outside that a statement has been...no, better, read it to them. Point out to them that they'll catch nothing but a cold standing on the pavement till morning. Get rid of them somehow. They make me nervous."

"I'll do my best." Winston consulted Dorabella's list of telephone numbers, and dialed United Press International. He read the statement, emphasized that he had nothing further to add, and rang off. Then, the paper still in his hand, he stood up.

Sir Edward had pulled back the curtains from the long window that overlooked the garden, and was standing, his back to the room, gazing out at the clear sky. Already, faint glimmers of light were diminishing the blackness, and the garden trees, still bare of leaves, could be made out as skeletal shapes behind the ghostly whiteness of a magnolia in bloom.

Winnie said, "I'll be off, then. I presume Dorabella's arranged for Duncan to be met at the airport?"

"She's going herself. The plane touches down at half-past seven. With any luck, he'll be here soon after eight. I'd appreciate it if you were too, Winnie."

"Of course."

"And meanwhile, get some rest."

"And what about you, Eddie?"

The Ambassador did not turn round. He had lit another cigar, and was raising it to his lips as Nelson spoke. For a moment, the movement was arrested, like a movie jammed in the projector. Then the dark hand continued its upward movement. Sir Edward said quietly, "I do not think that I shall sleep. Good night, Winnie."

It was a dismissal. Winston went out into the hall and through the front door to face the small cluster of journalists outside.

CHAPTER FIVE

THE PLANE FROM Antigua touched down at Dulles Airport exactly on time. While the other passengers—many of them incongruously dressed in their brilliant Caribbean resort clothes—waited for the mobile lounge to whisk them across the tarmac to the airport building, an elderly gentleman in a sober black suit was helped down the boarding ladder from the first-class section, and into a waiting limousine driven by a big, handsome black girl. There was no question of Customs or Immigration for Dr. Duncan. He was being given the full VIP treatment.

The young airport official who had organized the "special diplomatic welcome," and who now stood holding open the back door of the car, found himself somewhat shocked, both by the appearance and the behavior of this highly important personage. For a start, Dr. Duncan's black suit was patently ancient—and shiny where it was not threadbare. It must have been made at a time when he weighed considerably more than he did now, for it hung in shabby folds around his skinny body.

The old man had wispy, pure white hair and startlingly bright blue eyes, and his wrinkled skin was tanned to a deep chestnut color by years of exposure to the tropical sun. He looked more like a down-and-out beachcomber than anything else. A battered Gladstone bag seemed to be his only luggage.

Once on *terra firma*, he impatiently waved away the official and the open car door. Instead, he himself opened the door next to the driver, smiled with extraordinary sweetness, and said, "Hello, Dorrie, me darlin'. Got a kiss for a wicked old quack, then?" He climbed into the car, kissed the comely chauffeuse soundly on both cheeks, and turned to wave a feeble hand at the official.

"Thank 'ee, young man. Very civil."

The official slammed the back door of the car, took a pace backward and saluted smartly, feeling deeply insulted. Dr. Duncan wound down the car window and stuck his head out of it.

"Bit overweight, aren't you, sonny? Better cut down on the calories and take more exercise."

It was perhaps fortunate that the car moved off before the official had time to compose even a mental reply.

Like Michael Holder-Watts, Dr. Alfred Duncan was one of the few British residents to opt for Tampican nationality at the time of independence. He did not do so because he had his eye on any possible future benefit, but simply because he had made his life in Tampica for more years than he could remember, and had no other home, no other interest and no other place to go. He had arrived on the island more than forty years earlier, an impecunious, newly qualified doctor, amusing himself by signing on as ship's doctor on a freighter in order to see something of the world before settling down to a conventional practice in English suburbia.

He had fallen in love, first with Tampica itself and shortly afterwards with a Tampican girl, and had jumped ship with no qualms. He had married the girl and produced a family of beautiful, coffee-colored children, and the rest of his life had become a long and sometimes painful love affair with Tampica and its people.

He had soon made friends with a young curate named Matthew Barrington and his pretty blonde wife, Prudence, newly arrived from England. These three people had set out to tackle the problems of sickness, poverty and illiteracy on the island, armed only with faith and hope. Charity was conspicuously scarce, despite the generosity of an English spinster named Lucy Pontefract-Deacon, who had also made the island her home. Governmental aid was near zero, and opulent tourism only a dream for the future. What was achieved— and it was a great deal—came about by, as Matthew put it, a triumph of mind over money.

By the time that Matthew retired in all his episcopal glory, Tampica had three good schools and a modern hospital. For Alfred, there was no retirement. His Tampican wife had died, and his two sons were carving careers for themselves in England. Dr. Duncan continued his work at the Alfred Duncan Hospital, and if he was guilty of the sin of pride, it was because the well-equipped new building bore his name. He was the most deeply loved man on the island, and he had known Eddie Ironmonger, Sam Drake-Frobisher, Winston Nelson and Dorabella Hamilton all their lives—or in some cases rather longer, for he had brought most of them into the world. It was not surprising that Eddie Ironmonger should have turned instinctively to Doctor Duncan for help. Everybody on Tampica did.

As the limousine purred up the airport approach highway toward the Beltway, Dr. Duncan said, "My word, what a beautiful day. You have a pleasant climate here, no doubt about that." He glanced at Dorabella. She was looking straight ahead, concentrating on the road, her face expressionless. Duncan went on, "This sounds like a bad business, Dorrie." Still the girl did not speak. Gently, the doctor said, "Better tell me a bit about it. Sam was very vague and I wouldn't want to bother Eddie with too many questions."

Dorabella pressed her lips tightly together, and a single big tear ran down her black satin cheek. Then she sniffed and said, "I can't tell you much, Doc. I don't know."

"Tell me all you can."

"Well...it was the evening of our first official reception. You knew that?"

"I heard as much on the radio at Antigua. And Sam told me that Mavis's death was apparently not natural, and that there might have to be an inquiry. Outside of that, I'm in the dark."

"It's so unfair on Eddie!" Dorabella burst out suddenly. "He's always been so good and so patient, and trying to help her, and we thought she might show a little gratitude at last— and now she has to do this!"

"Do what?" Duncan prompted, softly.

"Kill herself, of course. In the middle of a reception, with maximum publicity! It'll ruin Eddie's career!"

Duncan said, "You mean, she actually committed suicide in front of all the guests?"

"Well...not exactly," Dorabella admitted. "She made some sort of a scene—I wasn't in the room at the time, but Michael says she got drunk and insulted an Israeli diplomat. Michael and...Mrs. Holder-Watts managed to get her away from the reception and up to her room, and they thought she'd just sleep it off. But oh, no. She'd stolen Eddie's revolver earlier in the day, and she simply shot herself."

Dr. Duncan was rubbing his chin thoughtfully. "What a very strange thing to do," he said. "You don't think it could have been...em...remorse for her bad behavior?"

Dorabella made a short, vulgar remark about remorse as she swung the car into the stream of traffic on the Beltway.

"Hm," said Duncan. "Well, perhaps you're right. In any case, I know now that she was shot, apparently by her own hand." He sighed. "Poor Mavis."

Dorabella took her eyes off the road for long enough to shoot him a glance. "Poor Eddie," she said bitterly.

"Oh, I know where your sympathies lie, my dear—and Winnie's, and many other people's. Still, you might try to find a little pity in your heart for her now."

Evenly, Dorabella said, "I always despised her. Now I hate her."

Dr. Duncan raised a gnarled brown hand as if to protest, then let it fall again, and sighed. The car turned off the Beltway to join the thickening traffic surging towards Washington along the lovely, wooded George Washington Memorial Parkway, and finally over the Potomac River and into Georgetown.

Sir Edward Ironmonger and Winston Horatio Nelson were both at the Embassy to meet Dr. Duncan. The three men greeted each other briefly, with subdued affection, and then Eddie and Winnie preceded the doctor upstairs. As the two of them stood silently, one on each side of the bedroom door, Dr. Duncan was suddenly and fleetingly reminded of the two life-size black statues that guarded Tutankhamen's burial chamber. Then Eddie produced a key from his pocket and opened the door.

He said, "The undertakers have been very efficient. She is already in her coffin, as you will see. When you have made your examination, I will have it closed. Then you must have break-fast and a short rest. An ambulance is waiting to take the coffin to the airport. A chartered plane will fly you back to Tampica. I would like the autopsy report by this evening."

Dr. Duncan glanced at the exquisite, pale face and the ugly wound. "I'll do my best, Eddie." His eyes took in the chalk marks on the floor, and the gun.

As if in answer to an unspoken comment, Eddie said, "As soon as she has gone, this room will be sealed until you have made your report. You will telephone me as soon as possible?"

"Of course. And now perhaps you will leave me with her. I won't be long."

There was only a handful of people—one journalist, a few passers-by and two policemen—outside the house to see

Mavis leave it for the last time. The coffin slid smoothly into the ambulance, Dr. Duncan climbed in beside the driver, the doors were closed and the vehicle moved off. The Ambassador did not appear, nor did any of his staff. The curtains of the Embassy remained drawn, and throughout the day the door was opened only briefly by an unseen hand to take in the telegrams and messages of condolence which arrived from Tampica, from the United States Government, from England and from other Washington embassies.

At seven o'clock that evening, the telephone rang in the Ambassador's study, where Ironmonger sat alone. He picked up the receiver. Dorabella's voice said, "Dr. Duncan is on the line from Tampica, Sir Edward."

"Put him through, please."

"Eddie? This is Doc Duncan." Sir Edward felt a little pulse of uneasiness. The use of a childhood nickname boded no good.

"What's the news, doctor?"

A pause. "Not very good, I'm afraid."

"Well, tell me."

Carefully, the doctor said, "Mavis died as a result of a bullet wound in her right temple."

"We all know that."

"Agreed. But there's something else, Eddie."

"What?"

Duncan hesitated. Then he said, "Tell me, Eddie, had Mavis been drinking heavily?"

For a moment, Ironmonger did not answer. Sitting with the telephone in his hand, he looked as though he had just been hit across the face. Then he said, "Surely your autopsy must have shown—?"

"No, no. You misunderstand me, Eddie. I meant—had Mavis had a…a drinking problem in recent months?"

Again a hesitation. Then—"Mavis enjoyed a drink, as you very well know, Doc. Sometimes she may have had a few too many. I don't think you could describe it as a problem."

"What I'm driving at is this, Eddie. Had Mavis been receiving medical treatment for alcoholism?"

"Good God, no!" Ironmonger sounded both outraged and amused. "What on earth gave you that idea?"

"She had not been taking disulfiram?"

"Taking what?"

"Disulfiram."

"Certainly not. What is it, anyway? I've never heard of it."

Duncan said, "It's a drug frequently used in the treatment of alcoholism, as a deterrent. The smallest amount of alcohol taken with or after it produces extremely unpleasant symptoms. This naturally discourages the patient from drinking."

"Are you trying to tell me that you found traces of this... whatever-you-call-it...in Mavis's body, Doc?".

"Yes, Eddie, I am."

"But that's ridiculous! I'd certainly have known if Mavis had been consulting a doctor."

"Would you? Are you sure?"

"In any case, I thought you said that it was impossible—or at least very unpleasant—to drink alcohol if one is being dosed with this stuff. Well, Mavis has certainly been putting away her fair share recently. Including yesterday evening, apparently, although she'd promised to stick to tomato juice. You must have found that out in your examination, too." Ironmonger paused, then went on, "Wait a moment. Unpleasant symptoms, you said. Well, why didn't the drug produce unpleasant symptoms last night?"

"It did," said Duncan, drily.

"You don't mean that—that it killed her? You just said she died of a bullet wound. You're not making sense, Doc."

Dr. Duncan sighed. "I'm afraid I'm making too much sense, Eddie. I'll explain, but I fear you won't relish the explanation. Well, here goes." He cleared his throat. "The autopsy showed that Mavis had taken a large amount of disulfiram—about twice the normal daily dose—not long before she died. She had also taken a small quantity of alcohol. A very small quantity. She had obviously been doing her best to keep her promise during the reception. Perhaps she thought a little sip wouldn't matter."

"But according to Michael and Eleanor, she was roaring drunk!"

"Exactly. The smallest amount of alcohol, taken in conjunction with all that disulfiram, would immediately produce the symptoms of drunkenness. It would then cause a lapse into deep unconsciousness."

"Eleanor said she seemed to pass out in the bedroom."

"Yes. The trouble is, Eddie...I'm truly sorry, but I have to tell you...the trouble is that there is no possibility that she regained consciousness before she died. You see what this means?"

Sir Edward Ironmonger let out his breath in a long sigh. He said, "I think I knew all along that Mavis was murdered."

"I'm afraid so, Eddie. What are you going to do now?"

"I don't know. I need a little time to think. Prepare a formal report of your findings in writing, please, and send a copy to the Prime Minister. A little later, I'll speak to Sam myself." Eddie Ironmonger paused, and then, with a trace of his usual humor, added, "This is one hell of a situation, isn't it, Doc?"

"It is, Eddie, my boy. By God, you're right. It is."

The ten o'clock television newscast that evening had a further announcement to make concerning the death of the Tampican Ambassadress. This time, however, the program producers had been ready and prepared, and the announcer had time to say no more than, "This evening, the Tampican Embassy issued a further statement..." before his amiable features faded from the screen, to give way to a blow-up of the photograph taken by *The Washington Post*'s photographer.

It was an exceptionally good picture. The French Ambassadress was just recognizable as a quarter-profile, back

to camera, in the foreground; in the background, Sir Edward
Ironmonger also appeared in quarter-profile, turning away
from his wife to exchange a parting remark with a guest who
was leaving the receiving line. Slap in the center of the frame,
dazzlingly lit by the flash-bulb in contrast to the darkness of
the other figures, stood Mavis—a faint smile on her lovely face,
leaning slightly forward and extending a tapering white hand to
her distinguished visitor.

Within seconds of the appearance of the picture on the
screen, Lady Ironmonger's death had become the hottest
news story in Washington. Up until then, only a handful of
people outside the small, enclosed world of diplomacy had had
any idea that the new Ambassadress was not a dark-skinned
Tampican lady, probably middle-aged, certainly charming
and admirable in every way, but hardly...well... It came as a
revelation that Lady Ironmonger had been young, white and
sensationally beautiful. Moreover, she had died in mysterious
circumstances only a matter of hours after the photograph had
been taken. Boy, was this a story!

The announcer's voice helped matters along, fanning the
flames.

"...a further statement concerning the sudden death
of Lady Ironmonger, the Tampican Ambassadress. Lady
Ironmonger's body was flown this morning to Tampica,
where doctors performed an autopsy. Their report states that
Lady Ironmonger died as a result of a gunshot wound in the
head. It is not yet known by whom the shot was fired, or
whether foul play is suspected. An embassy spokesman told
reporters that a full-scale inquiry will be held. Meanwhile,
Sir Edward Ironmonger, accompanied by British-born
Embassy Counsellor Michael Holder-Watts, has already left
Washington by air for Tampica, where he will attend his
wife's funeral..."

That night, both Winston Nelson and Dorabella Hamilton
left their respective apartments and moved into the Embassy,
which was experiencing a state of siege from the press and

other media, not to mention the rubber-necking public. But Eddie's careful strategy had been successful. He himself, together with what remained of poor Mavis, was safely out of the United States, and the whole affair was in Tampican hands. The situation was not good, but it could have been worse.

CHAPTER SIX

MAVIS IRONMONGER WAS buried the following afternoon in the cemetery of the square-set gray stone church—looking so much like an incongruously placed English village church—which stood up on the wooded slopes of Goat Hill, behind the town of Tampica Harbour.

The funeral was quiet, as Eddie Ironmonger had wished it to be—much to the frustration and fury of the battery of newsmen and women who had leapt on to the story as a result of the evening telecast.

To their cost, they found that Sir Edward had been too clever for them. Those who had not booked on the night flight to Antigua (and none of them had) found that they could only with difficulty get as far as Antigua Airport before the scheduled time of the funeral. After that, travel arrangements disintegrated into chaos. Those lucky enough to get on to the twenty-seater Heron biplane to St. Mark's Island found that only four of the twenty could be accommodated on the tiny Piper Aztec which was the largest aircraft capable of landing on the stretch of dust road which Tampica called its airport. Boats might be chartered, but would not arrive until late in the evening. The bars of Antigua and St. Mark's were crowded that night with embittered, hard-drinking journalists busy inventing spurious stories under the fictitious date line "Tampica."

Two mourners who did arrive in time, as honored guests of the Tampican government, were Mavis's parents—Mr. and Mrs. Hubert Watkins from Penge. Long before Dr. Duncan's telephone call, Michael Holder-Watts (on Sir Edward's instructions) had arranged for the Watkinses to be contacted through the Tampican High Commissioner in London. They had stepped off their first-class accommodation on a jumbo jet at Antigua the previous evening, to find a VIP welcome awaiting them, together with the Prime Minister's private motor yacht, on which they spent the night while it navigated the deep blue waters between the islands.

To tell the truth, Mr. and Mrs. Watkins hardly knew what to make of it all, for they had not set eyes on their daughter since she had (as Mrs. Watkins frequently remarked) broken her parents' hearts by successively going off to London to be a model, winning a beauty contest, and—horror of horrors— marrying a black man. Needless to say, the elder Watkinses had steadfastly refused to meet Eddie, and had not attended the wedding. As Pauline Watkins used to say bitterly to her friends at the bridge club—"Please don't mention Mavis to me. I don't have a daughter any more. It's just as if she was dead."

Eddie's knighthood had, of course, made a subtle difference—especially since Hubert had been promoted to Branch Manager of the Imperial Insurance Company and the couple had moved to a new neighborhood. A photograph of Mavis somehow found its way onto the mantelpiece in the lounge, and Pauline would say, off-handedly, to visitors—"Yes, that's my daughter...Lady Ironmonger, you know...yes, she is, isn't she? Sweetly pretty. Of course, we don't see much of them, I'm afraid...Eddie—that's her husband, Sir Edward—he has to be on the other side of the Atlantic most of the time..."

But now Mavis was dead, and the young man on the telephone—who had such a charming voice you really couldn't tell from it if he was black or white—had begged them to accept the hospitality of the Tampican Prime Minister, Sir Samuel Drake-Frobisher (that *sounded* all right—but what color was he?) and fly to Tampica for the funeral.

The young man had also suggested that while they were there, they might like to stay on for a week or so, as guests of the government: they should bring light clothes and beach wear, as the climate was really delightful at this time of the year.

The next thing had been the big black limousine with a uniformed chauffeur (black) and CD plates, which had whisked them from their suburban home under the admiring eyes of the neighbors. Then the VIP lounge at London Airport, the luxury trans-Atlantic flight, the private yacht. All well and good so far—but what next? Neither of them mentioned, even to each other, that they had never met their son-in-law. It all promised to be a little bit awkward.

They need not have worried. The yacht was met in Tampica Harbour by Michael Holder-Watts, who charmed the Watkinses on sight. This was their idea of a real diplomatic gentleman—and the right color, too. He escorted them off the yacht and into a waiting car, climbed in with them, and instructed the chauffeur to drive to the Victoria Hotel.

Then, as the car moved off, he said, "I'm afraid this is a terrible tragedy for both of you—you must feel it as keenly as Eddie does. I'm sure it will be a great comfort to him to know that you are here. I imagine your relationship is very close."

Mr. and Mrs. Watkins exchanged an uneasy glance. Mrs. Watkins said, "Well…that's to say…"

Smoothly, Michael added, "As close as could be expected, given the tremendous distance between England and Tampica."

"That's it!" said Mr. Watkins, with a sort of triumph. "That's just what Pauline meant."

"Then it makes my task easier," said Michael, with a practiced smile. "As Eddie's parents-in-law, you'll understand how he feels. He's anxious not to make a great show of mourning—it would be too painful. He has suggested that he should call for you at the hotel and drive you to the church for the funeral. Afterwards, he has to go to Government House for a conference with the Prime Minister—that's the penalty of being a public servant. Even private bereavement has to take a back seat to official work. So he suggests that you should move down to Pirate's Cave this evening, and we all hope that you'll manage to enjoy a little holiday, in spite of your grief. Eddie will have to get back to Washington almost at once."

"That seems a very sound scheme to me," pronounced Hubert. "Don't you agree, Pauline?"

"Oh, I do. Most thoughtful and convenient." Mrs. Watkins was thinking that she had seldom met a more delightful young man. And Pirate's Cave! Of course, they'd read about it in the papers—the place where all the film stars and such came to stay. The fabulous, American-owned resort hotel which had been instrumental in putting Tampica onto the tourist map. Wait till the neighbors in Penge heard about *that*!

Mrs. Watkins's favorable opinion of Michael Holder-Watts was not reciprocated. He regarded Mavis's parents as crass, ill-bred and a confounded nuisance. However, he had his instructions from Eddie—to preserve a flawless public façade at the funeral, to get rid of the Watkins couple as fast as possible afterwards, and to stop their mouths with the sweet sop of a week or so at Pirate's Cave. This would put them under a massive obligation to Eddie and the Tampican government, and also seclude them physically during what might be a sensitive period. Above all, they must be screened from the press, and prevented from putting their feet in things.

Meanwhile, Michael automatically switched on the effortless charm that was part of his job, and by the time he deposited them at the ugly, massive entrance to the Victoria Hotel in Tampica Harbour, both Watkinses were convinced that he had genuinely enjoyed their company, and was sorry to leave them.

Their meeting after lunch with Sir Edward was short, cold, formal and very correct. Few words were exchanged, either at the hotel or in the car on the way to the church. However, the bereaved widower was snapped by the local press solicitously escorting his parents-in-law through the lych-gate into the churchyard. Pauline Watkins felt the solemnity of the occasion more deeply with each flash of a photographer's bulb. She even shed a few quite genuine tears beside her daughter's coffin. She also felt gratified that she had recently bought a smart new black dress that would come out well in the pictures.

When it was all over, Sir Edward and the Watkinses shook hands with decorous expressions of grief, and were borne away in separate cars. By five o'clock, when the first and most enterprising journalists finally arrived from the United States, the excitement was over and the birds had flown.

The management of the Victoria Hotel told them— believing it to be true—that Lady Ironmonger's parents had already left the island on a small cargo ship which would take them by a leisurely route back to England. A few pressmen did attempt to contact Pirate's Cave, on the off-chance—but the staff were adept at defending the privacy and anonymity of their guests. They had never heard the name of Watkins. No, they never issued guest lists to the press. They were sorry, the hotel was fully booked. No, it was not possible for a nonresident to book a table for dinner. They deeply regretted...

As for Sir Edward Ironmonger and Mr. Holder-Watts, they were staying at the Prime Minister's residence, and there was no question of interviewing them. Dr. Duncan was in the operating theater at the hospital, and proposed to stay there.

Angry and frustrated, the journalists set about making bricks without straw, thumping out "atmosphere" pieces on the beauty of the island, the charm of the quiet hillside graveyard and the events leading up to the recent achievement of independence. They also, of course, set about digging up dirt on Mavis's character—but here, surprisingly, they met with scant success. The islanders, to a man and woman, loved Edward

Ironmonger. They certainly did not intend to pass on to strange newshounds gossip which might harm him—and besides, the wench was dead. As for the small remaining European community, it instinctively closed its ranks against outsiders. After all, you could say what you liked about Mavis, she had been *English*. Whatever hints the reporters might have picked up in Washington, they found no confirmation of them in Tampica.

In the bar of the Victoria Hotel, a journalist from New York gloomily ordered his third rum punch, and discussed his lack of progress with a colleague.

"I took a goddam jeep all the way over the hill to interview that crazy old woman—what's her name?"

"Miss Pontefract-Deacon," said his companion, heavily. "Pronounced Pumfrey-Doon. Yeah, so did I."

"The queen of Tampica, they call her. Eighty if she's a day, and bright as a button. And all she would say was 'Everybody loved Mavis.'"

The Tampican barmaid, arriving at that moment with the rum punch, broke into a peal of uninhibited laughter.

"Yo' can say *that* again!" she remarked, and swayed off down the bar, gyrating her shapely bottom. But what sort of a story, the reporters asked each other, could one make out of *that*? Besides, the woman was dead. "Lively...fun-loving... wide circle of friends..." that was about as far as one could go. Couldn't even say "gay" these days—and that, at least, was one activity of which nobody had ever accused Mavis Ironmonger... The newsmen ordered more rum, and sank deeper into depression.

Meanwhile, on a shady terrace outside the big drawing-room of the Prime Minister's residence, known as The Lodge, Sir Samuel Drake-Frobisher, Sir Edward Ironmonger and Michael Holder-Watts were engaged in an informal conference, as they watched the magnificence of a Caribbean sunset—the sky turning to deep red and burnished gold, as the blazing globe sank towards the darkening sea, outlining a string of small rocky islands like the humps of a sea serpent's back. The pale pink flowers of a spreading white cedar tree glimmered in the twilight beside the red blossoms of a leafless sword tree, and the huge buds of a Cinderella plant opened their white petals to the cool of the evening, to enjoy one night of beauty before the fierce morning sunshine smothered them with killing heat.

Sir Samuel, knocking the ash off his cigar into a silver ashtray, said, "This is a difficult business, Eddie."

"Eddie is doing splendidly," said Holder-Watts. "He is to be congratulated."

Ironmonger's mouth tightened. "A curious thing to say to a man who has just lost his wife, Michael."

"Oh, to hell with it, Eddie. You know what I mean."

"I do indeed. And I do not find it either amusing or in the best of taste."

"Now, let us not quarrel." Sir Samuel might not be Eddie's intellectual equal—indeed, he had never claimed to be—but he was many years older, and at moments like this seniority was a useful adjunct to rank. "What Michael meant—and I agree—is that things have been managed with great skill and diplomacy, so far. However, we're far from the end of this matter. There will have to be a full inquiry into Mavis's death. A police inquiry."

Eddie said, "You've read Doc Duncan's report?"

"I have. It could hardly be clearer. Mavis was murdered, and every effort must be made to bring her murderer to justice."

"Couldn't we—?" Holder-Watts began.

Sir Samuel shook his head, with a slight smile. "No, Michael. I know you only want to make things more agreeable for Eddie—and indeed for all of us. But we can't have any sort of cover-up. The case must be investigated and the truth established."

"Very noble, I'm sure, Sam," said Michael Holder-Watts, with a grin, "but you're among friends here. You can speak your mind. You don't seriously suggest allowing some flatfoot from the District of Columbia Homicide Squad to—"

"No, I do not suggest that." Sir Samuel's voice was quiet but very emphatic.

Michael exhaled, in relief. "Ah. That's good."

"Now, don't misunderstand me, either of you," Sir Samuel continued. "I'm opposed to calling in the U.S. authorities for several reasons. First, there's the question of precedent. We may be one of the newest and smallest sovereign states in the world, but our Embassy is Tampican territory, just as much as the British is British, or the Russian is Russian. It would create an unpopular and potentially dangerous precedent to call in the police force of the host nation. Then, there is the delicate situation between Tampica and the United States regarding the naval base."

"You mean, they won't pay up?"

The Prime Minister looked at Holder-Watts quizzically over the glowing tip of his cigar. "You have a deceptive way of oversimplifying complicated matters, Michael," he said. "You understand the situation very well, and I do not propose to insult your intelligence by expounding its finer points. The fact remains that, in view of the negotiations in progress between the two governments, and the upcoming talks with the leaders of the Senate Committee, it is highly desirable to keep Tampican affairs in Washington strictly under Tampican control. And there's the rub."

"What you mean is that however impressive it may look on paper, our police force boils down to a collection of traffic cops, headed by Sergeant Bartholomew and his bicycle," said Michael.

Sir Samuel said, seriously, "We must not forget our Commissioner, Major-General Forsyth." Even Eddie Ironmonger smiled at that, and the Prime Minister added, "Very well. Let us agree that the good Major-General's function is purely decorative. For a man of eighty-five, he holds himself as upright on parade as he did at Sandhurst, and his plumed hat is impressive on ceremonial occasions. Nevertheless—where does that leave us?"

"Up a gum tree," remarked Holder-Watts succinctly.

"Little did I think," said Sir Samuel, "that so soon after independence I should be looking back nostalgically to the good old days."

"What do you mean?"

"Simply that a month ago I would have been on the telephone to the High Commissioner in London by now, and a team from Scotland Yard would have been on its way. You remember the golf-course murders, ten years ago? The Chief Inspector they sent out was a most efficient man. Ah, well—no use trying to call back the past."

Sir Edward Ironmonger was leaning forward, his hands on his knees. He said, softly, "By God, Sam, I believe you've got it."

"Got it? Got what?"

"The answer. There's absolutely nothing to prevent us from calling in Scotland Yard this time."

"Don't be ridiculous, Eddie." Michael spoke sharply, and with displeasure, dropping any semblance of respect. "Out of the question. Tampica is a sovereign state."

"Of course she is, Michael." Sir Edward sounded mildly amused. "I would remind you that I am a lawyer, while you are a diplomat. Therefore, in some limited spheres, my experience and judgment may be superior to yours."

The Prime Minister was clearly intrigued. "You think we could do it, Eddie? It would certainly be the best solution."

"Of course we can do it. Nobody seems to dispute that if we wanted to we could ask for help from the American police. The fact that the crime occurred in Washington is neither here nor there—as you pointed out, Sam, a Tampican Embassy anywhere in the world is still Tampica. If we don't have the resources to carry out the investigation ourselves, we can turn for assistance to anybody we choose. We are newly independent and a member of the Commonwealth. It seems to me perfectly natural that we should ask for co-operation from the Mother Country. There's no political objection, I take it, Sam?"

"None whatsoever. Our relationship with Great Britain has never been better. She is delighted to have got us off her hands, and we are delighted to have lost our sense of inferiority towards her. It seems to me an excellent plan."

"Well, I disagree." Holder-Watts sounded sulky. "You talk about flat-footed Washington cops—or even Sergeant Bartholomew, with or without his bicycle. Do you think you'll get anything more sophisticated or discreet out of Victoria Street? This whole thing will need to be handled with extraordinary tact—especially by a non-American investigator. Surely you see that?" He appealed to Eddie.

"Certainly I do." Sir Edward was at his most urbane, most Oxford-high-table. "And for that reason I suggest, Sam, that you make a personal request for an individual, by name. I ate my dinners in Gray's Inn, in the company of one Michael Barker, who is now an eminent Queen's Counsel specializing in police prosecutions. It was through him that I made the acquaintance of a C.I.D. Inspector who is altogether out of the usual run. A very..." he hesitated, "a very superior person."

"Oh God," said Michael. "Spare us Lord Peter Wimsey."

"You misunderstand me, Michael," Sir Edward's calm good humor was quite unflappable. "This man is not an aristocrat by birth. On the other hand, he appears to be perfectly at ease with people at all social levels. He is a genuine person, and he is also extremely good at his job. I think you'll enjoy meeting him, Michael. His name is Henry Tibbett."

Since the next day was Sunday, everybody felt entitled to a little relaxation. Sir Edward slept late, sunned himself on the terrace, and after lunch went down to enjoy a swim in the limpid, reef-protected waters of the Prime Minister's private bay. He had not been in the sea for more than ten minutes when he was hailed from the beach by Howard, Sir Samuel's personal attendant. Reluctantly, he struck out for the shore, and was soon wading up the beach, shaking the water off his shining black skin.

Howard said, apologetically, "Very sorry, Sir Edward. Sir Samuel would appreciate it if you could spare him a moment." He picked up Eddie's beach towel from the sand, and held it out. "In his study...I've brought the Jeep to take you up. Very sorry, sir."

Eddie grinned as he briskly toweled himself dry. "Not your fault, Howard. O.K., let's go."

Sir Samuel was at his desk in the shady study overlooking the sea when Eddie arrived a few minutes later. Both men were informally dressed in pale, open-necked shirts and cotton slacks, which accentuated their ebony skins. They looked cool and comfortable in a way which few Europeans ever achieved in Tampica's climate.

Sir Samuel said, "Come in and sit down, Eddie. Sorry to disturb your swim. I have good news."

"What's that?"

"I have just been speaking on the telephone to our High Commissioner in London. I first contacted him at his home early this morning—of course, there is a five-hour time difference, so he was already up and about when we were still in bed. I inquired about your Henry Tibbett—who is now a Chief Superintendent, it seems. I told him about the delicacy of the mission. Now he has called me back."

"And the answer is 'yes'?"

"Better than that. It appears that Tibbett and his wife have friends—former neighbors from London—who live in Washington, only a few blocks from the Embassy in Georgetown. Their name is Colville—he is an economist at the World Bank. Strictly nonpolitical. It would be a very natural thing for the Tibbetts to pay a visit to the Colvilles, staying as house-guests."

"But—" Eddie was about to protest. The Prime Minister held up his hand.

"Yes, yes, I know. The inquiry must be seen to be made. Very well. We will send Sergeant Bartholomew from here to the Embassy in Washington—I have already arranged for his immediate promotion to Inspector. It sounds more impressive. We will announce that an officer of Tampica's C.I.D. is arriving to take charge of the case. Meanwhile, Bartholomew will have full authority to co-operate in every way with Tibbett, who will in fact be in charge of the investigation. Anything of a technical nature, like chemical analysis and so on, will be handled here by Doc Duncan. Tibbett will bring certain technical kit—but I feel that he is more likely to solve the problem by—how shall I put it?—by in-depth interviews."

"Exactly," said Sir Edward, who had vainly been trying to get a word in. "And on what authority is he to go round interviewing people? It won't just be Embassy staff, you know. Remember that there was a big reception going on that evening."

"There is no need to remind me, Eddie. Tibbett may interview whomever he likes. If it seems desirable, the interview will be arranged through Sergeant—I beg your pardon, Inspector Bartholomew, who will explain that Tibbett is acting officially at the request of Lady Ironmonger's English parents. By the way, I am arranging for them to prolong their stay at Pirate's Cave. I fancy they will have no objections."

"But—"

"If there is any trouble, or if any of the people concerned make a fuss or start invoking diplomatic privilege, I rely on you to handle the situation, Eddie. They will hardly refuse to talk to Tibbett if you ask them to, personally."

Slowly, a smile spread across Sir Edward's face. He said, "You're an old rogue, Sam, but I don't see why it shouldn't work. The case will be in Tampican hands, the Americans will not be involved in any way, the British will not be involved officially, and still we'll have the benefit of one of the best detective brains at the Yard. I congratulate you."

"No, no. The credit is yours, Eddie. It's just a question of knowing the right people." The two men smiled at each other. They were old friends. Then Sir Samuel said, "Michael has gone over to Sugar Mill Bay to have tea with Lucy Pontefract-

Deacon. You'd better explain the situation to him when he gets back. I'm afraid he may not be very pleased."

"I shall lose no sleep over that," replied Eddie.

"Good. And then I suggest that you both do your packing and get away on the night flight from Antigua. You will be needed in Washington as soon as possible."

CHAPTER SEVEN

THE JUMBO JET from London arrived at Dulles International Airport a few minutes earlier than the DC-10 from Antigua, but since the larger plane took longer to unload, the two sets of passengers dead-heated through Customs and out into the breezy sunshine. There was a sizable posse of journalists and photographers waiting, and it converged upon the huge, handsome figure of Inspector Bartholomew.

"Have you a statement to make, Inspector?"

"Was it murder?"

"Have you any suspects?"

"Hold it there, Inspector!"

"This way, Inspector!"

None of the pressmen even noticed the slight, sandy-haired man in the crumpled mackintosh who, with his plumpish dark-haired wife, had just arrived from London. They were greeted warmly by a slim, fair woman with an English accent, and whisked quietly away in her modest Volkswagen toward Washington, just like any other undistinguished travelers.

Meanwhile, Inspector Bartholomew held up an enormous black hand. He looked grave. The press fell more or less silent. He said, "I have no statement to make at this stage, ladies and gentlemen, except to say that the possibility of foul play in Lady Ironmonger's death cannot be ruled out. You will be kept informed as my investigations continue."

Some of the more persistent journalists seemed disinclined to leave it at that, but Inspector Bartholomew easily shouldered his way through the crowd to the waiting limousine. He climbed in amid more flashing of cameras, closed the door and relaxed thankfully as the car moved off.

Michael Holder-Watts had been less than fair when he jeered at Sergeant Bartholomew and his bicycle. It was true that the role of the Tampican police force was mainly ornamental. Officers were recruited on the basis of impressive physical statistics rather than mental ability, and with their gleaming white helmets and red-blue-and-gold uniforms, they were one of the island's biggest tourist attractions in every sense.

Major-General Forsyth (Ret'd), late of the Loyal Royal Loamshires, had done a fine job of instilling British parade-ground smartness and precision into the Tampican police, and, although no intellectual giant himself, he had had enough experience of judging men to recognize ability when he saw it. It was he who, some months before independence, had picked Robert Bartholomew out of the ranks of uniformed beefcake and sent him to London for an intensive course in criminal investigation. Constable Bartholomew had done extremely well on the course, and had returned with the rank of Sergeant as the only qualified C.I.D. officer in the Tampican police force. It was perfectly true that his normal form of transportation on the island was a bicycle, and that he had no facilities for conducting a full-scale murder investigation. Nevertheless, he was by no means a nonentity, and he looked forward with keen anticipation to working with Chief Superintendent Henry Tibbett.

His arrival in Washington gave a fillip to public interest in the case. Photographs of Inspector Bartholomew—six-feet-four and bearing a distinct resemblance to Harry Belafonte—were featured prominently in local newspapers and on television, while his remark about "foul play" gave rise to a further spate of speculative rumors. Bartholomew himself would have preferred a tight-lipped "no comment," but Sir Samuel and Sir Edward had given him his instructions, so he supposed they knew what they were about.

Now, lying back in the comfortable seat of the limousine as it sped along the airport approach motorway, Bartholomew braced himself, mentally and physically, for the encounter to come. He had never met Sir Edward personally—he knew him merely as the island's legend of the local boy who made good. Neither had he ever met Lady Ironmonger, but he was as well aware of her reputation as anybody else in Tampica. He also carried Doctor Duncan's report in his briefcase, and he had read it. Lady Ironmonger had been murdered, and he was supposed to bring her killer to justice—whoever it might be. He felt relieved that the full brunt of the investigation was supposed to fall upon Chief Superintendent Tibbett.

In the Volkswagen, Margaret Colville was saying, "It's simply marvelous to see you both again—but what's it all about? I mean, I don't flatter myself that you came all the way across the Atlantic just to see us. John's furious at missing you, but he has to be at this meeting in New York. Look over to the left—there's the Potomac River. And in a minute I'll show you the Watergate. Mind you, we've had a sensation closer to home recently—you heard about the murder of the Tampican Ambassadress? Just around the corner from us."

"Murder?" said Henry.

"Well, all right—death in suspicious circumstances. Everybody's saying it was murder. I mean, she was shot—look, there's the Watergate, that bulbous building beside the river, and beyond it is the Kennedy Center—I've got seats for us on Friday to see the New York City Ballet—what was I saying? Oh, yes—she was shot, so it must have been either suicide or murder, and nobody seems to think she was the suicidal type."

"Was she the murder victim type?" Henry asked.

"Ah, now that's an interesting question. People are saying—" Margaret broke off, as she maneuvered the car up the steep ramp from the riverside highway to the bridge. Then she added, "Why are you so curious, anyway? Professional interest?"

"Well, as a matter of fact—"

"I knew it!" said Margaret triumphantly. "I knew it was too much of a coincidence that you and Emmy should visit us just precisely now. I said so to John when he telephoned yesterday."

"I hope," said Henry, "that you haven't been saying it to anybody else."

"Of course not. Well, not really…no…"

"What does 'not really' mean?" Henry asked, with foreboding.

"Well, Ginny Schipmaker came in for coffee this morning, and of course we were talking about Lady Ironmonger, because Ginny was actually *there*, you see, and I did sort of mention that you were coming to stay and that perhaps you'd solve the crime, being at Scotland Yard and all that…" The car reached the far side of Key Bridge and turned right into M Street. "Welcome to Georgetown," said Margaret.

Soon the car had crossed Wisconsin Avenue, turned left, and was climbing toward Dumbarton Rock, up tree-lined streets and past fascinatingly assorted houses, from enormous mansions to tiny, brightly painted frame structures.

"That's the Tampican Embassy, where it happened," said Margaret suddenly. "The rather beautiful red-brick house on the left, with the flag outside it. It's still at half-mast, as you see. Now, we're just round the corner, if I can find somewhere to park…oh, good, there's a space right outside the door, just big enough for the beetle. It's a great advantage, I can slip her in where great American monsters would never fit."

She maneuvered the little car neatly into the space between a vast, gleaming Cadillac and a battered old van that had been painted in zebra stripes of vivid colors and had the words *Winnie-the-Pooh is love* daubed in white on its flanks. Looking at the three ill-assorted vehicles, Margaret said, "That about sums up Georgetown. The very rich, the penniless students and hippies, and the near-penniless..." She paused. "I can't say 'intellectuals,' can I? It sounds awful. But you know what I mean. People like us."

Henry said, "Since when has Winnie-the-Pooh been popular with hippies?"

"Oh, for quite a while now. It used to be Tolkien— *Gandalf lives* and all that. I doubt if Pooh will last much longer, though—smart advertisers are beginning to latch on to the idea, which means that the youngsters—what Marghanita Laski used to call the seminal group—will immediately drop him and find another symbol. There was a time when we thought Jesus Christ was due for a big comeback, but he's fallen a bit flat. A few months back people used to carry bumper stickers saying *Honk if you love Jesus*. Now there's a new crop saying 'Honk if you *are* Jesus'—which has quietened the streets considerably. I do love Georgetown. Now, come on in and see the doll's house."

The house was small, but also delightful. Its wooden clapboard exterior had been painted sky blue, with white window frames and black shutters, and a black-and-white front door. Inside, the kitchen, dining room and bedrooms were minuscule, but any feeling of being cramped was dissipated by the drawing-room, which occupied the whole of the first floor, and from which a little iron stairway led down into the garden.

"Only a back yard really," Margaret remarked. True, it was not large, but it was leafy and sunny and boasted two camellia trees in full bloom, one pale pink and the other deep red. Henry and Emmy felt very much at home—and Henry, for one, was extremely glad to have this friendly haven as his operational base. He foresaw considerable difficulties ahead.

For a start, his position was—to put it mildly—ambiguous. His presence was neither official nor unofficial, and although he had been assured of backing and co-operation from both the Embassy and Scotland Yard, he realized that his situation would be that of a man walking on eggs. To continue, his knowledge of the diplomatic world was rudimentary, but he was sufficiently informed to know that it was an ambience in which a raised eyebrow could spark off an incident. More eggs. Furthermore, he had met Edward Ironmonger only on a couple of fleeting occasions many years ago. He had very little idea of what to expect when he met him again.

To be sure, Michael Barker had entertained Henry with an excellent dinner and assured him that Eddie Ironmonger was still the salt of the earth, an outstanding personality, brilliant, urbane, civilized and with a great sense of humor. That, Henry felt, was all very well. Michael had known Eddie intimately when the latter had been a young, newly qualified lawyer living in a strange country. Now, he was a mature man, an ambassador, and—most importantly—a widower whose wife had died in suspicious circumstances. His acute intelligence and strong personality might well be more in evidence at the moment than his urbanity or sense of humor. Henry waited with some trepidation for the expected summons from the Tampican Embassy.

This arrived at five o'clock, in the form of a telephone call from a gentle-voiced female who identified herself as the Ambassador's secretary. Sir Edward would be pleased if Chief Superintendent Tibbett could spare him a little time that evening. Perhaps he could call at the Embassy in about half-an-hour? Henry replied, not quite truthfully, that he would be delighted to do so.

Sir Edward Ironmonger was waiting in his study. Henry barely recognized the handsome black giant of a man, whose impeccable upper-class English accent seemed somehow incongruous. The room itself—indeed the whole house—told Henry a lot about the person Ironmonger had become over the years.

The furniture and décor were too individual and nonhomog-
enous to be the work of a professional: this was the selection of
somebody who both knew and cared about fine and beautiful
things. A strong character, something of a perfectionist, a man
who knew his own mind.

"My dear Tibbett, I am extremely glad to see you again
after all these years." Henry's hand was engulfed in a huge,
powerful grip. "My congratulations on your promotion. Do sit
down. May I offer you a drink?"

Sir Edward poured two glasses of pale dry sherry from a
bar housed in an antique tallboy, gave one to Henry, and sat
down at the desk. After some polite small talk about mutual
friends in London, he said, "Well, to get to business. This is a
very sensitive matter, as I am sure you realize. A little later on,
I'll introduce you to Inspector Bartholomew. He's already been
interviewing members of the staff here—he should have some
reports for you. Before that, however, I would like to have a few
words with you alone, if you are agreeable?"

Henry murmured acquiescence, and Ironmonger went on.
"First of all, I want to make it absolutely clear that this matter
must be pursued to the utmost and solved—no matter where
the chips may fall, as they say," he added with a wry smile.
"There has been too much covering-up in this city. You have
read Dr. Duncan's report? Then you know that it is virtually
certain that my wife was murdered. I want her killer brought
to justice—no matter who it may be. You understand that?"

"I do, Sir Edward."

"All the same, some things must be said, in fairness." The
Ambassador hesitated. "My wife, Tibbett, was not a typical
ambassadress." ·

Henry smiled. "Is there such a thing?"

Ironmonger returned the smile. "Since I've been here,"
he said, "I've realized that they come in all shapes, sizes and
colors. However, most of them have certain things in common.
They are natives of their husbands' countries. They come
from upper-class families, often with a long tradition of public

service. They have spent years in more junior Foreign Service positions, and they know the *mores* of that world. They recognize each other by a subtle sort of radar. They do not like it when their ranks are infiltrated by an outsider."

Ironmonger stood up and walked over to the window, his back half turned to Henry. He said, "You will hear a great deal about my wife during the next few days, Tibbett, and most of it will be unpleasant. I merely want to give you a little of...of the other side of the picture."

Henry said nothing. Sir Edward gazed out at the garden. Then he squared his powerful shoulders and went on. "You will be told that Mavis was common and vulgar. That is largely true. She escaped from the vulgarity of suburban gentility into the commonness and pseudo-glamour of the exploitation of physical attraction. The wonder is that she remained so...so fresh and spontaneous. You will be told that she had many lovers. That is quite correct. She was too vital a person to be satisfied with just one partner. I knew about the others, of course. Or most of them. I think. But my relationship with Mavis was something different and special. I was her husband. Nobody ever really understood that."

There was a silence. Ironmonger, who had seemed almost to be talking to himself, suddenly drained his glass and turned to face Henry. In a hard voice he went on, "You will be told that Mavis was an alcoholic. That is totally untrue. Mavis loved life, and living. She loved parties and people. If you like, her judgment was sometimes poor. She never knew when to stop, with the result that sometimes she drank too much. I'm not attempting to deny that. But she certainly was not an alcoholic, and she wasn't being treated medically for that condition. You understand?"

"Dr. Duncan's report—" Henry began.

"I am not questioning it. It is up to you to find an explanation. I only know that my wife was not being treated for alcoholism." Ironmonger paused. Then, with an obvious effort, he said, "You will also be told that Mavis was a drag on my career. That is probably true. Had I been married to a woman of whom the Establishment approved, I might very well be Tampica's prime minister. I want you to understand that I'm well aware of all the facts that I've pointed out to you, Tibbett. I also want you to understand that I loved my wife, and I have no regrets about having married her. If other people choose to have regrets on my behalf, I really can't help it. Well, is there anything you want to say to me?"

Henry said, "Only that it occurs to me, Sir Edward, that you may well be Tampica's next prime minister."

For a moment, Ironmonger's face darkened with anger, and he glared at Henry with a frightening glimpse of violence in his eyes. Then, abruptly, he smiled. "Thank you, Tibbett. I see that we understand each other. You are quite right, of course. On the face of it, I had a strong motive to get rid of my wife, and there's no particular reason why you should believe me when I tell you the contrary. I won't even ask whether you do. I can only hope that your investigations will clear me."

"I have the same hope, Sir Edward," said Henry. For a moment, the two men looked straight at each other. Then, in a different tone, the Ambassador said, "And now you should talk to Bartholomew." He pressed a bell on his desk, and Dorabella came in, quickly and quietly. "Chief Superintendent Tibbett, this is my secretary, Miss Hamilton. Dorabella, please take Mr. Tibbett to see Inspector Bartholomew. My dear Tibbett, it has been a great pleasure to renew our acquaintance. Good luck."

Again the huge hand was extended, and engulfed Henry's. Henry said, "You've been very kind and helpful, Sir Edward."

"I hope to be more so in the future. If you have any questions to ask of me, don't hesitate. Dorabella will always arrange an interview. And I imagine that you may want to visit Tampica at some stage. That will be easy to arrange. Just let us know what facilities you need and we'll do our best to supply them."

The Ambassador gave Henry's hand a final, agonizing squeeze, and then relinquished it. The interview was over. Henry followed Dorabella out into the hall and across to the small library where Inspector Bartholomew was waiting.

The two men got along well together from the start. Before leaving London, Henry had looked up Bartholomew's record from his C.I.D. course, and had been impressed by the Tampican's obvious ability and common sense: now, face to face, he saw that these virtues were coupled with modesty, frankness and great charm. Bartholomew knew all about Chief Superintendent Tibbett's reputation, and was prepared to be overawed and even a little resentful. He was instantly disarmed by the small, sandy-haired man with dark blue eyes and diffident manner, who was obviously eager to tap Bartholomew's knowledge of Tampica and of the principal characters in the case.

Bartholomew's thumbnail sketches interested Henry particularly, because he judged them to represent the view of most intelligent Tampicans who were not on terms of personal contact with the people concerned—that is, they represented public images rather than inside knowledge.

It was quickly made clear that Eddie Ironmonger was a folk hero to the islanders. "Our greatest man," said Bartholomew earnestly. "He will lead our country one day, you will see. He is an inspiration to us all. He was born in a slum, you know, the son of a poor fisherman. He has made himself what he is, by his own efforts alone." He paused, then added, "With the help of Bishop Barrington, of course." He smiled at Henry. "We are independent now, and we are proud of it—it is the independence of a son who has grown to manhood. The British government was our mother, if you like—sometimes a stern and even harsh one, but individual British people, like the Bishop and Mrs. Barrington and Doctor Duncan—they are our uncles and aunts. We shall not forget what they did for Tampica."

Henry smiled back. "You put it very nicely, Inspector. I understand."

"Even people like Mr. Nelson," Bartholomew went on, "cannot bring themselves to dislike the Bishop."

"Mr. Nelson? You mean, the First Secretary here?"

"That's right. He has been a great fighter for independence, and he had no good words for the British government. Yet he regards the Barringtons almost as his own family. He was at their home when he heard the news of Lady Ironmonger's death."

"At their home? You mean, they live in Washington?"

"Oh, yes. They were at the reception and had invited Mr. Nelson to dinner afterwards, so Miss Hamilton tells me."

"And what about Mr. and Mrs. Holder-Watts?"

"They are respected. I would not say that they are loved."

"And Lady Ironmonger?"

There was a considerable pause. At last, Bartholomew said, "She was a very beautiful lady. She enjoyed life; she laughed a lot. We Tampicans laugh a lot. We understand. Also, she was greatly loved by Sir Edward."

Henry said, "Inspector Bartholomew, this is a police investigation. We must speak plainly."

"Yes, sir." Bartholomew's face had suddenly taken on a wooden look.

"For God's sake, man," said Henry, "the wretched woman was murdered. There must have been a reason."

"None that I know of, sir. It is a great mystery."

"And likely to remain one, if you maintain that attitude," said Henry. Bartholomew's mouth set in a stubborn line. He said nothing. "Oh, all right. Play it your own way, but it'll do no good in the end. Now, have you got the guest list of the reception?"

By the time he had concluded his talk with Inspector Bartholomew and walked back to Margaret's house, Henry was feeling depressed. He carried in his pocket a summary of the interviews already conducted with Embassy staff by Bartholomew, and also a list containing over a hundred and fifty names. Since nearly all of these were "Mr. and Mrs.," there must have been almost three hundred people at the Tampican reception, and any one of them might have been responsible for the death of Mavis Ironmonger.

Henry had, however, marked some names for personal interviews. These included Winston Nelson, Dorabella Hamilton, Bishop and Mrs. Barrington, Mr. and Mrs. Holder-Watts and Mr. and Mrs. Otis Schipmaker.

Margaret had given Henry a key to the little blue house, so that he could come and go as he wished. As he let himself into the narrow hallway, he was greeted by a wave of laughter from the drawing-room, and hesitated at the foot of the stairs. He could distinguish Emmy's voice, and Margaret's, but there was also a masculine voice taking part in the lively conversation. Margaret must have a visitor, and the last thing Henry wanted was to be dragged into a social occasion. However, there was no way of reaching the sanctuary of his bedroom except through the drawing-room. He decided that he would stay for the minimum time required by courtesy, and then escape to the upper floor. He climbed the stairs.

"Ah, Henry! There you are. You've got a visitor." Margaret called as she heard his step on the stairs.

"I have?" Henry stopped, taken aback, then came up into the room.

Sitting on the big sofa, flanked by Margaret and Emmy, was an elderly man with a shock of white hair and a lined face burnt brown as a chestnut. He wore an ancient and dilapidated suit. He rose to his feet as Henry approached, held out a gnarled but still beautiful hand, and said, "Chief Superintendent Tibbett, I presume? Forgive this intrusion, sir. I'm Doctor Duncan." Before Henry could reply, he added, "Twice in a week. Wouldn't have believed it. I've traveled in an aeroplane exactly three times in seventy years—and twice in four days! Don't tell Eddie."

Henry said, "I'm delighted to see you, sir. But I wasn't expecting—"

"Of course you weren't. Eddie has no idea I'm here, and in the ordinary way, nothing would have got me into that infernal machine again. But Sam told me you'd be here, and I thought I ought to come. How is Eddie?"

"Very unhappy," said Henry.

"Of course." Doctor Duncan turned to Margaret and Emmy. "Dear ladies, your delightful company has more than compensated for the discomfort of the journey from Tampica, but my time is short, and I must talk to the Chief Superintendent privately. If you would be so kind—?"

"Of course. We'll go and get supper..." Margaret and Emmy disappeared downstairs in a flurry of laughter. Dr. Duncan watched them go, beaming. "Charming," he said. "Enchanting. Both your wife and her friend. You are a very lucky man, sir."

"I know it," said Henry.

The doctor shook his head. "It's a lottery," he said. "Not everybody can win. I did." He sat down again, and looked at Henry. "I think we should have a talk."

CHAPTER EIGHT

HENRY GRINNED AT Dr. Duncan. "Where shall we start?" he said.

"Well, now," said Duncan, "that's always a problem, isn't it? However, since you are a policeman, and accustomed to conducting interviews, why don't you ask the first question? Like...why have you come here, Dr. Duncan?"

"That's a good question," said Henry, "but it wouldn't be my first one."

"It wouldn't? Then what would?"

Henry said, "Why did you look for disulfiram in Lady Ironmonger's body?"

There was a pause. Then Duncan shook his head with a wry smile, and said, "They told me you were a clever man."

"I don't think," said Henry, "that it required any great brilliance to ask that question. I'm no pathologist, but I suppose I'm more knowledgeable about autopsies than the general public is. Most people seem to think that a post-mortem examination is some sort of magic process, like an X-ray, which will inevitably show up anything and everything that was wrong with the deceased. I know that nothing will be found unless it's looked for. In a case of suspected poisoning, of course, tests will be made for every sort of toxin. But here, you had a bullet wound in the head—an obvious cause of death. Something must have made you look further, and I have a feeling that when you tell me what it was, you will also be telling me why you came here today."

Duncan hesitated. Then he said, "I was on the lookout for a dose or overdose of some sort of drug because of inconsistencies in the story I was told." As Henry seemed about to speak, he raised his hand in a silencing gesture. "Not inconsistencies of fact. Inconsistencies of character. You see, Mr. Tibbett, I know all these people very well. Known them all their lives. Except Mavis, of course, but I've known her ever since she came to Tampica as Eddie's wife. I felt certain from the beginning that Mavis had been killed—by somebody who had an ingenious idea for committing an undetectable murder but who did not know her very well."

"You are talking about Lady Ironmonger?"

"Yes. She was not the suicidal type."

"And yet," Henry said, "I understand that several people in what I might call the inner circle of the Embassy were convinced that she had killed herself, until you made your report."

"Exactly." The doctor took a gulp of his drink. "Winnie Nelson and Dorabella and Eleanor Holder-Watts. They all hated Mavis, and they all jumped at the suicide idea, for different reasons. Oh, I did quite a bit of nosing around and talking to people in my short stay here. All the reasons are wrong and the results of inflamed emotions."

"Would you explain, Doctor?"

"Certainly. All this is in strict confidence, of course. Let's take Dorabella first. She has been in love with Eddie for years. She hated and resented Mavis, and leapt at the idea that Mavis—for some extraordinary and undefined reason—planned a suicide during the reception in order to embarrass

Eddie and wreck his career. This notion is patently idiotic and illogical, but then, so is love. Or so they tell me."

He paused, then went on, "Winnie Nelson hated Mavis because he was, and is, fanatically devoted to Eddie. He knew that she deceived him—if that's the word, although I don't think Eddie was ever deceived—with a number of other men. He especially resented her liaison with Michael Holder-Watts, who is Winnie's career rival, and who also stands for the old colonial order. I have also heard it rumored, Tibbett—and I must warn you that I am a great old rumor-hound—that Winnie was one of the very few men with whom Mavis refused to go to bed. He therefore found it very opportune to impute her suicide to Holder-Watts's callous treatment of her. Illogical, again, but so is fanaticism.

"Eleanor's is an altogether simpler case. She was violently jealous of Mavis's affair with Michael, chiefly because she felt it humiliated her. Now, a suggestion of murder might bring the whole thing out into the light of a public inquiry, whereas a suicide not only removed her rival, but did so quietly. So, like Dorabella, she opted for the notion that Mavis had committed suicide out of spite and a desire to 'get her own back.' Also illogical, but so is jealousy. I realized at once that none of these stories was viable and that Mavis had probably been killed."

"I still don't get the disulfiram connection," Henry said.

"I'm coming to that, young man. Be patient." Dr. Duncan took another drink and mused a little. "Of course, Mavis was a pushover for murder. She was not, as far as I know, an alcoholic—but she liked to drink and she had a weak head for liquor. I think it was Ernest Hemingway who remarked rather bitchily that both Scott and Zelda Fitzgerald would pass out after even a moderate amount of alcohol—moderate by Hemingway's standards, that is—in order to avoid a difficult situation. Mavis was very much like that. If someone had been feeding her vodka that evening, and she suddenly realized she was getting drunk, her instinctive defense mechanism would be to pass out. After which, it would be simple for her murderer to shoot her and stage a suicide. On this assumption, I expected the autopsy to show that she had drunk a considerable amount. To my surprise, there was very little alcohol. About the equivalent of one stiffish drink. And yet, I was told that she could barely stand when Eleanor got her upstairs."

"You mean, she was pretending to be drunk?"

"That was a possible explanation, and would have reinforced the suicide theory—but I didn't believe it."

"You mean," Henry said, "that Lady Ironmonger wouldn't have committed suicide under any circumstances whatsoever?"

"I didn't say that. I can imagine one such circumstance."

"What would that be?"

"If she had been incurably ill, or was about to lose her beauty—or both. I almost hoped to find indications of cancer or some other fatal disease. But no. Mavis was perfectly healthy when she was shot. So, if her passing out was not faked, it must have been chemically induced by something other than alcohol. Naturally, disulfiram suggested itself. You know the stuff?"

"I've heard of it," Henry said. "And naturally I boned up on it when I heard your report. I presumed that Lady Ironmonger was being treated for alcoholism, and that somebody who knew about it slipped some vodka into her fruit juice, knowing that it would have a drastic effect."

"That's what I thought," said Duncan. "And now we are getting near the answer to the second question. Why I came all this way to talk to you." He paused. "Eddie Ironmonger is almost like a son to me, Tibbett. It would break my heart to see his career smashed and his reputation shattered. Nevertheless, I have to tell you what I know. First of all, Eddie has emphatically denied to me that Mavis was having any such treatment."

"He might not have known," Henry pointed out.

"I suggested that. He at once replied that she had been in the habit of drinking her usual amount of alcohol during the last days of her life—which would have been impossible if she had been taking regular doses of disulfiram. It is also a sad but undeniable fact that, from the point of view of his career, Eddie is very much better off without Mavis."

"This is all very interesting, Doctor," Henry said, "but it still doesn't explain why you made this journey to see me."

"I'm coming to that. You know that Eddie sent for me, so that I could make an examination and take the body back to Tampica?"

"Yes, I know that."

"The room where Mavis died was locked. Eddie himself had the key and let me in. He assured me that the room was sealed. As far as I know—and I admit I cannot be sure—nobody had been in there except Eddie himself, Michael Holder-Watts and the American doctor who certified death. I am an inquisitive old man, Tibbett. While I was in there alone, I not only examined the body. I also snooped in Mavis's bathroom. And in the cabinet, I found a half-full bottle of a well-known brand of disulfiram tablets—Alcodym. It didn't look as though anybody had tried to hide it—it was just standing there on the shelf. You will now understand why it was not difficult for me to decide to look for that particular drug in the body, and why I felt I must talk to you."

"You mean that Sir Edward was lying?"

"That's for you to decide, Tibbett. At least, you know the facts now. I would suggest you search the room as soon as possible. I didn't touch the bottle of tablets. It will be interesting to see if it is still there."

"And from this you infer—?"

Duncan stood up, slowly. "I infer nothing, young man. That's your job. I've told you what I came to tell you because I did not care to say it over the telephone. Also, I wanted to meet you. The futures of many of my friends are in your hands. I feel sure they are secure."

"Thank you, sir."

"And now, if you would be kind enough to call me a cab, I shall return to the airport and board that dreadful machine once again. I hope that you will come to Tampica. I look forward to meeting you again."

Dr. Duncan was still on the doorstep, taking obvious pleasure in kissing both Margaret and Emmy good-bye, when Henry contacted Inspector Bartholomew by telephone.

"The bedroom? Well, as a matter of fact, no, Chief Superintendent. Sir Edward has the key, and I was waiting until you... I was just packing up to go home...yes, in a hotel round the corner... I really don't know, I think he's going to some sort of a reception...yes, I think it would be best if you spoke to her..."

Dorabella was displeased. "It is six o'clock, Chief Superintendent," she said, as tartly as her gentle Caribbean voice could manage. "Sir Edward is about to leave the Embassy. I really don't think I can—"

At this moment, she was interrupted by Ironmonger's deep voice. He must have been listening on another line. "Tibbett? What is it? You wanted to speak with me?"

"Yes, Sir Edward. I wondered if it would be possible for me to examine Lady Ironmonger's bedroom this evening."

There was a tiny pause. Then Ironmonger said, "Of course, my dear fellow. No problem at all. I have the key—I intended to give it to you this afternoon, but I'm afraid it slipped my mind. Can you come over at once? I have to leave in a few minutes, but I would like to hand the key over to you personally. You understand?"

"Perfectly, Sir Edward."

Edward Ironmonger was waiting in the hallway of the Embassy when Henry arrived. He made an impressive figure in evening dress with decorations—which included several colorful ribbons bestowed by the new-born state of Tampica, as well as several more restrained and more highly prized honors from the United Kingdom.

He said, "Ah, there you are, Tibbett. I have the key here. I'll come up with you."

The curtains in the bedroom were drawn and the windows closed, creating a warm, scented and yet depressing atmosphere, like a deserted love nest. Mavis's bed had been neatly covered with a clean white sheet, the pillows plumped to remove the indentation where her lifeless head had rested. However, the revolver still lay on the lime-green carpet and so did the angora-cat nightdress case, each still surrounded by blurred chalk marks.

Sir Edward said, "Everything has been left exactly as it was found, Tibbett. That is to say—as it was when I first saw it after my wife's death. Mr. Holder-Watts was the first to come in and find the body, but there's no reason to think he tampered with anything. The gun is mine. My secretary noticed earlier in the day that it was missing from my desk drawer, but did not think of remarking on it, as we had been discussing keeping it up here. This you know, of course."

"I've read Inspector Bartholomew's preliminary reports," said Henry.

"These marks," Ironmonger went on, "show where Mavis's right hand and foot touched the ground. She was lying on her back, on the right-hand side of her bed, with her right arm and leg sprawled over the edge. You see that the gun is in the position where it would naturally have fallen if she had been holding it in her right hand. I've no doubt at all that you will find her fingerprints on it. The scene was set with great care. I expect you'll want to take the gun away with you."

Ironmonger's voice was completely impersonal, but Henry had the impression of deep emotion held on an almost impossibly tight rein. He said, "Yes, Sir Edward, I'll take it eventually. Inspector Bartholomew and I will do some fingerprinting later on, and meanwhile I've brought a camera. I'd like to get pictures before anything is moved. For the moment, though, could I take a look in the bathroom?"

"The bathroom?" Ironmonger sounded faintly amused. "Which one?"

"There's more than one?"

"Yes, indeed. That door over there leads to my dressing room and bathroom. Mavis's bathroom is through this door here."

"I'll look at them both, if I may," Henry said.

"Of course, my dear fellow. Look at anything you like." Sir Edward glanced at his watch. "Forgive me, I really must go. Here is the key. Please keep it. Don't give it to anybody. You understand?"

He handed Henry the big old-fashioned key and went out quickly, closing the door behind him. Henry slipped his small flash-bulb camera out of its case, and began to photograph the room systematically—the empty bed, the gun, the nylon cat, the chalk marks. He took great care not to touch anything. Then he went into Lady Ironmonger's bathroom.

It smelt overpoweringly feminine—scent and bath essence and expensive soap and dusting powder had left their mingled fragrances hanging like smog in the air. The fluffy pink bath mat was rumpled and spattered with talcum powder, and a filmy white negligée had been tossed carelessly onto the carpet. Obviously, Mavis had taken a bath before dressing for the reception, and Henry remembered that she had been late getting downstairs—according to Inspector Bartholomew's report on interviews with the Embassy staff. There had been no chance to clean up the bathroom after her.

Stepping with extreme care so as to avoid the bath mat and the traces of powder on the carpet, Henry reached the hand basin and very delicately, with a handkerchief over his fingers, opened the door of the bathroom cabinet. Not, he reflected, that these precautions were of the least use. Dr. Duncan, that inquisitive old man, had already marched into the bathroom, as a masculine footprint clearly visible in the powder on the mat bore witness. His fingerprints would be all over the handle of the cabinet door, masking any others which might have been useful. Henry had taken a liking to the doctor, and in one way his curiosity had been invaluable. In others, however, it was a great nuisance. The cupboard door swung open.

Inside, on a couple of glass shelves, stood a bottle of aspirin tablets, some Alka-Seltzer, a jar of mouthwash and a supply of contraceptive pills. There were also some assorted face creams and lotions, a spare tube of toothpaste and a bottle of cough syrup. Not only was there no sign of Alcodym, but no sleeping pills, no tranquilizers, no pep pills. The contents of the cupboard suggested a normal, unneurotic woman with no problems other than avoiding unwanted pregnancies and the occasional morning-after headache. The fact remained, however, that a bottle of Alcodym had been removed since Dr. Duncan visited the bathroom—in which case, other things might also have disappeared. Henry took some more photographs and then went downstairs, having carefully locked the bedroom door behind him.

He was greeted in the hall by Dorabella, who did not appear to be in a very good temper. "Mr. Tibbett, I believe you have the key to Lady Ironmonger's bedroom."

"That's right. Sir Edward gave it to me."

Dorabella gave a little sigh of impatience and annoyance. "He is so absent-minded sometimes. I am supposed to be in charge of that key. May I have it, please?"

"No, I'm afraid not, Miss Hamilton," said Henry agreeably.

They faced each other—eye to eye. In fact, with her wedge-heeled shoes, Dorabella stood a good inch taller than Henry. He said, "Sir Edward specifically asked me to keep it. I'm afraid I can't give it to anybody without his consent." Mentally, he added, "Nor with it, come to that." Aloud, he added, "I really can't see that there's any reason for you to go into that room, Miss Hamilton. Inspector Bartholomew and I will be busy there tomorrow, and nothing must be touched."

"There are some of her things—"

"When the police investigation is finished," Henry said, "you'll be able to go in as much as you like. But not until then."

Dorabella tossed her head. "Oh, well, if you're going to take that attitude... Sir Edward will be very angry, you'll see."

"I don't think so."

Dorabella sniffed, and swiveled on her two-inch cork wedges.

Henry said, "Tell me about the chalk marks, Miss Hamilton."

Dorabella, who had started on an angry and ostentatious mince back toward the study, suddenly stood still. Then she wheeled to face Henry, and said, "What chalk?"

"In the bedroom," Henry said. "Chalk marks have been made on the carpet to indicate the position of various objects. I wondered who made them, and when—was it you?"

There was a tiny hesitation, and then Dorabella said, "It's not chalk. It's talcum powder. It was all we could find."

"We?"

"Eddie—I mean, Sir Edward—and me. As soon as Michael...told us...he—Eddie, I mean—he ran up the stairs on his own. He told me to wait. He must have been in there about two or three minutes. Then he came out and beckoned me to come up." Dorabella had forgotten her irritation. She was reliving an experience which had moved her deeply. "He said...'It's true, Dorrie...she's dead...you'd better come up...' I felt sort of numb. I can't even remember going up the stairs. The next thing, I was just standing there, looking down at her. She didn't look dead, somehow. Just as though she'd passed out. I thought she'd look ugly, but she didn't. Not even then."

Dorabella paused, sniffed, and pulled herself together. When she spoke again, it was in her calm, efficient, secretarial voice. "Sir Edward pointed out that we ought to mark the position of the gun, and so on. He asked me to find something that would make marks on the carpet. So I went into the bathroom and looked in the cupboard—I thought there might be some tinted foundation lotion, or something like that—but Lady Ironmonger didn't use it. All I could find was the talcum powder, so I brought it, and we outlined the gun, and the nightdress case, and Lady Ironmonger's hand and foot—the ones that were touching the carpet. Then Sir Edward told me to go and telephone for the doctor."

"Mr. Holder-Watts hadn't done so already?" Henry asked.

"No. He was going to, but Eddie—Sir Edward—stopped him. He was quite sharp about it." Henry thought he detected a note of satisfaction in Dorabella's voice. "He wanted to see Lady Ironmonger for himself first. Then he asked *me* to telephone."

"And so you left Sir Edward alone in the bedroom?"

"Only for a minute or so. I telephoned the doctor from the study, and Sir Edward came and joined me there even before the number was answered."

"Miss Hamilton," said Henry, "when you looked through the bathroom cupboard, what did you see in it?"

"Oh—just the ordinary things."

"Can you remember what was there?"

Dorabella shook her head. "Aspirin and things. Pills...you know."

"Was there a bottle of tablets marked Alcodym?"

"No, there wasn't." To Henry's surprise, Dorabella answered quickly and decisively.

"How can you be sure?"

"I'd have certainly noticed anything—like that, Chief Superintendent. I can assure you there was no such bottle."

"How well did you know Lady Ironmonger, Miss Hamilton?" Henry asked.

Dorabella tossed her dark, curly head. "I am Sir Edward's secretary," she said. "I've never interfered in his private life."

"But surely here—with the residence and the Embassy all under the same roof—"

"I had been doing a little secretarial work for Lady Ironmonger recently," Dorabella admitted. "As a favor to Sir Edward, until we could get a social secretary. I explained to Lady Ironmonger that I was far too busy to take on any extra work permanently."

"You didn't like Lady Ironmonger very much, did you, Miss Hamilton?" Henry said it with a smile. He got an icy stare in return.

"It was not my position to like or dislike her," said Dorabella primly.

"All right, skip it. You were at the reception, of course, Miss Hamilton?"

Dorabella made a *moue.* "You can say that again. I organized it. By the time the guests started to arrive, I was exhausted. It was our first official reception, you know. It was terribly important that it should go well."

"And I gather that it did," said Henry. "Up until Lady Ironmonger's unfortunate outburst, that is."

Quietly, Dorabella said, "I shall never forgive her for that. Never. I don't care if she is dead."

"No, you don't, do you?" Henry was being deliberately provocative, and Dorabella was provoked.

"I didn't mean that. I never said I wanted her to die, and if anybody says I did, it's a lie! I simply meant that it would be utterly hypocritical if I now pretended I'd forgiven her for... what she did."

"Just what did she do, Miss Hamilton?"

"You must have heard about it, over and over."

"No, I haven't. I've only read about it in Inspector Bartholomew's report. I'd like your first-hand account."

Dorabella hesitated. "Well," she admitted, "I wasn't actually in the room at the time."

"You weren't? Where were you?"

"I was in the kitchen. There was some confusion about the serving of the hot snacks—our staff isn't very experienced, you see. When I came back to the reception, Lady Ironmonger had disappeared. It wasn't until later that I heard what had happened."

"Who told you?"

"Mr. Holder-Watts. But as soon as I saw she had gone, I could guess."

"Guess what?"

"That she was drunk," said Dorabella, with deep distaste.

"What made you so sure of that?"

"Well...look what she did...what she said to poor Mr. Finkelstein..."

"But you didn't actually see or hear—"

"No. But it was all around the room in no time. Among us Embassy people, I mean. We tried to keep it from the guests, of course. Anyway," Dorabella added, defensively, "she was always getting drunk. We were quite used to it."

"Lady Ironmonger frequently got drunk in public, did she?" Henry asked, just too innocently.

Dorabella froze him with a stare. "I am not public," she said. "Sir Edward is not public. The Embassy is not public. I said that *we* were used to it."

"So," said Henry, "you think that Lady Ironmonger drank too much at the reception, insulted an Israeli diplomat and was then helped up to her bedroom, where she shot herself with her husband's gun. Is that a fair statement of your opinion, Miss Hamilton?"

"It is not my opinion, Mr. Tibbett. It is what happened."

Henry let this go. He said, "To get back to this famous key for a moment. Who has had charge of it or access to it since Lady Ironmonger's death?"

Promptly, Dorabella replied, "Sir Edward and myself. Nobody else."

"You're quite certain of that?"

"Of course."

"But surely Sir Edward might have handed the key to—"

Dorabella glanced ostentatiously at her watch. "It is half-past six, Chief Superintendent. If you will excuse me, I have to close up the official rooms of the Embassy before I go home..."

Henry smiled. "Oh, well. In that case—good evening to you. Please tell Sir Edward that I have the key and will take good care of it. Don't bother to see me out."

CHAPTER NINE

HENRY'S IDEA HAD been to interview the Holder-Wattses, Winston Nelson, the Otis Schipmakers and the Barringtons, in that order and as soon as possible, but the busy social life of Washington intervened. Michael and Eleanor were attending the same diplomatic function as Eddie Ironmonger. The Schipmakers were gracing a charity ballet performance at the Kennedy Center. Winnie Nelson was representing Sir Edward at the opening of a new civic center in a predominantly black quarter of the city. The only people available for interviewing that evening were Prudence and Matthew Barrington.

Inspector Bartholomew had telephoned the Barrington home earlier from the Embassy, and had been engulfed in a typically warmhearted welcome from Prudence. "Why, Bobby Bartholomew! How are you, dear? We were just looking at your picture in the evening paper, arriving at the airport. My, how you've grown! How's your mother these days?... Well, of course, we're none of us getting any younger, but you tell her from me that she ought to go and see Dr. Duncan, just for a check-up…yes, I know what she's like, dear—stubborn and self-opinionated and she will *not* take proper care of herself, and you are to go home right now and tell her…oh, no, of course, you can't, can you?… How's the investigation going?… Scotland Yard?… No, of course I'm not surprised. Naturally Eddie would want to call in the very best people…oh, don't be silly, Bobby, what does independence have to do with it?… Oh, does he? I can't think why… What's the name again? Tibbett?… Yes, by all means, tell him we'll be delighted to see him for supper this evening, around seven-thirty…Jean and Homer are coming, but nobody else, just family…and you must come and see us soon, Bobby. Muriel will be so pleased to see you. You remember Muriel?… And when you write to your mother, dear, remember me to all your brothers and sisters… and their fathers, of course…"

Henry's cab made good time out to Chevy Chase, despite the remnants of rush-hour traffic still streaming toward suburbia. He was glad to see that there were no cars in the driveway of the Barrington house, indicating that he had arrived before Jean and Homer—who were, he gathered, the Barringtons' daughter and son-in-law. With any luck there would be time to talk to the Bishop and his wife alone before the family evening set in.

Matthew Barrington greeted Henry with a glass of sweetish sherry and a rather surprising air of formality which Prudence at once dispelled.

"We're so very pleased to meet you, Mr. Tibbett, and to know that this sad affair is in good hands. So sensible of Eddie to call in the Yard—he always was a bright boy. You must tell us all about London—dear old London, such a long time since we've been there, but we do try to keep in touch—"

"The Chief Superintendent," said Matthew ponderously, "has not come all this way to gossip about London, Prudence."

"Well, perhaps not, but it's always nice to hear news from home. What a pity your wife couldn't come over here with you, Mr. Tibbett."

"As a matter of fact, she did," said Henry. "We're both staying with Mrs. Colville."

"Then you are very naughty not to have told me," said Prudence. "You should have brought her this evening. Next time, you must promise—"

"Prudence!" Matthew was as brusque as he ever could be. "Please let us get to the point. The children will be here soon."

"Oh, dear." Prudence smiled enchantingly at Henry, shedding thirty years with no effort. "I'm afraid Matthew is going to make a speech. Or deliver a sermon. I know the signs."

Matthew cleared his throat. "My wife exaggerates, like all women," he said. "Nevertheless, Chief Superintendent, I do wish to—to make a statement. Just for the record."

"By all means, sir," said Henry.

"Well..." For a moment, Bishop Barrington seemed at a loss for words. Then he pulled himself together, and said, "I do not wish to be hypocritical, Tibbett. Consequently, I have decided to tell you straight away that I thoroughly disliked Mavis Ironmonger. Not as a person, but on account of her marriage to Eddie. I love Tampica, and I regarded that marriage as no less than a national disaster, which might have had dire consequences for generations of Tampicans as yet unborn. I won't hide from you the fact that I consider her disappearance as an unmixed blessing. I suppose you find this shocking."

"On the contrary," said Henry, "I find it refreshing."

"Well, I find it disgusting!" Two pink spots had appeared on Prudence's cheeks, and her eyes were sparkling with anger. "I'm ashamed of you, Matthew. And there's no need to be so pompous. 'Generations as yet unborn' indeed!"

More gently, Matthew said, "I am trying to be honest, my dear. I am thinking of Tampica."

"And I'm thinking of Eddie, and that poor girl. People don't kill themselves for no reason, you know."

Henry said, "I do appreciate your frankness, Bishop Barrington—just as I appreciate Mrs. Barrington's warmheartedness. But, really, what would help me most would be a simple account of exactly what you both did on the evening that Lady Ironmonger died."

Prudence and Matthew looked at each other for a moment, and then Matthew said, "No problem there. Perfectly straightforward. We arrived at the Embassy by taxicab at... what time was it, dear?"

"I really don't know, Matthew, but it must have been well after six, because a great many people had arrived already. And there were those demonstrators with banners outside—you remember, Matthew?"

"I do."

"Well," Prudence went on, "we went in and I left my coat in the cloakroom and we joined the receiving line and shook hands with Eddie and Mavis. He was charming, as usual. I thought she seemed rather quiet and withdrawn. Didn't you, Matthew?"

"She was behaving herself," said the Bishop.

Prudence went on, a little hurriedly. "We talked to some other people...Dorrie Hamilton...Michael...we didn't really know many of the people there..."

"My wife," said the Bishop, "means to say that we do not move in the social swim of diplomatic Washington, and I for one am thankful for it. We occasionally get invited to parties by Ginny and Otis Schipmaker—that's Jean's brother-in-law and his wife—if they wish to present a façade of unimpeachable respectability. Even retired bishops have their uses at times."

Prudence beamed. "Matthew says the silliest things," she remarked. "We have a very nice little circle of friends, and we don't lack social life in Chevy Chase, I can assure you. What with the Chevy Chase Episcopal Ladies' Club, and charity coffee parties and—"

"Could we please get back to the Tampican reception?" Henry asked.

"Of course. Forgive me, Mr. Tibbett, I'm afraid I tend to run on. Where was I?"

"You'd shaken hands with Sir Edward and Lady Ironmonger, and you had spoken to Miss Hamilton and Mr. Holder-Watts."

"That's right. Then we had another glass of sherry, just chatting to each other, and it was after that that I noticed the receiving line had broken up and that Eddie was circulating among the guests. I saw Mavis standing by herself, looking...I don't know...out of things..."

"Not surprising," growled Matthew, almost inaudibly.

Prudence ignored him, and went on. "Well, Mr. Tibbett, I don't care who anybody is or what people say about them. The poor girl looked quite abandoned...don't snort like that, Matthew, you know perfectly well what I mean...and I insisted that we go over and talk to her."

"How did she seem?" Henry asked.

"Seem? Why—perfectly all right. A little stiff and shy, but that would only be natural, wouldn't it? In any case, we only had a moment with her, before Eleanor Holder-Watts came up and suggested showing us the garden. Of course, we jumped at the chance. Georgetown is famous for its gardens, you know—a little paradise in the middle of the city, as I always call it. But ordinary people like us only get to see the private gardens during a couple of days in the spring when people open them to the public, for charity. Yes, it really was a treat. There's a most unusual rockery with some *iris reticulata* of a color which I have never—"

"Prudence," remonstrated Matthew, "I really don't think that Mr. Tibbett is interested in a horticultural catalogue of the Embassy garden."

"No, no, of course not. You're quite right, Matthew. To put it in a nutshell, then, Mr. Tibbett—we became quite absorbed in the garden. I don't know how long we spent there. After a little while Eleanor explained that she had to go back to the reception—well, of course we understood, she was on duty, as it were. So we simply puttered around the garden on our own until Matthew said that it was time to go and meet Winnie.

Actually, we thought that we were already late, but fortunately Matthew's watch is always wrong so we were just on time. Winnie was waiting for us, and he drove us home. That's about all I can tell you, Mr. Tibbett."

"And Lady Ironmonger was still behaving quite normally when you left the Embassy?"

"I presume so, Mr. Tibbett. We didn't go back into the reception room—we came straight from the garden through the hall and into the small library, so we really can't tell you anything more about the reception. The only other thing I do recall is that some of the demonstrators were quite rude to poor Winnie. Most extraordinary. They seemed to resent him far more than they did us, and yet he is one of their own people. Really, I find modern politics very confusing."

"You have always found politics confusing, my dear," remarked the Bishop. "The militant blacks dislike people like Eddie and Winnie because they have chosen to live in our world."

"What other world is there?" Prudence was genuinely baffled. "After all, they're independent now, and taking their place in the great family of nations. Isn't that what they want?"

"It's still predominantly a white man's world," Barrington persisted. "Our world."

"Oh, well," said Prudence, tartly, "if they don't like it, let them go and make another one for themselves. I should have thought they'd be quite glad to take advantage of all the hard work and experience that we've put into—"

The Bishop held up his hand "I think we should get back to Mr. Tibbett's questions, Prudence, and not become involved in a political discussion."

Prudence turned to Henry. "Isn't that just like a man? As soon as I make a good point, he changes the subject. Ah, I think I hear the doorbell. Jean and Homer must have arrived. Do forgive me, Mr. Tibbett..."

Henry had no difficulty in recognizing the dark-haired woman who came into the drawing-room on a wave of lively

chatter as one of the brides from the twin wedding photographs. A little plumper, perhaps, a few incipient wrinkles
in the fine, fair skin—but Jean Barrington Schipmaker had
changed little in ten years. The question of which twin it was
was resolved the moment her husband joined her. Comfortably
rotund, wearing gold-edged spectacles and a bow tie, Homer
Schipmaker gave the impression of a thoroughly pleasant,
rather ordinary American who has been varnished with the
patina of great wealth. Neither of the Schipmakers was dressed
ostentatiously, or even very fashionably, yet their clothes
exuded an aura of custom-made, real-silk-and-leather, hand-
stitched quality.

"...and Ginny was really quite snappy on the telephone;
she simply refused to discuss it at all, didn't she, Homer?" Jean
appealed to her husband, who smiled blandly.

"I guess she's bugged by people calling up every hour of
the day, fishing for a tidbit of gossip," he said. Both Schipmakers
spoke just fractionally louder than the norm, which Henry had
noticed was a characteristic of many wealthy Americans. Rich
English people, on the other hand, tend to speak more and
more quietly in direct relation to their money, so that the few
real multimillionaires are virtually inaudible.

"Well, of course," Jean went on, "lots of people were
invited and didn't go because they thought it was just another
tinpot little embassy, and now they're *furious* at missing it.
Anyhow, Mother, you were there and you can tell us *all*."

"I'm afraid I can't, dear. Sherry for you, too, Homer? Here
we are. You see, Daddy and I left before anything happened.
We only heard about it on the ten o'clock news."

"Oh, really, Mummy, isn't that just like you? Trust you to
miss all the fun. You can be maddening." There was affection
in Jean's voice, which had retained all its relentless Englishness,
both in accent and idiom.

"Ah," said Prudence, "but I do have a treat for you. Come
and meet Chief Superintendent Tibbett of Scotland Yard, who
is investigating the whole affair."

At once, Henry was overwhelmed by a tide of questions, compliments and the genuine interest in other people which is characteristic of the United States. At last Jean said, almost triumphantly, "So she *was* murdered! I was sure of it!"

Prudence looked shocked. "I can't think why you say that, dear. Mr. Tibbett is investigating Mavis's suicide. Isn't that right, Mr. Tibbett?"

Henry said, "I'm investigating her death. We don't yet know very much about it. I think the communiqué from the Embassy made that clear."

"But she was, wasn't she?" Jean persisted.

"What makes you so sure, Mrs. Schipmaker?"

"Well, for one thing, Mavis would *never* kill herself. *Never.* And then, think of all the people who had good reasons for wanting her out of the way—"

Homer Schipmaker said, uneasily, "Honey, I really don't think you ought to—"

"Oh, don't be silly, Homer. Everybody on Tampica knew all about Mavis." She turned to Henry. "Don't tell me nobody's told you how she slept with every man on the island?"

Prudence Barrington let out a small, shocked squeak of protest, but Jean went on, unperturbed. "Why, Homer, you remember the business of Mavis and Otis—and he was just one of a crowd." Before her husband could speak, Jean had turned back to Henry. "Otis is Homer's younger brother. The whole family used to come to Tampica for a holiday every year. It was all long before Otis met Ginny—ten years ago, in fact, because it was the year Homer and I got married. Mavis had just married Eddie and come to live on Tampica—she was very young and absolutely stunning to look at, and of course Otis took a real shine to her. Then Eddie had to go to New York on some legal case or other, and once she was left alone—"

"Jean!" Bishop Barrington's voice was commanding and resonant, as if from the pulpit. "That is quite enough of that. You know I abominate tittle-tattle, and I will not have it in my house."

"Oh, don't be, stupid, Daddy." Jean was quite unintimidated. "Everybody knows—"

"I think you are wrong, dear." Prudence spoke quietly, but with unusual firmness.

"Wrong? About what?"

"Virginia," said Prudence, "does not know. And I think this would be a most unfortunate moment for her to find out."

"Oh, Mummy. Ginny *must* have heard the story."

"I think not. She's never been to Tampica, you know. She and Otis met here in Washington when her family came back from Europe. She could only have heard about Mavis from a member of the Schipmaker family, and I can't believe that any of them would have been so cruel as to rake up an old scandal for her benefit."

Prudence ended on a note of interrogation, addressed to Homer, who had gone slightly pink. He said, "I guess your mother's right, honey. There was no reason for anybody to put Ginny wise, unless Otis told her himself—"

"Which he didn't," remarked Prudence, with serene confidence.

"How can you be sure?" Jean demanded.

"My dear Jean, would she have agreed to go to the reception if she had known?"

Jean considered, her head on one side. "She might have, just for the hell of it."

"No way." Homer put an arm round his wife's shoulder. "I didn't mean to mention this, baby, but since the subject's come up—well, here goes. Fact is, Otis called me the day before the reception. Boy, was he steamed up! They'd gotten this invitation—trust Mavis, she wouldn't miss a trick like that—and Ginny was determined to accept. Nothing Otis could say would change her mind. Well, what with Otis's political ideas..." He turned to Henry, whose presence and right to know the facts he seemed to accept without question, and added, in parentheses, "Otis has some big political ambitions these days—got his eye on a senate seat. His biggest clout comes from Ginny's family—her father's been a presidential adviser, an ambassador in several European countries and so on. He's what's called an elder statesman. Otis reckons that with his father-in-law's political influence and the Schipmaker bread behind him, he's got the nomination just about sewn up. He's running in the primary this spring. He needed Mavis Ironmonger to turn up in Washington at this moment in time like he needed a hole in the head. If Ginny and her family found out about the old scandal…or worse, if Mavis created a new one…hey, honey, you didn't say anything to Ginny on the telephone, did you? About Mavis and Otis, I mean."

"No, I didn't." Jean sounded subdued at last. "I didn't get a chance. She practically hung up on me. Gosh, I'm sorry, Homer. It never occurred to me…but actually, Mavis behaved very well, didn't she, at the reception? With Otis, I mean. It wasn't until later—"

"Sure. Otis says he had his heart in his mouth as they stood in the receiving line, but all she said was 'Pleased to meet you'—just as if he'd been a total stranger. She did give him a wicked little wink, he says, just as he was moving away—but Ginny certainly didn't see it, and he doesn't think Sir Edward did, either."

"And then we're asked to believe that half-an-hour later she went and shot herself!" Jean had recovered her spirits. "What rubbish! Anyhow, Bobby Bartholomew said that foul play couldn't be ruled out. I read it in the *Post*. And once a policeman says that, you can be sure it's murder."

It was not a direct question to Henry, but close enough to warrant a defensive parry. He said, "Tell me, Mrs. Schipmaker— did Sir Edward know about this old scandal…about his wife and Otis Schipmaker?"

Jean and Homer exchanged a brief glance. Then she said, "I really don't know. Eddie's a…well, a secret sort of person, isn't he, Mummy? He doesn't talk about…that is, he talks about everything under the sun except his private life. All I can say is that everybody on Tampica was convinced he must know about her various adventures—it's difficult to keep secrets on a small island. But I've never known anybody who ever got him to say so. Eddie's attitude was that he loved Mavis, Mavis loved him, it was a very happy marriage, and—finish. Not another word."

"You knew Sir Edward well, did you?" Henry gestured to encompass the elder Barringtons. "That's to say—your families were friendly on Tampica?"

Prudence said, "Matthew and I knew Eddie as a small boy, of course. Matthew helped him a great deal. Then he went off to university in England—and when he came back with Mavis, he was like a stranger."

Sharply, Matthew said, "That is less than fair, Prudence. Eddie has always been most charming."

"Yes—but you couldn't call him a real friend, Matthew. One couldn't get close to him. Even Doc Duncan said so."

"That was really what I was getting at," Henry said. "Did he have any really close friends in Tampica, after his marriage?"

There was a little silence. Then Matthew said, "If he had a friend, it was Winnie Nelson. And then, of course, there's Dorabella..." He paused, and added, "He certainly had an enemy."

"An enemy?"

"Michael Holder-Watts. They hate each other."

"Then why on earth," said Henry, "is Holder-Watts Sir Edward's Counsellor at the Embassy?"

Matthew said, "That's simple. Expediency. Pragmatism. Eddie's a lawyer, not a diplomat. He's got a very important job here, and he needs Michael. That doesn't make him like him any better."

The silence that followed was broken by the drawing-room door being flung open.

"Dinnah," said Muriel, ringingly, "is served."

CHAPTER TEN

"**T**ELL ME," said Henry, "about the naval base."

It was shortly before lunchtime on the following day. Henry had spent most of the morning with Inspector Bartholomew in Mavis's bedroom, fingerprinting, photographing and analyzing—all to very little effect, but it had to be done. He had then interviewed Winnie Nelson, whose account of the evening of the reception tallied exactly with that of the Barringtons; and now at last he had run Michael Holder-Watts to earth in his office at the Embassy—a room on the first floor which had once been a guest bedroom.

Michael told him, deftly and in detail, about the events at the reception, and his subsequent discovery of Lady Ironmonger's body.

"At first I thought she'd just passed out, and I can't say I was surprised. But then I saw the gun...and the wound...no, I didn't touch anything. It was obvious she was dead. I ran downstairs again, got rid of the last stragglers and then told Eddie. It wasn't very pleasant."

"He must have been very upset."

"He was more than that. He was in a white rage. Or perhaps I should say a black rage. You see, I also had to tell him about Mavis and Mr. Finkelstein, and what Eleanor and I had done, and he seemed to think that we had stepped beyond the line of duty—to put it mildly. He didn't actually accuse me of murdering Mavis, but he did imply... I can't remember his exact words...he suggested very strongly that I'd driven her to suicide. We all took it for granted that she'd killed herself. Of course, now that we know she was murdered, my position is even worse."

Michael looked at Henry quizzically, poised for a spate of awkward questions, like a tennis player preparing to receive a sizzling service. But the awkward questions did not come. Instead, Henry said, "Tell me about the naval base."

"The naval base? What about it?" Michael had been jolted out of his usual effortless command of the situation. Having quickly decided that this detective was far from unintelligent, he was forced to conclude that the switch from an obvious and tempting line of questioning must be deliberate—the probable purpose: to regain initiative and prevent him, Michael, from directing the course of the interview. He looked at Henry with renewed respect.

Henry did not appear to notice. He said, "I've heard a lot about it, but in a vague and confused way, as if everybody expected me to know all about the situation, which I don't. I gathered in London that it was one of the main reasons I was being sent for. Can you elucidate?"

"Very well." Michael considered for a moment. "To start at the beginning. The United States has had a naval base at Barracuda Bay for nearly thirty years. It so happens that it's the only well-protected deep-water anchorage in the area, and it's strategically placed with regard not only to Cuba, but to certain South American countries on which Uncle Sam is keeping a more or less benevolent eye. The base was leased to the United States by Britain at a fixed rental and under an all-or-nothing lease arrangement."

"What's that?"

"It means that the lease came up for review every five years—but only on the basis of whether or not it should continue in force. Either side could cancel the lease completely, and the U.S. Navy would depart, but if they stayed, the terms of the contract remained unchanged."

"In fact, there was no possibility of raising the rent? A sort of controlled tenancy."

"Right." Michael picked up a pencil and began to doodle as he spoke. "The British and Americans were both happy about the arrangement. The yearly rental provided the island's main source of revenue, and the sailors on shore leave spent a lot of lovely dollars. The Americans felt they had a permanent base at reasonable cost, and they put a lot of money into building harbor facilities, docks, warehouses, shore installations and so on. There seemed no reason why the *status quo* should ever change. But, of course, independence has altered everything."

"Why?"

"Well..." Michael hesitated. "I don't suppose you know much about international law..."

Henry smiled. "It just so happens that I know a certain amount. I was on a case in Holland which involved...never mind. I think I know what you're going to say. The Tampican government doesn't consider itself bound by a treaty entered into on its behalf by the previous colonial government."

Michael smiled back. "You certainly pick up the oddest bits of information, for a bobby. Yes, you're right. Our position—that is, the Tampican government's position—is that the existing arrangement is invalid, and that a whole new agreement must be worked out."

"With a hike in the rent?"

"That," said Michael primly, "would be for the conference to decide. In any case, Eddie has advised Sam—that's Sir Samuel Drake-Frobisher, our Prime Minister—that in his view the United States is occupying Barracuda Bay illegally.

He's prepared to take the case to The Hague, and Washington knows it. That's our position—negotiate or get out."

"And supposing," said Henry, "that they call your bluff?"

"Our bluff?"

"Supposing they simply up anchor and go?"

Michael leant back in his chair, smiling. "My dear Tibbett, that is what a great many Tampicans would like to see them do. That is why we are bargaining from a position of strength."

"But the revenue—"

"Let me put it this way. When the original agreement was drawn up, tourism on Tampica was minimal. In fact, it hardly existed anywhere in the Caribbean. The boom started in Bermuda and the Bahamas, and then spread to the Virgin Islands. It began to touch Tampica when a big American hotel consortium opened up Pirate's Cave Hotel and made it one of the great luxury resorts of the world. But Pirate's Cave is just one hotel, and it's not Tampican-owned. We are still missing out on the most lucrative tourist source of all."

"What's that?" Henry asked.

"Cruise liners, old man. Have you ever been to St. Thomas? Well, you should see the little town of Charlotte Amalie when four or five big liners are in port. You can hardly move on the streets for wealthy tourists, just begging to be allowed to spend their money. That's what we want in Tampica. And Barracuda Bay is our only deep-water anchorage."

"I see," said Henry. "So if the U.S. Navy went, and left all their harbor facilities behind..."

"Exactly. The American shore establishment buildings are grouped around one of the most beautiful beaches on the island. Everything is there—plumbing, electricity, water. It wouldn't take a great deal of reconstruction to turn those buildings into hotels—less expensive and therefore more popular than Pirate's Cave. And Tampican-owned, of course. No, old man—the U.S. will have to come up with a pretty sensational offer, and they know it. To put it bluntly, we have them over a barrel."

"Except," said Henry, "for the fact that they are there. Possession is nine points of—"

"I know, I know. The process of eviction may be a little complicated. And, of course, there are some Tampicans who actively want the Navy to stay."

"Really? From what you said it sounds as though the whole island would benefit from the extra tourist trade."

"Materially, yes," said Michael. "But I'm talking about the ecologists. Or the sentimentalists, if you prefer. They've seen what has happened to islands like St. Thomas, and they don't want the same thing in Tampica. They reckon that if the States will up the ante, the island can get more money and still remain unspoiled. Don't tell anybody, but I'm a bit of an ecologist myself. Unofficially, of course. Officially, I must support Eddie."

"I'd have thought," Henry said, "that Sir Edward might be an ecologist, too."

"Then you'd have thought wrong," said Michael. "One of the reasons that Eddie is here is that he's a hard-liner on the question of the base. Remember, he's an Oxford man. It may be a city of dreaming spires, but it also turns out a pretty shrewd breed of businessman. Those who dream, stay on and teach; those who don't—corner the market in pig iron, or some other unattractive commodity. No, Eddie's first and foremost a Tampican. He wants prosperity for the island, and he sees it coming better and faster from tourism than any other source. We need that harbor—and Eddie is here to see we get it, or else." He paused and smiled. "No, funnily enough, the sentimentalists are people like Winnie Nelson and Sam Drake-Frobisher. I'm not giving away any state secrets when I tell you that Eddie is the ramrod that's keeping Sam hard-lining on the question of the base. To be honest, Sam has always regarded himself as something of a caretaker Prime Minister. And now that Mavis is no longer a problem...well, it's just a matter of time before Eddie takes over. That's why Sam will leave most of the talking at the conference to Eddie."

"Oh, there's a conference scheduled, is there?"

"Certainly there is. Didn't you know? Next week. Sam was bright enough to insist on holding it in Tampica, and the delegates will be accommodated at Pirate's Cave, at government expense. I need hardly tell you that the Americans accepted with alacrity. Perhaps you should be there, too."

"Perhaps I should," said Henry.

"I won't be there myself," Michael added. "I'm minding the shop here for Eddie—naturally, he'll be there. I'd be disappointed not to be going, if it wasn't for the Watkinses."

"The who?"

"Mr. and Mrs. Hubert Watkins of Penge, England. Mavis's parents. Eddie stashed them away at Pirate's Cave after the funeral, to keep the press off them, and I gather they show no signs of wanting to leave. We may have to prod them a little before too long."

"You were having a love affair with Lady Ironmonger, weren't you?" said Henry, casually.

Michael raised his eyebrows. "My, how you do hop about from topic to topic. Guilty, Inspector. I'm sorry, guilty, Chief Superintendent. No, that doesn't sound right—let's leave it at Inspector. There's absolutely no reason why I should deny it. It wasn't a very great distinction, you know. There were a number of other men in the same happy position, and Eddie knew all about it."

"There were others here in Washington?" Henry asked.

"There were certainly some exes, as you might say. I don't think Mavis had had time to get around to anything new. Besides, I kept her fairly well occupied."

"You say Sir Edward knew. Didn't he object?"

Michael made a small gesture, indicating hopelessness. "My dear chap, you might just as well object to the sun shining. Mavis was a dear, sweet, completely amoral girl. To the point, in fact, of being rather touchingly innocent. I don't know if you understand what I mean."

"Whether or not I understand it hardly matters," Henry said. "The question is—did Sir Edward, and did your wife?"

"Let's not confuse the two cases," said Michael. "Eddie knew and did not object. Eleanor would certainly have objected, but she did not know."

"You're sure of that?"

"Positive. Eleanor only knows what she wishes to know."

"Did she like Lady Ironmonger, personally?"

Michael smiled. "Don't ask for miracles, old man. Eleanor is a doctor's daughter, raised in a small English country town. She could never, under any circumstances, have liked Mavis—whether or not I was involved. Most of the time, Eleanor tried to pretend that Mavis didn't exist. And now, of course…she doesn't."

Henry said, "You knew Lady Ironmonger very well, Mr. Holder-Watts. Did she have a drinking problem?"

"I wouldn't have said so. She just liked to drink. I don't call that a problem."

"Would you have known if she was being treated for alcoholism, medically?"

"If being treated implies that she would have cut out drinking altogether—I can tell you that she wasn't. She put away several large martinis in my company the evening before she died. She did promise Eddie and me that she'd stick to tomato juice at the reception. Of course, when she made that scene, I assumed that she'd been tippling on the quiet all evening—but it seems that I was wrong. Somebody had slipped her something."

"Would that have been difficult to do?"

"The easiest thing in the world. It's impossible to hold a glass and shake hands at the same time, so she had her drink on a small table behind her. Anybody in the room could have switched it for a doctored glass without being noticed."

"How many people," Henry asked, "know the contents of Dr. Duncan's report?"

Promptly, Michael replied, "Sam, Eddie, Nelson, Bartholomew, myself—and you, of course."

"Nobody else?"

"Not as far as I know. We agreed to keep it secret for the time being."

"Not even your wife?" Michael shook his head. "Or Miss Hamilton?"

Michael said, "I suppose Eddie might have told Dorrie, but I doubt it. He gave his word, and he is very scrupulous."

"I see. Thank you. Now..." Henry had pulled a notebook out of his pocket and was studying it. "I think you may be able to help me. I've been trying to make a rough timetable of events on the evening of the reception. The guests were invited from six to eight, I believe?"

"That's right. We were all here well before six—except Mavis, of course, who was late as usual. We were in our best bibs and tuckers, and feeling somewhat nervous. Actually, the guests began arriving very early—even before six. At about ten past, Eddie told me to go upstairs and tell Mavis to hurry, before too many people arrived. I found her all ready, gazing out of the window at those inefficient demonstrators who were just marching up." He smiled. "She wanted to invite them all in for a drink—quite seriously. That was the sort of thing that made it impossible for anybody to dislike her."

"Except for your wife."

"We're not talking about my wife. She—Eleanor—wanted to call the F.B.I. and have all the demonstrators arrested. Obviously, neither suggestion was viable. Demonstrators in Washington are part of its scenic charm."

"O.K.," said Henry. "That handles the beginning of the reception. Are there any other details of timing that you can remember?"

"Well," Michael said, "funnily enough, I can pinpoint pretty accurately the moment when Mavis sounded off. At a function like that, one doesn't go around looking at one's watch—but it so happened that I did. The last guests had arrived, and the reception line had broken up. Mavis and Eddie were circulating, dispensing charm. You know the sort of thing. Winnie Nelson came over to me and remarked on how well everything was going. I agreed, but said we'd have to keep a sharp eye on things—I didn't know just how right I was. Anyhow, he said that he would soon be leaving, as he had an appointment with Bishop and Mrs. Barrington at seven. It was then that I looked at my watch and remarked that he'd better hurry, as it was two minutes to."

"Your watch is accurate, I presume," said Henry. "Unlike Bishop Barrington's."

"My watch is accurate," said Michael. He looked at Henry levelly. "Winnie went off to his rendezvous, and it must have been about five minutes later that Mavis took leave of her senses. So you can pinpoint that little episode at just about seven-oh-three. Eleanor must have got her upstairs and locked in by five or six minutes past. It all happened very quickly."

"Right," said Henry. He made a note. "Now—with the exception of Nelson and the Barringtons—was there anybody who could *not* have subsequently slipped away from the reception and upstairs to the bedroom, and killed Lady Ironmonger?"

"That's a big question, isn't it?" Michael considered. "First, you've got to narrow it down to the people who realized that Mavis had been removed. I can't give you a complete list, but there's Eleanor and myself, of course. Dorabella—I told her as soon as she came back to the reception room. Mr. Finkelstein, Otis Schipmaker...let's see, who else? Mrs. Ngomo might have noticed something, and so might the Dutch Ambassador. There were other people around, of course, but I really can't remember exactly who they were."

"You don't include Sir Edward?"

"No, I don't. He was on the other side of the room, talking to Senator Belmont, and his reaction afterwards, when he found out—"

"All the same," Henry persisted, "he *could* have seen the incident and pretended to ignore it, couldn't he?"

"I suppose he *could* have," Michael conceded.

"All right. Now, to whittle that list down still further, the murderer must have known which was the Ironmongers' bedroom. That would seem to rule out the visiting diplomats, who were in the house for the first time."

"Dear God," said Michael. "You don't have to spell it all out. The obvious suspects are Eleanor and myself and Dorabella and Eddie."

"And can any of you be eliminated for sure?"

Michael thought for a moment. "No, not really. Eleanor and I clearly had the best opportunities. Dorabella was in and out of the reception room all evening—nothing simpler. Eddie—well, I've told you that I don't believe he saw what happened, and I also think that his absence from the room would have been spotted...but that's conjecture, of course. I didn't have my eye on him all the time."

"Would Otis Schipmaker know which was Lady Ironmonger's bedroom?" Henry asked.

"What an extraordinary question, Inspector. Why on earth should he?"

"It occurred to me. I believe he was an old friend of hers."

"I think," said Michael, "that you are brighter than you look. Yes, Otis Schipmaker might have known."

"Had he visited Lady Ironmonger here in Washington?"

"I really don't know. Let's say it's possible. I spoke to Schipmaker myself just after the Finkelstein incident, with the object of making sure he kept his mouth shut."

"Blackmail?"

"In a gentlemanly fashion. It's known as diplomatic pressure."

Henry said, "Then there's the question of the gun. I believe Miss Hamilton noticed it was missing earlier in the day."

"So she says now," Michael leant back in his chair. "Of course, it's open to doubt. Or, if Dorrie is telling the truth, Mavis may well have taken the gun herself—there'd been discussion about keeping it in the bedroom instead of the study."

"Let's consider another angle," Henry said. "How many people here at the Embassy are teetotalers?"

"My wife doesn't drink," said Michael promptly. "Nor does Dorabella. Eddie…well…"

"Sir Edward doesn't drink at all?"

"Oh, yes, he does—but not much and not often. Smoking is his vice. Great big rich-smelling cigars."

"Any more names for the teetotal list?"

"Not that I can think of. Most people enjoy a modest tipple. Mavis was the only one who was inclined to overindulge." Michael picked up a pencil and twirled it between his long fingers. "Poor Mavis. She simply didn't realize that one cannot go through life doing precisely what one pleases, and not make enemies. However beautiful one may be."

"Mr. Holder-Watts," Henry said, "I'm going to ask you a very indiscreet question, but please answer it truthfully. Remember, this is a murder investigation."

"How very alarming," said Michael, mildly. "O.K. Fire away."

"Of those two people you mentioned who don't drink, did either one have a drinking problem in the past?"

There was a long silence. At last, Michael said, "This is confidential, isn't it?"

"For the moment," said Henry. "I can't promise what might have to come out in a court of law."

Another silence. Then, "Well, I hate to tell you this—but, yes. Eleanor did. Many years ago, before we went to Tampica. I was in the Colonial Service, and stationed in a God-forsaken corner of Africa—and to make it worse, I had a huge area to cover and was away from home most of the time. You can imagine what Eleanor's life was like. She's never been an outdoor person—she hates physical sports, and discomfort, and dirt, and the lack of what Jane Austen called 'the decencies of a private gentlewoman'—and there weren't many of those around, I can assure you. She was lonely, bored and miserable. You can imagine the rest."

Henry said, "How was she cured?"

"'Cured'" is rather a strong word, old man. The problem

was never that serious. I found out about it, and fortunately we were posted home, and then transferred to Tampica. Eleanor went to a doctor in London, I believe. I thought it tactful not to ask too many questions. In any case, she simply gave up drinking altogether, and that was that."

"Did this London doctor give her any medication to help her?" Henry asked.

Michael smiled faintly. "I've no idea. I see what you're driving at, of course, but I can't help you. You'll have to ask Eleanor."

"Yes," said Henry. "Yes, I'll have to ask Eleanor."

"Certainly not! How dared he tell you such a thing!"

It was mid-afternoon, and Henry was in the drawing-room of the Holder-Wattses' rented house, trying to get some information from Eleanor. He was not being very successful. She stood facing him, trembling with fury, two bright spots on her normally pale cheeks. Then she began to cry, pressing an inadequate handkerchief to her eyes. "It's typical of him…trying to put me in a bad light…telling you lies about me…"

"But you did have a drinking problem, didn't you?" Henry persisted.

"Of course not. I admit I used to take a drink now and again when I was so…so terribly lonely and depressed…but as soon as we moved to Tampica, everything was different. I simply stopped drinking because I'd never really enjoyed it…"

"You didn't consult a doctor in London, then?"

"I consulted nobody." Eleanor was recovering from her tears, and the anger was coming back. "Why Michael should go out of his way to discuss such a thing with you, and to tell you such lies…"

"I asked him because I thought it might have some bearing on Lady Ironmonger's death—but it's not important." Henry glanced at the sheet of paper in his hand. "Now, to get back to the reception. There's one small thing puzzling me, Mrs. Holder-Watts. If I've understood correctly, you took the Barringtons out into the garden at about a quarter to seven."

"I suppose so. I didn't make a special note of the time."

"You then left them in the garden, saying you had to return to the reception."

"That's right," said Eleanor.

"Now—" Henry tapped the paper. "I don't want to split hairs, but the Barringtons arrived in the small library at seven, whereas you didn't get back to the reception until about five past—after Lady Ironmonger's outburst. Can you tell me how you spent that ten minutes or so?"

Eleanor Holder-Watts looked coldly at Henry. "Since this is a police investigation, I suppose I must answer impertinent questions, even though they have nothing to do with Mavis's suicide. I went to the bathroom, as the Americans say. Does that satisfy you?"

"It'll have to, won't it?" said Henry.

At that moment, the telephone rang. Eleanor said, "Excuse me—" and went to answer it. Henry watched her as she walked across the room. She was thin, pale and parched, like a sheet of paper. Her feet seemed so light that the deep pile of the carpet did not register her tread. She picked up the telephone, and said, "Hello...yes, he is...yes, I'll tell him...at once...yes, I understand...thank you..."

She rang off, and turned to face Henry. "That was a Mrs. Colville," she said. "I believe you are staying with her. She's been notified that there's a call coming through for you in about ten minutes, from Dr. Duncan in Tampica. The Embassy told her you were here with me."

"Oh, well," said Henry cheerfully, "then I'd better get back to Margaret's place right away. Dr. Duncan, you say? I wonder if it's important."

"Anything that would induce Dr. Duncan to make a long distance telephone call would have to be important," said Eleanor, icily. "He'd almost as soon get on an aeroplane."

"In that case," said Henry, "I'll say good-bye. I'm sorry we had to cut short our talk. Perhaps we can resume it another time."

Eleanor stood up a little straighter. "I very much hope not," she said. "I will, of course, tell you anything I know which is relevant, but if you are interested in somebody with a drinking problem, I think you will find more fruitful avenues to explore. You must know what I mean."

"Perhaps I do, Mrs. Holder-Watts."

CHAPTER ELEVEN

"**M**R. HENRY TIBBETT! Please put Mr. Henry Tibbett on the line!**" the long distance operator was displaying the near-incomprehensible bossiness characteristic of her profession.

"Speaking," said Henry.

"I have a person-to-person call for Mr. Tibbett from Tampica."

"I know you do," said Henry. "I'm waiting."

"Tampica? Is Dr. Duncan there? Kindly tell Dr. Duncan that his party is waiting." The operator was behaving like an overanxious sheep dog, and with the same results.

"Tibbett? Are you there, Tibbett? Duncan here!" The doctor's voice came loud and clear down the line, but before Henry could answer, the operator said tetchily, "Please do not speak at this time. I am trying to connect you."

"We are connected," Henry protested. "Hello, Duncan!"

"Tibbett—"

But the operator was not going to let them get away so easily. Henry just had time to hear her say, "Tampica! Please give me your area code and number"—before a switch was thrown which disconnected his line from that of Dr. Duncan, and substituted a cacophony of clicks and buzzes. Then the operator returned to Henry, demanding his identity, his current telephone number and address, and other irrelevant information, before she announced triumphantly, "I'm putting you through now!"—and Henry found himself talking to Sir Samuel Drake-Frobisher's secretary, who was trying to make a call to the State Department in Washington. The operator, like a games' mistress trying to control an unruly hockey game, ordered everybody to hang up and start again from the beginning. And at long last Henry found himself talking to Dr. Duncan.

"Tibbett. Duncan. Thought I must call you."

"Why? What's happened?"

"Information. Disturbing information. Such a dear girl, and I don't like to tell tales, but there it is. You'll have to know."

"Tell me, then," suggested Henry.

"I hardly know how to. These people are my friends, you see. That's the whole trouble."

"What's the whole trouble, Dr. Duncan?"

"Why, that I knew her too well. And her family. That's why she went to another island."

"Who did?"

"Are you connected?" broke in the fluting tones of the operator.

"Yes, by the grace of God, so don't interfere!" shouted Duncan. "Now, where was I?"

"Somebody went to another island. Who?"

"Dorrie Hamilton, of course. Because she wouldn't have wanted to come to me, you see."

"But Miss Hamilton is here in Washington," said Henry, raising his voice against what sounded like the waters of the Atlantic Ocean pounding down the line.

"I'm talking about a couple of years ago. When she had a serious drinking problem. Can you hear me, Tibbett?"

"Yes, I can. Go on."

"Well, if she'd come to me for help, it would have been all round the island in no time, professional secrecy or no," said the doctor. "You can't hush things up in a small, enclosed society like that. So she went off to a doctor on St. Mark's—there's a plane every day, only takes a quarter of an hour—and he put her on disulfiram. Alcodym, to be precise. So there's your source of the stuff, right in the Embassy."

Henry said, "If she was drinking so heavily, surely people on the island must have known about it?"

Duncan hesitated. "I don't think so," he said. "Some may have, but I never heard of it, and I know most things that go on. Seems she was a solitary drinker. Of course, she was all broken up by Eddie's marriage. That'll have been the root of it all."

"So how did you finally find out?" Henry asked.

"Pure luck. If you can call it that. I was round at the Hamilton house taking a look at one of the smaller children—suspected measles. I said the child should be isolated—they all live in each other's pockets, these big families—and Dorrie's mother said that fortunately Dorrie's room was now free, and that she'd clear it out for the kid. Well, the clearing out must have been pretty rudimentary, because when I called this morning to see the child, it was obvious that most of Dorrie's things were still there. And the first thing I set eyes on was this empty Alcodym bottle on the dressing table. I asked Cassie about it—that's the mother—and after a bit the whole story came out.

"Dorrie's cured now, and very seldom needs to use the Alcodym, but she keeps a bottle with her, just in case." Dr. Duncan paused, and sighed. "I really can't believe that Dorrie would have...she was jealous, of course, and that creates tensions...all the same...somebody might have taken the bottle from her room...oh, well. I'll have to leave all that to you, Tibbett." Suddenly, the doctor sounded very old and tired. "Give my love to Dorrie and—please be gentle with her."

"I'll do my best," said Henry.

"Yes...well...there it is. Let me know what happens. Good-bye, Tibbett."

The line went dead. For a moment, Henry sat quite still, frowning to himself. Then he picked up the telephone again, called the Tampican Embassy and asked to speak to Inspector Bartholomew.

"Good afternoon, Inspector. Hope I'm not interrupting your work."

"No, no, sir. I have already made the inquiries, as you asked me to."

"Any result?"

"Just what we expected. I have questioned every one of the waiters who served food and drinks at the reception. Including those who were hired from outside. They all agree Lady Ironmonger was served nothing but straight tomato juice."

"How can they be so sure?"

"Well...the fact is that only one waiter served her. He's a member of the Embassy staff, by the name of...just a minute..." Henry could hear the rustle of paper as Bartholomew thumbed through his notes. "Ah...here we are...Walter Jenkins. It seems that the staff was briefed by Dorrie—by Miss Hamilton, I should say—before the reception. They were all told that Lady Ironmonger would be drinking nothing but tomato juice throughout the evening, and that if she asked for a drink, only tomato juice was to be served her. However, Jenkins was allotted the special task of looking after His Excellency and Lady Ironmonger, to make sure they had everything they wanted and wouldn't need to ask for anything."

"Jenkins came with the Ironmongers from Tampica, did he?"

"That's right, sir."

"Then presumably you must have known him back home," Henry said.

There was a little pause. Then Bartholomew said, "Not really, sir. He's not Tampican, you see. He's from St. Mark's.

Came over to work for Miss Pontefract-Deacon—the English lady who lives out on Sugar Mill Bay, and that's far out, I can tell you. Jenkins didn't come into town much. He seems a nice enough guy—when you consider that he's from St. Mark's."

Henry tried to keep the smile out of his voice. "I see. And what did he tell you?"

"He says he served three glasses of plain tomato juice to Lady Ironmonger in the course of the evening. While the receiving line was going on, she kept her glass on a small table behind her, and took a sip from it every so often. He kept an eye on it, and when it was empty he replaced it with a fresh one, without waiting to be asked. Those were his orders. When the receiving line broke up, Lady Ironmonger picked up her glass and carried it with her while she talked to the guests. Jenkins noticed it was full. It was some time since he'd given her a fresh drink, so he concluded that she had simply not touched it. It seems more likely to me that somebody else substituted a doctored drink when Jenkins wasn't looking. He was in and out of the room, naturally, fetching drinks and food from the kitchen. It would have been easy enough to do, heaven knows. Just a question of picking up an ordinary Bloody Mary, adding the Alcodym and doing a switch while nobody was looking. Anybody in the room could have done it." Bartholomew sounded distinctly glum.

"Things may not be as hopeless as you think," said Henry. "I think we've got a lead at last."

"We have? What's that, sir?"

"I'll tell you a little later on, Inspector. Meanwhile, can you put me through to Miss Hamilton?"

"I'll try, sir. I'm not quite sure if I know how to—"

"You'll find a push button on your telephone receiver, Inspector. I think you push it twice to alert Miss Hamilton's extensions." Henry had noticed, while visiting the Embassy, that there appeared to be only one outside telephone line, but many extensions to various rooms and offices. The button system enabled anybody who answered the phone to draw the attention of an occupant in another part of the house that the call was for him.

"Oh…I see…that's right…thank you, sir…"

There was a buzzing noise, and a moment later Dorabella was saying, "Sir Edward Ironmonger's office. May I help you?"

Henry said, "Ah, Miss Hamilton. This is Henry Tibbett."

"Good afternoon. What do you want, Chief Superintendent?" Dorabella's voice was correct but not friendly.

"A word with you, if I may. I believe that you use Alcodym, Miss Hamilton."

Henry was taking a calculated risk, and he knew it. Nobody from the Embassy could have overheard his conversation with Dr. Duncan, but any of them might know of the doctor's intention to call, for Margaret had telephoned the Embassy in search of Henry. If Dorabella knew of the call, and was guilty, she would have guessed the gist of Duncan's information—or at least suspected it. She would be on her guard, and Henry's only hope was to spring the word "Alcodym" on her without warning and pray to get an instinctive reaction. However, he was aware of the dangers involved.

For a moment there was dead silence. Then Dorabella said, "How on earth did you know that?" She sounded scared.

"Never mind how. It's true, isn't it?"

"Well…yes…that is, I used to take it. I don't need it any more, thank goodness."

"But you keep a bottle of it, just the same?"

Another long pause.

Henry said, "Please don't try to deny it, because I know you do."

"Very well. I do."

"Have you checked the bottle lately? Is it emptier than it ought to be?"

This time, the silence seemed endless. At last Dorabella said, "I don't think we should discuss this on the telephone, Chief Superintendent. I finish work in an hour's time, at five o'clock. Why don't you come along to my apartment at half-past five? 2581 P Street, near the bridge. Third floor. I'll talk to you there. You see, the day before the reception...oh, excuse me. Sir Edward wants me. I must go. See you at half-past five." The line went dead.

Henry put down the telephone and sighed. There was no definite proof, of course, but it was depressingly obvious that Dorabella Hamilton had opportunity, means and motive to kill Mavis Ironmonger. Also, she had sounded frightened on the telephone. On the other hand, she had also sounded puzzled. Whatever the outcome, Henry felt sure that she would keep her appointment with him at half-past five and that she would have interesting information for him.

One of the features which keeps Georgetown such a well-defined entity, a village within a city, is that its eastern and southern boundaries have been indelibly pegged out by nature. To the south, the Potomac River separates it from Virginia. To the east, the escarpment of Dumbarton Rock falls precipitously down to the narrow gorge known as Rock Creek Park. The creek itself tumbles and cascades along the bed of the valley, followed now in its windings and twisting by the motorway known as Rock Creek Parkway. On the far side, the ground rises again to become downtown Washington.

Two hundred years ago, the abyss of Rock Creek effectively severed any easy communication between Georgetown and the rest of urban Washington—a fact which isolated and annoyed the Georgetowners. Now, several bridges span the valley, some distinguished by fine animal sculptures and known as the Buffalo Bridge or the Lion Bridge, others more mundanely as the M Street or P Street bridges. In any event, it is impossible to get to or from Georgetown without crossing a bridge, and taking a brief look down at the rushing waters of the creek below. This fact creates a psychological gulf between Georgetown and Washington, quite as deep as the physical one.

It also makes it impossible for even the most honey-tongued real estate agent to describe a house as being in Georgetown when in fact it is in Foggy Bottom.

Right up as far as the bridges on the Georgetown side, however, property can be and is described as Georgetown—but the last few blocks are definitely on the fringe. Only here will you find the occasional high-rise apartment block, for the area is not protected by a law to preserve its historic character. Many of these apartments are large, modern and comfortable, and have beautiful views down to Rock Creek. It is, of course, pure snobbery for people to maintain that they prefer a tumbledown frame cottage with a leaky basement and a dank back yard in the heart of Georgetown. Nevertheless, this attitude persists.

The address which Dorabella Hamilton had given Henry proved to be one of these apartment blocks near the P Street bridge. It struck Henry as being an eminently suitable choice of residence for a single girl in Dorabella's position. It was within easy walking distance of her work, modern and therefore easy to run, and without the endless disadvantages of a rickety if historic house. The clerk at the desk in the foyer informed Henry that Miss Hamilton's apartment was No. 416, on the fourth floor—which Henry now knew enough to interpret into English as the third floor. He inquired where he might find the lift, and encountered a moment of blank incomprehension until the clerk realized that he wanted the elevator. It was twenty-nine minutes past five.

He could hear the insistent buzz of the doorbell inside the apartment as he pressed the button with his finger. A second and a third time the beelike summons rang, but to no effect. Dorabella was not at home.

It certainly would not have taken her a full half-hour to walk from the Embassy to 2581 P Street, Henry reflected. Sir Edward must have asked her to stay on and work late. Henry lit a cigarette, leaned against the door jamb, and waited.

After ten minutes, he went downstairs again and telephoned the Tampican Embassy from a public call box in the foyer. The phone was answered almost at once by Winston Nelson, who sounded surprised.

"Yes, Mr. Tibbett…yes, as a matter of fact, I can…she left here just a little late, at ten past five… Well, yes, I am sure, because she looked into my office to see if I was still here. She said, 'It's ten past five, Winnie, and I'm leaving now. Will you be here for a while?' I told her I had at least another hour of work to get through, and she said, 'Oh, good, then you can take any outside calls, because Eddie's out and everyone else has gone home.' That's why I answered your call, Mr. Tibbett."

"It's strange," Henry said. "I'm at her apartment building now. We had a date at half-past five."

Winston said, "It wouldn't have taken her that long to walk home. Perhaps she stopped to do some shopping on the way."

"Perhaps she did," said Henry thoughtfully. "Well, thank you very much, Mr. Nelson. I'll just wait here and hope she arrives."

It was about ten minutes later that the telephone on the clerk's desk rang. "Yes…yes, there is a gentleman waiting for Miss Hamilton, but…oh…" The clerk's ebony face registered shock, and he lowered his voice to a respectful murmur. "Yes, sir…yes, of course…just a moment…" He put his hand over the mouthpiece of the telephone, and said to Henry, "Are you Mr. Tibbett?"

"I am."

"It's the Tampican Embassy on the telephone for you, sir. I'm afraid…I'm afraid it's bad news. About Miss Hamilton."

Henry was at the desk in an instant, snatching the telephone from the clerk's hand. At the other end of the line, Winston Nelson was making a great effort to be calm, but failing. In his emotion, a West Indian accent broke through the façade of his B.B.C. English.

"Mr. Tibbett…worst possible news, I'm afraid…an accident…hit and run…yes, that's what is so terrible…only just around the corner from the Embassy…there's a quiet little street, makes a good short cut, Exeter Place…must have happened soon after she left…the hospital just called…"

"Why?" asked Henry.

"Why? Mr. Tibbett, don't you understand? Dorrie's dead… run over by some bastard of a—"

"What I meant," said Henry, "was why have they only just called you from the hospital? Didn't they find her for some time, or…what?"

Winnie was becoming more agitated by the moment. "Oh, yes, sure they found her. A lady living in Exeter Place heard a scream and ran out and saw Dorrie lying in the road. But the car was gone. The lady says she heard it drive off—but what's the use of that? No one'll catch that son-of-a—"

"For heaven's sake," said Henry, "get a grip on yourself and listen to me. Did somebody call an ambulance right away?"

"Oh, yes. The lady called right away…ambulance and police…Dorrie was dead at the hospital…"

"Then," said Henry patiently, "why did they take so long to get in touch with you? She must have had identification on her—"

"No."

"What was that?"

"I say 'No.' No identification. Only just discovered who she is."

"But that's ridiculous," said Henry. "She must have had something in her handbag…driving license…diplomatic identity card…"

"No handbag."

"Talk sense, man." Henry was becoming exasperated. "She was on her way home to meet me. She must have had her handbag with her."

"No. I looked in her office, after the hospital called. Her handbag was there. I have it now."

"Well, for God's sake don't touch it."

"Have touched it, Mr. Tibbett."

"God give me strength. Is Inspector Bartholomew there?"

"No. Nobody. Only me."

"Now, listen carefully, Mr. Nelson. Call Inspector Bartholomew, get him round to the Embassy, explain what has happened and give him the handbag—he'll know what to do with it. And tell him to seal off Miss Hamilton's office and keep guard on it. Got that?"

"Yes, Mr. Tibbett."

"And now, perhaps you can at least tell me the name of the hospital?"

"Of course. Thomas Jefferson Memorial Hospital."

"I'll be there if anybody wants me. Have you told Sir Edward yet?"

"I can't. I don't know where he is."

"Somebody at the Embassy must know!"

"Dorrie knows..."

"Well, stop sniveling and find him," said Henry, and rang off.

Henry had anticipated that he might run into a certain amount of trouble at the hospital, owing to his unofficial status. However, the trim black receptionist agreed to put in a call to the doctor who had handled the case, and a moment later she looked up from the telephone with a wide smile.

"Dr. Miles would like to talk to you, Mr. Tibbett. You can take the call in that booth over there."

"Mr. Tibbett? I'm Dr. Miles. I'm sure glad you're here."

"Why? You don't know me."

"Right. But Miss Hamilton was asking for you, just before she died."

"I thought she was dead on arrival at the hospital," Henry said.

"No. She was unconscious, and there was never any real hope of recovery. However, she did have a moment of lucidity, and she mentioned your name. I've got Officer Stanton of the D.C. Police with me here, and he'd like a word with you, too. Could you come up? Room 962."

The doctor and the police officer were both young men—the policeman white, with neatly cropped hair and a clean cut jawline, the doctor black, with a carefully tended Afro hairstyle. Officer Stanton sat at a desk in the small office, compiling his official report of the accident. Dr. Miles stood by the window, gazing out over the rooftops toward the green grass of the Mall and the slender needle of the Washington Monument.

The doctor said, "Glad to know you, Mr. Tibbett. This is a bad, sad business. You knew Miss Hamilton well, of course?"

"No. Only slightly."

Stanton intervened. "Have you any idea what reason she might have had for mentioning your name before she died?"

"Yes, but it may be the wrong one. What did she say?"

Stanton moved a paper to consult his notes, but Dr. Miles forestalled him. "I can tell you exactly. She was barely conscious, just murmuring. She said, 'Tell Tibbett...Mavis...my fault...I did it...' After that she mumbled some more, but I couldn't make out the words. Then she died. Does that make any sense to you?"

"I'm afraid it does," said Henry. "You know that Miss Hamilton worked at the Tampican Embassy?"

"We do now," Stanton said. "It took quite some fancy detective work. She had no pocketbook, you see—no identification. Just stepped out to mail a letter, I guess. We traced her by a dry cleaner's receipt in her pocket made out in the name of Hamilton, and the fact that her dress had a label of a shop in Tampica Harbour. My department checked out the diplomatic list, and sure enough, there was Miss Dorabella Hamilton, secretary to the Tampican Ambassador. Lady Ironmonger's first name was Mavis, wasn't it? I've been following the story on TV..." He paused, on a distinctly interrogative note.

Henry said, "Yes. I'd better explain." When he had done so—going into no details, but explaining how Tampica was handling Lady Ironmonger's death, and his role in the matter—Stanton said, "Well, they can't keep this one out of our hands. This took place on a public highway in the District of Columbia."

Dr. Miles turned back to the window. He said, "It's all academic. You'll never catch the hit-and-run driver. The girl is dead, and there's the end of it. All we can do is make reports and tie up legal loose ends."

"Can you tell me," Henry asked, "who the witnesses were, and what they said?"

Stanton pushed a sheaf of papers across the desk. "It's all there. Nobody actually saw the accident. Exeter Place is dangerous—we've been saying so for years. It's a useful short cut for traffic, and motorists take it much too fast. Two children have been injured there this past year. The houses on the street are all very large, and set back among trees and gardens—and several of them are empty. People can't afford these Georgetown mansions any more. There was nobody around to see what happened. However, the housekeeper from No. 3021 happened to be in the garden, and she heard Miss Hamilton scream, and then the sound of a car accelerating down the road. By the time she got to the gate, the car had gone. She saw Miss Hamilton lying in the middle of the road, and ran to call the ambulance—and us."

Henry said, "In the middle of the road?"

"That's what Mrs. Drayton said."

"Isn't that rather strange?"

"Well, I suppose she was crossing over when the car hit her."

"Is there a letter-box—a mail box—on that street?"

Dr. Miles said at once, "No. I often walk down Exeter Place. There's no mail box."

"Then there's no earthly reason why she should have been crossing the road," Henry said. "She had an appointment with me at her apartment on P Street, and she was coming from the Embassy. She didn't need to cross to the south side of the road at any point."

"She can't have been on her way home," Stanton objected. "She didn't have her pocketbook with her."

"Her what?" Henry asked.

The officer looked puzzled. "Her pocketbook. Like all women carry."

"Oh, you mean her handbag. We really are divided by a common language, aren't we?" Henry grinned at Stanton, and then said, "What hope do you have of catching the hit-and-run driver?"

The doctor and the policeman looked at each other. Stanton shrugged. "Virtually none, if you want the truth. The car would have suffered only minimal damage—nothing we could ever prove. There'd be no traces of blood on it—the Doc here says her injuries were consistent with being picked up and hurled into the air, as it were, not run over."

"Could that account for her being in the middle of the road?" Henry asked. And then, answering his own question, "No…if she'd been walking along the pavement—"

"Why should she do that?" Miles demanded. "Why wouldn't she use the sidewalk?"

Henry smiled. "Here we go again. What we call the pavement is what you call the sidewalk."

"Then what do you call the pavement?"

"The roadway."

Stanton shook his head. "Beats me. Go on. If she'd been walking on the sidewalk—"

"Well, the car would have had to swerve off the road—off the pavement—either deliberately or out of control, in order to hit her. In which case, it would either have pushed or tossed her *away* from the street, toward the garden wall of the house. I think we have to accept the fact that for some reason she was in the middle of the road when the car struck her."

"Without a pocketbook," said Stanton, very deliberately. "And she said to tell you that something about Mavis was her fault—that she did it. It adds up, doesn't it, Mr. Tibbett?"

"I'm very much afraid it does," said Henry. "As it happens, I have another piece of evidence—something I was going to discuss with Miss Hamilton—which just about clinches it. I'm afraid she threw herself deliberately under that car…that she never intended to reach home or talk to me. Of course, we can't prove it—and for the sake of the Embassy and Miss Hamilton's family, it's better just to announce that she was the victim of a hit-and-run accident, which is perfectly true."

Stanton nodded, slowly. "I'll put in my report," he said. "You'll be around for a bit, will you, Mr. Tibbett? Just in case…"

The telephone rang, and the doctor picked it up. "Dr. Miles speaking…yes, sure, he's here…just a moment, Sir Ironmonger…" He turned to Henry. "The Tampican Ambassador for you."

Ironmonger's voice was grave. "Tibbett? Winnie Nelson has just told me the dreadful news…I suppose she was killed instantly, poor girl…"

"Not instantly," said Henry. "She regained consciousness for a while in hospital."

"Enough to speak?" Henry thought he detected a sharp note of anxiety.

"Yes."

"Could she identify the car that hit her?"

"That would be asking rather too much, Sir Edward. I don't suppose she even saw it."

"Then what did she say?"

"If you can meet me at the Embassy in half-an-hour, I'll tell you. Meantime…" Henry hesitated. "You leave for Tampica tomorrow, don't you? For the conference?"

"No, not tomorrow. Friday. And what I shall do without Dorabella…however, that's a very selfish viewpoint. I can tell you, Tibbett, that I'd be happier about going if you could clear up the mystery of Mavis's death before I leave here."

"I think," said Henry, "that that has been attended to."

CHAPTER TWELVE

IT WAS TWELVE noon on the following day, Wednesday. Henry sat facing the Tampican Ambassador in the latter's study at the Embassy.

"A tragic matter," Sir Edward Ironmonger was saying, shaking his handsome head. "Tragic, but not, I suppose wholly unexpected. At least it is better to know the truth."

"Yes, it is," said Henry.

Ironmonger rose from his desk and walked to the window. He lit a big cigar and gazed out at the trimly tended garden. With his back to Henry, he said, "Dorrie was the obvious person. There's no getting away from it. I knew that she disliked Mavis, and of course she had ample opportunity to take the gun and doctor the tomato juice. What I did not know about was her drinking problem. She certainly concealed it very well."

"I don't think it had been a problem for some time," Henry said. "She kept a bottle of Alcodym with her, but she wasn't using it. Unfortunately, she knew what effect a double dose of it would have with a stiff drink." He paused. "You must have known, Sir Edward, that she was in love with you?"

Ironmonger's shoulders stiffened. Without turning round, he said, "I consider that an impertinent remark, Mr. Tibbett."

"I'm sorry. It is also relevant."

"I knew that she was...fond of me. Intensely loyal. I certainly never encouraged her in a sexual manner, if that is what you are implying."

Henry thought, "The man's frightened. I wonder why." Aloud, he said, "Of course I'm not implying any such thing, Sir Edward. I'm simply trying to sort out Miss Hamilton's motives. She was deeply attached to you personally, and she seems to have convinced herself that Lady Ironmonger was an impediment to your career. I imagine her first idea was merely to create the sort of scandalous scene which she hoped would persuade you to break up your marriage. I know it sounds ridiculous, but people under great tension can rationalize almost anything. Then, with the talk about the gun the other day, a more drastic plot evolved."

Sir Edward said, "You are sure of your conclusions, Tibbett? You will put in a report—you and Bartholomew—to the effect that Miss Hamilton was responsible for my wife's death, and then took her own life?"

"I don't see what else we can do," said Henry. "Especially in view of what was virtually a deathbed confession. Not to mention that she had left the Embassy without her handbag, and was in the middle of the road when she was hit. We have no choice."

Sir Edward sighed and took a long pull on his cigar. Then he turned to face Henry, seeming to change mental gears as he did so. His voice was smooth and urbane as he said, "Well, now the matter is resolved, and for that I am extremely grateful, Tibbett. It is an enormous relief to be able to go to Tampica for a difficult conference without an unsolved problem hanging over our heads." He sat down at the desk again, facing Henry. "As a small token of my government's gratitude to you in this sad business, I hope that you and your wife can find time for a short holiday on our island before you go back to London. Pirate's Cave is a pleasant hotel, and we would like to welcome you as official guests."

"It's very kind of you, Sir Edward," Henry said, "but I'm afraid we must get back to England as soon as possible. We've no possible reason for staying on. The case is closed."

❀ ❀ ❀

"So the case is closed," said Emmy Tibbett. She, Henry and Margaret Colville were sitting round the crackling log fire which Margaret had lit in the drawing-room, sooner than turn on the central heating against the slight chill of the April evening.

"It seems so," said Henry.

"Well, I think you've been splendid," said Margaret. "You've only been here a few days, and everything is solved and sorted out. Sheer genius."

"Sheer nothing," said Henry. "I've been as much good as a sick headache. The only detective work that's been done at all was done by old Duncan, and that's been more luck than judgment." He paused and rubbed the back of his neck with his left hand—a sign which Emmy recognized.

"You're not happy about it, are you, Henry?" she said.

"I'm never happy if I've made a lousy job of something."

"I mean—you don't really believe that Dorabella Hamilton was guilty. Or that she killed herself."

"Of course I do," said Henry, irritably. "You can't get away from the facts, and there they are—staring you in the face. Together with an explicit confession to a total outsider—the doctor." He paused, and smiled. "You're absolutely right, of course. My nose... I mean, I find it difficult to believe that things happened so conveniently and neatly. Or, let's say, I don't want to believe it. Also, there are certain inconsistencies... but what's the use? As long as I've no shred of evidence to the contrary, and a completely independent witness testified to a deathbed confession…how can I argue with the obvious?"

"Isn't there anybody else you could talk to?" Margaret asked. "Anybody who might shed some new light on—anything?"

Henry opened the file on his lap, and turned the pages slowly. He said, "Between us, Bartholomew and I have interviewed everybody. All the Embassy people, the doctor, the police, the waiters at the reception, the Barringtons, the Schipmakers…no, that's true, I haven't actually met Otis and Virginia. But there seems little point to that now."

"Isn't there anybody else?" Emmy persisted. "In connection with Dorabella Hamilton, I mean?"

Henry was thumbing through reports. "The only other person who gave evidence was the housekeeper from Exeter Place…Mrs.…where is it?…Mrs. Belinda Drayton. She's the one who heard the scream and called the police."

"You don't think she might help?"

"I can't think how," Henry said. "I've got a transcript of her evidence here, and it couldn't be clearer. She was in the garden of the Exeter Place house, heard the car and the scream, and ran to investigate. That's all there is to it."

"You don't think she might have seen or heard something more—something she didn't think of mentioning to the police?"

Henry smiled at his wife. "No, Emmy, I don't. But since you are obviously determined not to let me off the hook, I'll walk around to Exeter Place in the morning and have a word with the lady, just to make you happy. And then we'll get on the next plane and go home."

Thirty-twenty-one Exeter Place was a house so imposing that Henry would have been tempted to classify it as a mansion, had it not stood across the street from 3018, which was surrounded by acres of garden and boasted a curved carriage drive, a classical portico, graceful bow windows, clusters of coach houses and garages, and fifteen bedrooms (if you don't count the guest annex). 3021 was a more modest establishment, built of rose-red brick in the latter half of the eighteenth century. About half an acre of garden protected the house from prying passers-by, and the garden in its turn sheltered behind a tall, ivy-covered wall. In the wall were two gates—the main entrance, a pair of finely wrought iron gates giving onto a graveled drive leading to the front door; and the tradesmen's entrance, around the corner on 30th Street, which was a stout wooden door, painted black. Henry made for the tradesmen's entrance.

A narrow paved path led up to the kitchen door. Before Henry had time to ring the bell, the door opened and a sturdy black woman in her sixties came out, vigorously shaking a small rug. She stopped when she saw Henry, and said politely, "May I help you, sir? The front entrance is right around the corner, on Exeter Place—but I'm 'fraid Mrs. Blair isn't home right now. She's in Europe." Her voice had the soft, pleasant lilt of the South.

Henry said, "As a matter of fact, I'm looking for Mrs. Drayton."

"Drayton? Why, that's me, sir. What can I do for you, then?" Mrs. Drayton smiled, revealing a blaze of white teeth.

"I'm sorry to bother you, Mrs. Drayton," Henry said, "but I'm a policeman, working with Officer Stanton. I believe you made a statement to him about the accident in Exeter Place on Tuesday."

Mrs. Drayton's merry face clouded. "That poor girl," she said. "I can see her now, lying right there in the street. I'll not never forget that, I tell you, sir. And I can still hear it...the way she did scream. I didn't sleep all night, thinking of it."

"But you weren't able to tell Officer Stanton anything about the car?"

"No, sir. He was off too quick for me. Besides, I couldn't think on nothin' 'cept the poor young lady."

"But you heard the car?"

"I sure did. And like I said, if I'd bin watchin' that car instead of the girl in the road, I'd like as not have seen him 'fore he got off roun' the corner. Enough to see his color, anyways."

"Well," Henry said, "it's a pity, but it can't be helped. It was perfectly natural for you to give all your attention to Miss Hamilton. We appreciate how promptly you called for help."

Mrs. Drayton shook the rug again. "If I hadn't have happened to be out in the garden," she said, punctuating her words with vigorous shakes, "that poor chile might've laid there in the road a long, long time. But there I was, gathering some parsley for dinner, so I heard her and come runnin'. But I was too late."

"She was unconscious when you got to her? She didn't say anything?"

"Not nuthin', sir. Not nuthin'."

"And that's all you can tell me?"

"I tole Officer Stanton all I knows, and now I tole you, sir."

"You noticed that Miss Hamilton wasn't carrying a handbag?"

"I didn't see no handbag, that's true. Never thought about it at the time."

Henry sighed. "Well, that seems to be that. Thank you very much, Mrs. Drayton."

"Y'all welcome sir, I'm sure. Have a good day now."

Mrs. Drayton went back into the kitchen, closing the door behind her. Henry was walking slowly back down the path to the tradesmen's entrance when his eye was caught by a patch of bright green, down the garden to his right. A fine crop of curly parsley, planted out neatly in a bed of other herbs, convenient to the kitchen. So Mrs. Drayton had been there, picking parsley, when... Henry stopped dead. Then he ran back and knocked on the kitchen door.

Mrs. Drayton opened it almost at once. "Y'all forget somethin'?"

"Mrs. Drayton," said Henry, "that's your parsley bed over there, isn't it?"

The black woman looked puzzled. "Sure is."

"So that's where you were when you heard the scream. Now, that's well away from Exeter Place, on the 30th Street side of the garden. I don't know how fast you can run, Mrs. Drayton, but I can't see any way you could have got to the front gate from there, and out into Exeter Place, in time to hear and very nearly see the hit-and-run car. Do you think there might have been two cars?"

Mrs. Drayton was regarding him with a gentle smile, nodding to herself, her arms crossed. "You got it wrong, sir. Surely I was out to pick parsley, but when the young lady scream, I was on my way to the front already."

"You were? Why?"

"I don't hear so good these days as when I was a girl," Mrs. Drayton admitted. "I just done make a mistake. I done think I hear somebody callin' my name out in Ex'ter Place. I think maybe it's Walt—he's the chauffeur from 3018, over the street. So I come over to see what he want—and then there's the scream, and the car, and no sign of Walt, so I just made a mistake, like I said."

Hardly daring to breathe, Henry said, "You thought you heard a voice calling your name?"

"That's right, sir."

"A voice calling 'Mrs. Drayton'?"

Mrs. Drayton beamed. "Lordy, no, sir. We're all good friends round this block. We don't use no Mister and Missus."

"So you thought somebody called 'Belinda'?"

"Belinda's my name, sir, sure enough, but folks find it bothersome long. No, sir—what I'm called around here is Bella."

Henry said, "You thought it was a man's voice. Would you recognize it again?"

"There wasn't any voice, sir. Like I said, my ears aren't what they were. Stand to reason nobody done call me, 'cause nobody was there in the street excepting the poor young lady. Must have been that old mockingbird—he can imitate 'bout any sound you can name."

"Yes," said Henry. "Yes, you're right. It must have been the mockingbird. I'd forget all about it if I were you."

"That's just what I aim to do, sir. I wouldn't have mentioned it, if you hadn't brought it up. I wouldn't like folks to know an ole mockingbird can make a fool out of me."

"Of course you wouldn't," said Henry. "I promise I'll keep my mouth shut. And you do the same."

"Sure will, sir. That ole mockingbird..." Shaking her head, Mrs. Drayton went back into the house. Henry beat a decorous retreat through the garden gate, and then sprinted for the nearest public telephone booth.

Dr. Miles was not at all surprised. In answer to Henry's question, he said, "She had severe concussion, you know, as well as internal injuries. It's highly unlikely that when she regained consciousness in the hospital she had any recollection at all of the accident. She would probably remember nothing after leaving the Embassy for her meeting with you."

Officer Stanton agreed. "That's the trouble with these hit-and-run cases. Even if the victim survives, after concussion he usually has a permanent memory blank covering the actual accident. He can't help us with descriptions of the car or the driver. Of course, in a suicide case like this, one wouldn't expect the lady to do anything except try to make her confession, if that's what it was. But if it had been an accident, I doubt she'd have been able to tell us anything about it."

The telephone rang in Sir Edward Ironmonger's study. The Ambassador broke off the discussion on the upcoming conference which he was holding with Michael Holder-Watts, picked up the receiver, and said, "Ironmonger."

"Oh, Sir Edward, I'm so glad I got you. I keep getting wrong numbers." The young Tampican filing clerk who was now occupying Dorabella's office sounded near tears. "There's a Mr. Tibbett on the line for you. Shall I put him through—if I can, sir?"

"Yes, put him on," said Ironmonger gravely. He put a hand over the mouthpiece and twinkled a smile at Michael. For the moment, at least, his animosity towards the Counsellor seemed to have disappeared. He said, "I think our policeman may have had second thoughts about Pirate's Cave." Into the telephone, he said, "Chief Superintendent? What can I do for you?... You have? Well, I'm very glad to hear it...no, no trouble at all...yes, of course you and Inspector Bartholomew should be together for the writing of the report...yes, that's correct, he left this morning...no, no, I think it is an excellent decision, and I hope you'll find time for a little play between working sessions... Our party leaves for Tampica tomorrow morning...I'll arrange seats on the afternoon plane for you—that'll give us time to get things organized at the other end...there'll be a car to meet you and Mrs. Tibbett at the airport...think nothing of it, old man, it's our pleasure and privilege..."

He rang off and grinned hugely at Michael, who remarked, "I didn't think he'd be able to resist it. Poor devil, he'd never be able to afford a holiday at Pirate's Cave if he worked overtime for a hundred years. You really can't blame him."

Thoughtfully, Sir Edward said, "He seemed very definite about refusing yesterday."

"Maybe," said Michael, "but in the meantime he probably mentioned your offer to his wife. Hence the change of heart. How does it feel to be Father Christmas, Eddie?"

Ironmonger said, a little stiffly, "He deserves our gratitude. It's tragic about Dorabella, but at least the matter is settled and we can concentrate on the conference. By the way, Michael, you'd better call Tampica and fix up the hotel and the car for the Tibbetts. Winnie will be too busy, even though he's on the spot." He paused, and added, "I'm sorry you're not coming with us,

Michael, but I really don't feel there's anybody else I can leave in charge here. That's why I sent Winnie on ahead to Tampica and why he'll be my aide at the conference. You do understand?"

"Of course, Eddie." Michael lit a cigarette and gave the Ambassador a quizzical stare. "We ex-British are secure enough not to carry chips on our shoulders. I'm sure Winnie will be very useful to you."

Ironmonger grinned. "I hope you're right," he said. "However, I like to think that you'll be at the end of a telephone line, if necessary. Meanwhile, I'd like to go over those figures again...this is the sum I'm suggesting to Sam that he should demand over a five-year period, and it's essential that he shouldn't weaken his case by..." The dark head and the fair one came close as the two men pored over the document. Murder is murder, personal dislike is personal dislike, but politics is something else again.

When Henry got back to the little blue frame house, it appeared deserted, and he assumed that Margaret and Emmy were both out; but then, through the French windows of the drawing-room, he saw his wife in the garden. She was standing on tiptoe, reaching up to the top of the fence to stroke and converse with the excessively handsome Siamese cat from next door. Around her, forsythia blossomed in a golden cascade, a camellia tree blazed with dark red flowers among thick, shiny leaves, and the ground at her feet was blue with violets. She turned at the sound of the opening door.

"Oh, hello, darling. I was just making a new friend." The cat gave Henry a disdainful look, and jumped down on his own side of the fence. Emmy said, "How did you get on? Don't tell me. If you'd found out anything useful, you wouldn't be home so soon. Oh, well. It was worth a try. I suppose I'd better start packing." She looked around the little garden. "I shall miss Georgetown. I hope we can come back one day."

"Yes," said Henry. "I'll miss Georgetown, too. And certainly we should start packing. But first of all, we've some shopping to do."

"Shopping? Oh—you mean, presents for people back home?"

"I mean," said Henry, "that we'll both need at least one swimsuit, and some shorts and light shirts, not to mention dark glasses and suntan oil and—"

"Henry, have you gone completely bananas, as Margaret says? What on earth are you talking about? Swimsuits and dark glasses in London in April—?"

Henry grinned. "If you'd allowed me to get a word in edgewise," he said, "I'd have told you that we're not going to London. We're going to Tampica."

"To Tampica? Whatever for?"

"To have a free holiday at one of the world's most famous hotels, as guests of the Tampican government."

Emmy's face clouded. "Oh, don't be silly, Henry."

"What d'you mean—don't be silly?"

"Well—we agreed we couldn't possibly accept. I'm not saying I wouldn't adore to go—I'm only human—but obviously we can't put ourselves under that sort of an obligation, and you know it."

Henry said, "Where's Margaret?"

"Out shopping. What has that to do with it?"

"Come inside and I'll tell you."

Emmy looked quickly at her husband's face, but she said nothing until they were both inside the drawing-room, and the door was closed. Then she said, "So you did find something."

Henry said, "Yes. That is, something happened to make me change my mind about the Tampican invitation. Now, listen, Emmy. Nobody—but *nobody*—must know that we're in Tampica for anything except a holiday. Since I turned down the offer very firmly yesterday, the implication must be that you talked me into going after all. You won't deny it—just giggle and say that you may have had something to do with it. Fortunately, some people are always ready to believe that any woman is selfish and stupid, whatever the evidence to the contrary. O.K.?"

"Of course. But what did you find out?"

Henry hesitated. Then he said, "Darling, you know my rule—what you don't know can't hurt you. I really would rather not tell you what I'll be looking for in Tampica."

Emmy sighed, then smiled, and put her arms round Henry's neck. "O.K. I should have known better than to ask. Come on—let's go to Wisconsin Avenue and buy those swimsuits."

Henry and Emmy arrived back from their shopping expedition to find Margaret cooking lunch, and a message for Chief Superintendent Tibbett to call Officer Stanton at the M Street Station.

"Tibbett? Stanton here. Just to let you know we've got the results in on that pocketbook that Inspector Bartholomew turned over for fingerprinting...yeah, the Hamilton girl's pocketbook... Well, all I can tell you is that there was just one set of prints...no, no, it had been extensively handled, but by just one person...nothing to match anything in our files...no, definitely not Miss Hamilton herself...yes, quite positive... I dare say you'll be wanting to collect the pocketbook...yes, surely, why don't you come along to the station this afternoon...be glad to see you..."

Officer Stanton's office was just like every other office in every other police station in the western world. It occurred to Henry that a number of governments must simultaneously have ordered large surplus quantities of green and cream semi-gloss paint, which they proceeded to unload on their law enforcement establishments. On Stanton's desk lay a new-looking, shiny black patent leather handbag. Stanton welcomed Henry genially.

"Good to see you, Superintendent. Well, there it is—just about perfect for fingerprints." He paused, ripped the paper off a slice of gum, and began to chew reflectively. "Funny they weren't her prints. Got any idea whose they could be?"

"I know whose they are," Henry said. "A First Secretary at the Embassy found the handbag in her office, and pawed all over it before I could stop him. We'll have to check, of course, but there's not much doubt—"

"Then why weren't her prints on it as well as his?" Stanton demanded.

Henry said lightly, "Oh, I expect she'd been polishing it. It's obviously very new."

"I guess you're right," Stanton said, with a grin. "Every time an ordinary cop like me gets a bright idea, it turns out there's an obvious explanation that he's too goddam stupid to see, right under his nose. Well, it's all yours...excuse me a moment..." He broke off to answer the insistent buzz of the desk telephone. "M Street, Officer Stanton...who?...ah, dammit, not again...why can't that guy keep his nose out of trouble, for Chrissakes?... O.K. bring him along here and book him...sure, I'd like him off the back of my neck, he's nothing but a pain in the ass..." He hung up and looked at Henry, shaking his head sadly. "Some guys..." he said.

"What was all that about?" Henry asked. He really did not care, but Stanton was clearly about to unburden himself, or burst.

"Franklin D. Martin," said Stanton. "Demonstrator without a cause. Boy, does he get in our hair. Just been arrested for streaking outside the White House, wearing a white mask—he's black, of course—and carrying a banner saying 'Impeach Ralph Nader.'" He shook his head. "Boy, oh boy, oh boy. I wish I'd seen it." He looked up. "Come to think of it, last time we busted him, it was outside the Tampican Embassy, the night Lady Ironmonger got shot."

Henry was intrigued. "Holder-Watts mentioned a demonstration," he said. "What was it in aid of?"

"Goddam nothing," said Stanton. "That's what I mean about Martin. Demonstrating's become a profession with him. As far as I remember, the banners said 'Go home Uncle Eddie' and 'Kill the White Bitch'—plus the usual anti-police signs, of course."

On an impulse, Henry said, "If he's being brought in here, could I see him?"

"See him? You can tango with him for all I care. You'll get nothing out of him, though. He's a jailhouse lawyer—knows his rights."

"What about plea-bargaining?" Henry said.

"What?"

"We've heard a lot about it lately," Henry said. "You've got some...what's it called...some clout around here, haven't you?"

"Some," admitted Stanton, through rotating jaws.

"Well, supposing you told Martin that the police would only ask for a nominal fine on the streaking charge...or indecent exposure or whatever it's legally called..."

"Obstructing the traffic," muttered Stanton.

"...if in return Martin would talk to me about the evening of Lady Ironmonger's death. Could you do that?"

Stanton meditated. "Sure could. What's in it for you? I thought that case was all sewn up."

"It is," said Henry. "It's just a question of tying up loose ends, and I think Martin could be helpful and save me a lot of time, if he'll co-operate."

Outside in the corridor, sounds of scuffles, shouts, protests and snatches of song grew louder as a posse of some sort approached, and then faded as it passed down the passage toward the cells.

"There he goes," Stanton remarked gloomily. "He's yours and welcome. I'll just go do that bargaining you spoke of. Then we can let him go on bond so he won't keep us awake all night. Be seeing you." He rose to his feet and went out of the office. Five minutes later he was back.

"O.K. Come with me. He's all yours."

Franklin D. Martin was sitting on a wooden bench in a cell, wearing nothing but a gray army blanket and a broad grin. He seemed highly delighted, both with his prowess as a streaker and by the legal arrangements which had been made. As to the motivation of the Tampican Embassy demonstration, however, he was less than lucid.

"Because, man...like...well, man...there it was...we don't miss a chance...well, man...like this Ironmonger is in Whitey's pocket, like, with a white woman in his bed...you dig?...like, man...here's a chance, I said...like..."

"What you mean," said Henry, "is that it was a good chance to get your name in the papers. There were a lot of famous people at the reception, weren't there?"

"Right. Right on, man."

"You know most of these people by sight, don't you?" Henry asked.

"Saw a fair lot I knew... Senator Belmont, I sure know him...fascist racist pig..."

"You saw him that evening?"

"Sure did. Drove up in a big fat Cadillac, I'm telling you, man, like he was the King of England."

"Mr. Finkelstein?"

"The Jew boy? Sure, sure, I know him. Sure, I saw him. He rides around in a Volkswagen. He's O.K., man."

"The Otis Schipmakers?"

"Do me a favor, man," pleaded Martin. "Don't make me throw up."

"You saw them?"

"Sure. They arrived in a Lincoln. Con-tin-ent-al, man. And with a black brother hu-mil-i-ated by driving them in a fancy outfit." Martin spat on the ground.

Henry said, "You seem to have seen a lot of people arriving. I'm more interested in when they left."

"Most I didn't see, man, thanks to the pigs busting me."

"What did they bust you for?"

"Nothing, man. Just a matter of a blade of grass, like."

Henry grinned. "O.K. But I suppose you saw Winston Nelson and the Barringtons leave?"

"That the black guy with the silver Chevelle and the two old white folks?"

"That's right."

"Sure, I saw them leave. Just before I got busted."

"You know Sir Edward Ironmonger?"

"Man, he's my best friend."

Henry found himself smiling. Martin was undeniably endearing. "I mean, you know him by sight. Did you see him that evening?"

"I did not. Nor that fancy black whore of his. Seems she shot the white bitch and then did herself in, man, and good riddance to both."

Surprised, Henry said, "Where did you hear that?"

"Don't ask me no questions, man. Just don't. You got a fix?"

Henry judged it was time to leave. Back in Officer Stanton's office, he glanced through a file, and made some quick notes. Police reports indicated that Franklin D. Martin and his protesters had arrived outside the Embassy in Oxford Gardens at 6:10 P.M. on the evening of the reception. They had behaved themselves reasonably well, and no action had been taken against them. By a quarter to seven, most of the demonstrators had dispersed, and the rest were sitting on the sidewalk. Everything appeared to be quiet and orderly until a policeman noticed what he judged to be the smell of marijuana.

Several demonstrators who were smoking quickly stubbed out their cigarettes when the officer approached. Two of them, of whom one was Martin, were clever enough to drop them through the grating of a street drain, so that they could not be recovered. Four demonstrators in all were arrested, and arrived at M Street Police Station at 7:28 P.M. The two whose reefers were retrieved and analyzed were charged with illegal possession of the drug. The other two, including Martin, claimed that the police had no proof except the allegation that the smell of marijuana still clung to their clothes, and that this would not be enough to convince a court. Reluctantly, the police agreed and the two men were released.

Henry thanked Stanton, signed a receipt for Dorabella's handbag and a copy of the fingerprint report, and took a cab back to Georgetown.

CHAPTER THIRTEEN

THE LITTLE PIPER Aztec aircraft rose smoothly from the runway at St. Mark's, and headed out over the Caribbean, whose waters gleamed in the bright sunlight like a carpet of jewels—sapphire, aquamarine, emerald and amethyst. Small islands of brown rock and green scrub rose here and there to break the shimmering surface, ringed with curved sandy beaches and creamy white breakers. Sometimes, a protective coral reef was clearly visible beneath the water a little off-shore, taking the buffeting of the waves upon itself, and creating a calm lagoon whose shallow waters were pale and transparent as green tourmaline.

The goodlooking young black pilot turned in his seat every so often to point out a particular island or strait to his passengers, who occupied the four seats in the tiny cabin behind him. Two of the passengers were Henry and Emmy Tibbett. The others were a handsome and obviously wealthy couple in their thirties, who—unlike the rubber-necking Tibbetts—seemed to know the area well and to find it unremarkable.

The man's face was vaguely familiar, and Henry felt reasonably sure of his identity. His hunch was soon confirmed. After a few minutes in the air, the man said, "You folks headed for Tampica?"—a rhetorical question, since Tampica was the aircraft's sole destination.

Henry and Emmy agreed that they were.

"Going to stay at Pirate's Cave?"

"Yes."

The man beamed. Henry and Emmy had passed the wealth test, and were now members of the club. "Well, since we're about to be fellow-guests, I reckon we should introduce ourselves. I'm Otis Schipmaker, and this is my wife, Ginny."

"Glad to know you," said Henry, who picked up local idiom as a magnet picks up iron filings. "We're Henry and Emmy Tibbett. I believe I met your brother Homer at the Barringtons' house back in Washington, D.C."

"And you're friends of Margaret Colville's," Emmy chimed in. "We've been staying with her."

"Well, well, well. It's a small world, isn't it?" Otis Schipmaker was now thoroughly relaxed, having well and truly established the Tibbetts' credentials. "You from England?"

"Yes, we are."

"Well, you'll be quite a rarity in Tampica—certainly at Pirate's Cave. Apart from a few government officials, you don't get to hear many British voices on the island. What with the naval base and tourists, it's just about all American—and of course the currency is in dollars."

"You know Tampica well, do you, Mr. Schipmaker?" Emmy asked, quite innocently. Henry had not repeated to her the conversation at the Barrington home.

There was a little pause. Then Otis cleared his throat and said, "I've been there before, yes. Some years ago. This is Ginny's first visit. We usually go to St. John's, but we thought we'd like a change of scenery this time."

"And of course, the naval base conference this week makes it a particularly interesting place to visit just now," said Henry, rather less innocently.

Ginny Schipmaker laughed. "You've hit it right on the head, Mr. Tibbett," she said. "Otis is running in the primary this spring."

"What's that?" Emmy was mystified. "Some sort of race?"

"Race for nomination to fight for a senate seat," Ginny explained. "He's about to make the issue of the naval base a plank in his platform, so of course he has to be here. The U.S. delegates are all staying at Pirate's Cave. But would you believe it, I had to talk him into it? He wanted to go and sit on his fanny in Caneel Bay, just like every other year."

Schipmaker looked uncomfortable. "I'm supposed to be on vacation," he muttered.

"Honey," said his wife, "politicians are never on vacation, and well you know it. Besides, I want to see Tampica."

"There it is now." The pilot's voice broke into the conversation. "See? Ahead and slightly to the right. That's Tampica."

Henry and Emmy craned to look out of the window. Tampica was a comparatively large island, some fifteen miles long by five miles wide. In the center, it rose to a swelling scrub-covered mountain, devoid of human habitation, over which they could see a narrow dirt track winding its precipitous way. A couple of Jeeps were making their way over the mountain, from one end of the island to the other. Immediately below the plane, Henry and Emmy saw a sizable township clustered round a harbor crammed with yachts and fishing boats, looking like toys in a child's bathtub.

"Tampica Harbour, capital of Tampica," explained the pilot. "That big building up on the hill is The Lodge, the Prime Minister's official residence. And just around the point there, you can see the naval base at Barracuda Bay."

The naval base was impressive. It was situated on a beautiful bay whose twin curving headlands promised excellent protection and whose sapphire-dark water was clearly deep to within a few yards of the shore. Several big, gray naval vessels rode at anchor, while others were tied up at the dock-side. A complex of large buildings clustered around the docks, while others—less official-looking—climbed the green hill-side behind the waterfront. Henry saw at once what Michael Holder-Watts had meant. It was easy to imagine the somber warships replaced by white-painted, flag-fluttering cruise liners, and the barracks converted from military austerity to luxury hotels.

The pilot went on, "And now you can see Pirate's Cave Bay, and the hotel."

It did not look like a hotel. It looked like a crescent of firm golden beach, edged with palm trees and dotted with small cottages. Then, as the little airplane lost height, it became plain that the palm trees on the beach were in fact artificial structures, like giant umbrellas, and that beneath them on canvas beach-beds lay probably the most expensive expanse of near-naked flesh in the world, tanning itself to perfection in preparation for an evening of dancing under the tropical stars. The beautiful people were making sure that they remained just that.

The aircraft swung left in a tight circle, and Emmy exclaimed, "What's that bit of dirt road going nowhere?"

The pilot grinned. "That's the airport, ma'am."

"It can't be!"

"It certainly is. That's why we use these little airplanes."

"But you couldn't land a helicopter on that!"

"Want to bet, lady?" The pilot flashed a huge smile at Emmy, and put the Piper's nose down. The airstrip was no wider than a country road, unpaved and extremely short, and the farther end of it terminated in a nasty-looking wall of rock. Nevertheless, the plane came gently down to a smooth landing, and had lost all but minimal speed long before the rock wall loomed. The pilot taxied around to the left and there was the Terminal Building—a small concrete shed, over which the green and purple flag of Tampica fluttered in the trade wind blowing in from the purple sea.

Inside, along with Tampican customs and immigration officers, were several personable young white Americans, dressed in spotless white shorts and wearing tee shirts embroidered with the Pirate's Cave emblem—a pirate with skull and crossbones on his hat, dancing a hornpipe. The same device was painted on the small fleet of Jeeps and the minibus which stood in the parking lot, waiting to transport guests to the hotel. It seemed that a slightly larger plane from St. Thomas had recently landed, as well as another Aztec from Tortola, so that a group of ten brightly dressed tourists were waiting for the arrival of the Antigua plane to complete the party for the drive to Pirate's Cave.

One of the young men hurried up to greet the Schipmakers and the Tibbetts, his apparently informal and relaxed manner cleverly disguising the fact that he was very much on duty, and was coping with official forms and passenger lists and immigration regulations in such a way as to make the whole procedure absolutely painless for the new arrivals. This done, he turned to Otis Schipmaker and said, "Mr. Tibbett? The official car is waiting outside. If you and Mrs. Tibbett..."

"You've got the wrong guy." Henry could not decide whether Schipmaker was merely amused, or whether there was a hint of annoyance. In any case, there was a new respect in his voice as he said to Henry, "You must forgive me, Mr. Tibbett. I didn't realize you were here officially for the conference."

"I'm not," said Henry quickly. "This car business is quite unnecessary, but Sir Edward Ironmonger insisted. We'll see you at the hotel later on, I hope."

He shepherded Emmy out to the parking lot, where a sleek black limousine waited with the Tampican pennant fluttering from its hood and a uniformed black chauffeur holding the door open. Meanwhile, with a lot of speculative and some envious looks, the mere millionaires were ushered into the minibus for the short drive to Pirate's Cave.

It was the same story at the hotel. The manager himself, a dapper New Englander, hurried to greet Henry and Emmy, and to escort them to their cottage, where a big bowl of purple and yellow hibiscus and sweet-scented frangipani stood on the table, flanked by a bottle of excellent champagne in an ice bucket. Feeling a little overwhelmed, Henry and Emmy set about unpacking and exploring.

Each cottage consisted of two adjoining apartments, surrounded by lawns and shaded by exotically flowering tropical trees. Both large bedrooms gave on to adjoining verandahs, whence paths meandered down to a bank of scrublike trees. Between them, the Tibbetts caught tantalizing glimpses of sand and sea. Quickly, they changed into their newly bought swimsuits and ran down to the beach.

They emerged from the shade of the trees into a brilliant world of sun, sand and water. The sea was fresh and sparkling, cool but by no means cold, and crystal clear as a tropical fish tank. Little Swordfish sailing dinghies with blue-and-white striped sails scudded over the reef-protected water, responding to the steady, refreshing breeze. Near the reef, many bright orange breathing tubes showed the presence of a school of snorkelers, as they cruised above the coral, entranced in their submarine world of brilliantly colored fish. Occasionally, their black rubber flippers and variously-garbed posteriors would break the surface as they swam, giving the impression of a bizarre herd of porpoises. Henry and Emmy watched them enviously, and decided to borrow masks and flippers and try the sport for themselves the next day.

For the moment, they enjoyed a swim and a lazy bask in the sun, until suddenly it was five o'clock; the sun sank with tropical swiftness, and they joined the general exodus from the beach and made their way back toward their cottage.

Approaching from the seaward side, they were able to get a good view of the neighboring verandah, and to see that the next-door suite was a mirror image of their own. A light glowed outside the cottage, and in the rapidly deepening twilight they could see that a woman was sitting on the other verandah. She wore some sort of white flowing caftan, and had her feet up on a chaise-longue, and a drink at her elbow. As the Tibbetts approached, she stood up and switched on the outside light of the cottage, illuminating both her verandah and the path. She said, "Hi. Y'all must be our new neighbors. Come on over and have a drink." Her voice had an attractive southern drawl.

A few minutes later, Henry and Emmy were sitting on canvas chairs on the next-door patio, watching the golden Chinese lanterns in the gardens come on one by one, transforming Pirate's Cave into a pantomime fairyland (and also enabling the cottage dwellers to find their way to the dining room with some degree of certainty). Their hostess busied herself with the mixing of drinks, chattering away the while.

"I'm Magnolia Belmont. No sense in being neighbors if you can't be friends. So you're Henry and Emmy—that's what I call good, old-fashioned, no-nonsense names. And from England... well, y'all have certainly come a long ways. Y'all on vacation?"

"Yes, we are," said Henry.

"Sure are fortunate," remarked Magnolia. "Here, taste that for size." She handed out brimming tumblers of rum punch.

"Delicious, thank you," said Emmy. "Does that mean that you're not on holi—on vacation?"

"Well, George isn't. That's my husband. He's here for the naval base conference. Senator George Belmont, y'all surely have heard of him. My, but they're sitting late this evening. I just hope it means my poor Georgie will be able to have an easy ole time of it in the morning. He sure needs a little sun and sea while he's here." Magnolia rejoined the Tibbetts, carrying her drink. "Y'all come here every year, I guess."

"I wish we did," said Henry. "I'm afraid this is a once-in-a-lifetime trip for us."

"Well, fancy that, now," said Magnolia. "I didn't think it was that difficult to reach from England."

"It's not so much the difficulty as the expense," Henry explained.

Magnolia looked at him with wide-open eyes, as if she had never heard the word "expense" before. She was, Henry decided, still a very beautiful woman, for all her half-century of birthdays. Slim and huge-eyed, with fine long-fingered hands and a drift of blonde ringlets. Certainly, she was spoilt: always had been, and always would be, because that was the tradition in which she had been born and bred. But stupid? Henry doubted it. Under the "little me" exterior, he suspected, lay a shrewd businesswoman, and also one who had old-fashioned ideas about the duties of beautiful women and the rights of the men who provided for them and pampered them. In Magnolia's Dixieland, the lives of the beautiful people were really an exquisitely staged and dressed performance of a strictly audited balance sheet.

"Why, there's George now, I do declare!" Magnolia jumped up as a tall, shambling figure approached the cottage through the trees, his white linen suit glimmering in the twilight. Magnolia ran to her husband and took his arm, chattering busily as she led him to the verandah.

"Honeybee, you must be worn out, they've no business working you so hard…come on in and sit down and I'll fix you a drink… Meet our new neighbors, Henry and Emmy, they're from England, just imagine… I've been telling them how much we love this little ole island of theirs…"

"Glad to know you," said Senator Belmont, in the overstatement of the year. He sat down heavily on a canvas chair and bent forward to remove his shoes. When that operation had been successfully concluded, with a certain amount of grunting, he accepted a drink from Magnolia and said, "Well, I sure am glad we're through for today. That was quite a session."

"I just hope they're letting you off a bit tomorrow," said Magnolia, with a charming pout. "It's Saturday, after all, and it's no fun on the beach all by myself."

"We're not meeting again till three, officially," said Belmont. "I dare say I'll be able to fix it to take a swim, but I've a get-together with the guys from the Pentagon at eleven. That's the idea of the schedule, you see. Preliminary, exploratory meeting today. Time tomorrow to let the delegations consult among themselves. Short get-together tomorrow afternoon. Then come Monday—wham!" He took a long pull at his drink. "Boy, these Tampicans sure know how to talk tough!"

"Well, I just don't follow it at all," said Magnolia. "What ever would they do without our naval base? They're just playing possum, trying to bluff poor old Uncle Sam into paying up, as usual. Y'all call their bluff, honey. Y'all talk tough right back. That's the only thing these...these people understand."

"It's not that simple, honey," said her husband. "Fact is, they're bargaining from strength, and they know it. Come right down to it, we need that base more than they need us here, and they reckon to name their own price."

"Why, that's blackmail!" Magnolia exclaimed indignantly.

Belmont grinned ruefully. "Blackmail's not a polite word around international conferences, honey," he said. "In any case, we're here to see it doesn't work. Sure, we need the base and we're prepared to pay a good price for it. But we're sure as hell not about to be held over a barrel for it."

"Oh, it's all so silly," said Magnolia. "What would they do with the base if we went away? They don't even *have* a navy."

"And very fortunate they are, too," remarked George. "Ours costs us billions a year, whereas Tampica would make a very nice tidy profit out of Barracuda Bay if it were turned over to tourism. Why, I've heard rumors there's a company been formed already, and people are buying up stock as fast as they can, on the off-chance." He chuckled. "If the negotiations look as though they're heading the wrong way, I'd be tempted to buy some myself."

"Why, George, how can you say such a thing? That would *not* be ethical."

"I was only fooling, honey." Belmont sighed. "That guy Ironmonger—the Ambassador—he's the tough nut to crack. Brain as quick as a knife, and boy, does he know what he wants, and is he going to get it! I reckon we could make a deal with Drake-Frobisher and the others, but Ironmonger keeps whipping them along and pouring concrete into their backbones.

That'll be just how he'll spend tomorrow morning—undoing any progress toward a deal that we made today."

"But what does he want?" Magnolia demanded.

"He wants out of the contract," said Belmont bluntly. "That's obvious, although of course he's not saying so. So what does he do? I'll tell you. He persuades Drake-Frobisher to make the price so steep that whichever way things go, Tampica will be the winner." He shook his gray head, then looked up and grinned at Henry. "Gee, folks, I'm sorry to talk shop like this. You're here on vacation, and you want to relax, not talk politics."

"It's fascinating," said Henry. "I'll follow the news reports with much more interest now that I know something about the issues. By the way, you don't know the name of that real estate development company, do you?"

George and Magnolia exchanged a quick, wary glance. Then Belmont said, "No, sir, I don't. Don't even know for sure it exists. It's just a rumor, and I guess I was indiscreet to mention it. You weren't thinking of buying stock yourself, were you?" There was a note of anxiety in his voice.

"Good heavens, no," said Henry. "In any case, as an Englishman I very much doubt if I'd be allowed to. No—I just wondered."

"Sorry I can't help you. And now, if you'll excuse me, I'll go change out of this city suit and into something more comfortable. See y'all in the bar before dinner." He stood up, indicating that the party was over. Henry and Emmy took the hint.

"We have to change too," said Emmy. "Thanks for the drink. Be seeing you."

The bar at Pirate's Cave was literally on the beach, open to the sea and sand, with a steeply raked roof of wooden tiles and a floor of natural stone. Chinese lanterns hung from the roofbeams, echoing the bobbing lights of yachts anchored in the bay. From the dance floor above came the throbbing, foot-tapping rhythm of a steel band miraculously beating the melody of "Yellow Bird" out of a battery of tuned oil drums. The night was warm and soft, and the stars looked polished and larger than life against the blue-black sky, like diamonds on display in Tiffany's.

Competing with the remote, insistent beat of the drums, the nearby palm trees rubbed their dry leaves together in the gentle wind, making a sound like the claws of a small animal on stony ground. And in the bar itself, ice tinkled merrily in tall glasses of rum punch and piña colada, and smooth, suntanned men and women sipped and chatted and made plans to take a cruise in a sailing boat or go scuba diving or horseback riding in the morning.

The first people that Henry and Emmy noticed in the bar stood out because of their incongruity. A middle-aged couple, red-faced rather than tanned, the man wearing a sober blue suit with a collar and tie, and the woman in an overelaborate cocktail dress made of white lace and satin. She was still very lovely, Henry thought—but why, oh why, did her blonde hair glitter so unconvincingly, why had it been elaborately dressed and sprayed until it resembled a plastic crash helmet? And why was her face so familiar? The two of them sat stiffly on stools at the bar, grasping their rum punches—a bizarre contrast to the informal, relaxed, loose-limbed elegance of the other drinkers, who looked like the world's most expensive collection of castaways.

The only two unoccupied bar stools were next to the overformal couple—a fact which Henry did not find surprising. He pulled one of them out for Emmy, climbed onto the other himself, and said, "What will you have, darling? A rum punch?"

The man in the blue suit swung round with an exaggerated gesture, held out his hand, and boomed, "Dr. Livingstone, I presume?"

"I beg your pardon?" said Henry.

"What Hubert means," said the woman, "is that you don't often hear an English accent round here. Makes quite a nice change."

"You're English, then?"

"Oh, yes. May we introduce ourselves. I'm Pauline Watkins, and this is my husband, Hubert. We're just here for a little bit of a holiday."

"Watkins?" The card index in Henry's mind did a quick flip and came up with a fact. He had only seen Mavis in photographs, but the combination of the name and Pauline's profile was enough. "Then you must be Lady Ironmonger's parents. I thought I read that you had gone back to England."

Hubert and Pauline exchanged a quick look. Then Hubert said, "Eddie…that is, Sir Edward, my son-in-law—he suggested we come here for a few days. The whole thing has been a severe shock to my wife, hasn't it, dear?"

"A nasty shock," Pauline agreed. "Poor little Mavis. Such a sweetly pretty girl, and doing so well for herself. Still, at least it's all cleared up now." To the barman, a stoutish, sober-faced black man, she added, "I'll have another Pirate's Special, Francis, and go easy on the Tabasco, will you?" Then, to Henry again, "Yes, I dare say you've heard, it was some black woman killed our Mavis. From this very island. Jealous, you see. Well, what can you expect, they're all half-savage, aren't they? Just can't control themselves like civilized people. I don't mean Eddie, of course. There's a real gentleman for you. But he got away from this place, you see, and bettered himself. But the others…thank you, Francis…yes, that's very nice…now, just you remember the way I like it…yes, as I was saying, it's no use expecting them to behave like us, because they never have and they never will. Not that I'm bitter—you can ask anybody…"

Emmy felt her stomach turning over, and instinctively drew away from Pauline. Is it possible, she thought, that the woman really imagines that Francis can only hear her when she's actually talking to him? Is it possible that she is so insensitive as not to realize what she's saying? Doesn't she think he's human? Oh God, let's get away from them…

But Henry seemed to have developed an unaccountable appetite for the company of the Watkinses. He insisted on introductions, he bought another round of drinks and before long all thoughts of Mavis were buried under great spadefuls of laughter, as Hubert Watkins roared at his own jokes.

At length, he said, "Well, it's certainly cheered this place up a bit, meeting a couple of kindred spirits from the old country. Between ourselves, old man, the Yankees here are a bit...well...stand-offish, if you know what I mean. Pauline's noticed it, haven't you, dear?"

"Well, some of them," said Pauline. "But there's that nice Mrs. Belmont who arrived yesterday—her husband's a senator, you know, something to do with the conference. We had a most interesting talk about the Color Problem—somehow, I never realized they had it in America, and she seemed quite surprised when I told her about places like Wolverhampton, back home. It just goes to show how travel can broaden the mind... Francis! Mr. Watkins is ready for another drink!"

"Point of fact, old man," Hubert Watkins confided, "you're just about the only English people we've seen since we've been here. After the Embassy crowd went back to Washington, that is. We were told there was an old English lady, a Miss Pontefract-Deacon, living out at Sugar Mill Bay, and we thought it would be civil to go and call on her. The Queen of Tampica, they call her. Well, I can only tell you, we had one hell of a ride over there in a mini-moke—and then she was almost rude to us. Talk about Lady High-and-Mighty. Knew all about us and who we were, of course. They say there's nothing that goes on on this island that she doesn't know. But we definitely got the feeling that we weren't welcome, didn't we, Pauline?"

"Especially," said Pauline bitterly, "when she told us she'd no water to flush the toilet, so we'd better go behind a palm tree. I thought that was really coarse, for a woman of her age. And very uncomfortable, too. I must say, I shan't be too sorry to go home tomorrow. Not that we haven't had a wonderful time," she added quickly. "I'm sure everybody at home in Penge will be ever so interested to hear all about it. And Magnolia has promised to write. Mrs. Belmont, that is. She likes me to call her Magnolia."

"I didn't realize you were leaving so soon." Henry sounded completely guileless.

"Well, yes... Hubert can't stay away from the office forever, and now that the case has been solved, Eddie—Sir Edward, that is—felt we'd rather be off back to Penge. Ah, here come Magnolia and the Senator now!" Pauline waved energetically. "Hullo, there! Over here!"

It was with inexpressible relief that Emmy saw Otis and Virginia Schipmaker coming down the steps from the dining room to the bar, and raising their hands in greeting. She and Henry quickly excused themselves and made their way towards Ginny and Otis, leaving the Belmonts and the Watkinses to broaden their minds on their own.

"It's a real pleasure," said Otis Schipmaker, "just to sit here and relax and have a quiet drink before Ginny starts hounding me off to work."

"To work?" Emmy echoed.

Otis Schipmaker grinned. "Making contact with the conference delegates," he explained. "I see Belmont over there—he hates my guts anyhow, so I won't waste much time on him. But there are the Pentagon people and the special assistant from the State Department and so on. I should be able to get a line on how things are going."

"I can tell you a little," Henry said. "Gleaned from Senator Belmont, who has the other half of our cottage. The Tampicans are going to hold out for a ridiculously high rent for the base, because they don't really want the U.S. Navy here. They'd rather have the bay and its facilities for tourism."

"That's common knowledge," said Otis. "Point is—how are the negotiations going?"

"Tough on both sides, I gather," said Henry. "And there's one rather interesting thing."

"What's that?" Virginia Schipmaker leaned forward, her attractive, intelligent face outlined against the light of a Chinese lantern.

Henry said, "There's been a lot of talk about developing Barracuda Bay for tourism, but up to now I understood it was only talk. Today, I heard that a real estate development company has already been formed, and that stock is selling fast."

Schipmaker regarded the glowing tip of his cigar. He said, "Are you sure about that? It would be quite a story."

"No, I'm not sure," said Henry. "I haven't been able to find out the name of the company, or who holds the stock."

"Could be interesting."

"If you should happen to hear…"

Henry let his remark hang unresolved in the air. Then Virginia Schipmaker leaned back, lit a cigarette, and said decisively, "Sure, Henry. If Otis finds out, he'll tell you."

CHAPTER FOURTEEN

AFTER DINNER, WHICH was served on the big, palm-roofed open terrace overlooking the bay, Henry and Emmy danced to the compelling Caribbean beat of the steel band as a huge moon soared up over the horizon and laid a pathway of silver across the dark sea. The warm night air was full of the sweet scent of frangipani; coconut palms, spiky aloes and stubby cactuses stood in exotic silhouette against the silver of the moonlight; Henry and Emmy marveled that ordinary people like themselves should be here, in this fabled place.

As they returned to their table after a particularly energetic session on the dance floor, they were surprised to see that a man was already sitting there, almost hidden in the shadows. He raised his hands as they approached, and clapped them in gently ironic applause.

"Very pretty indeed," said Dr. Duncan. "I had no idea you two were such accomplished dancers."

"Dr. Duncan!" Emmy exclaimed. "What are you doing here?"

"Looking for you, of course, my dear. What else?"

"How did you know we were on the island?" Henry asked.

Duncan smiled in the darkness. "From Lucy Pontefract-Deacon, of course. Who else?"

"And how in heaven's name did she know?"

"That," said Duncan, "I have no idea. I can only tell you that she knows everything that goes on on this island, very often before it actually happens. She wants to meet you."

"We shall be honored," said Henry.

"Good. Why don't you hire a moke from Barney and drive over to Sugar Mill Bay for tea tomorrow afternoon. You'll enjoy the drive, apart from anything else."

"How will we find the way?" Emmy asked.

"Don't worry about that. There's only one road over the mountain, and it goes nowhere except to Sugar Mill."

"That must be the track we saw from the air," Emmy said. "You remember, Henry? It looked a bit dangerous to me."

"It's a lot better than it used to be," Duncan assured them. "Bits of it are even paved—up as far as The Lodge, anyway. And the views are spectacular."

"O.K. then," said Henry, "we'll do that. How do we set about finding this chap Barney and hiring the car?"

Duncan glanced at his watch. "As a matter of fact," he said, "I was thinking of dropping in at Barney's Bar on my way home, for a nightcap. Perhaps you'd care to come along with me? See a little of the other side of island life—and you can fix up the moke at the same time."

As the doctor's ancient Jeep trundled between the manicured lawns of Pirate's Cave toward the main gate, Duncan said, "I think you'll find Barney's Bar amusing. It's almost like an extension of Pirate's Cave, except that it's largely patronized by the staff when they're off-duty. Only the most adventurous of the guests ever go there. It's not at all like the smart bars and night clubs in Tampica Harbour, which are highly tourist-orientated. Barney's is a real local affair. Barney himself is a good fellow. He runs the local garage in the daytime and the bar at night."

He drove on in silence for a few moments, and then added, "I should warn you, the atmosphere at Barney's may not be as cheerful as usual tonight. Dorabella Hamilton was buried today, and the whole island attended her funeral. They're...bewildered, I think. They don't doubt that she killed Mavis Ironmonger and then committed suicide—but they can't comprehend it properly. There's even some resentment against Eddie, which is unheard of among these people. Suddenly, he seems to represent the Establishment, and Dorabella the ordinary people. That's one reason I'm going to Barney's. Just to keep an eye, you know."

They heard Barney's Bar long before they saw it. A deafening, cacophonous wave of music swept down the lane as if to attack them. It was rougher and less expert than the tamed steel drums of Pirate's Cave. It also thrummed with vitality and zest. Raising his voice, the doctor said, "I hope you have strong eardrums. Fortunately, the music is not continuous."

He pulled the Jeep to a halt outside the source of the din—a smallish concrete building, painted pistachio green and surrounded by hibiscus and oleander bushes. Through the open door, Henry and Emmy could see a brightly dressed, gyrating crowd of islanders, dancing with that almost static energy and rhythm that few non-Caribbean people can imitate. Mercifully, just as Dr. Duncan ushered the Tibbetts into the bar, the band decided to take a beer break, and blessed peace descended.

Henry noticed that they were not the only white people in the bar. He recognized a few faces from Pirate's Cave—a handful of youngsters who had been dining with staid-looking parents, and had now escaped to a more congenial ambience; plus a couple of the clean cut young Americans who had met them at the airfield. There were also two bearded characters in blue jeans, unmistakably off a boat. However, the predominance and mood of the place was obviously black and local, and it was at once clear that the doctor had been right. Once the music stopped, so did any semblance of gaiety. People stood and talked quietly as they drank their beer or rum, and saluted each other gravely, without any of the islanders' usual ebullience.

Dr. Duncan was greeted warmly, and with obvious affection—and Henry and Emmy, as his guests, felt themselves under the friendly protection of his aegis. Nobody mentioned Dorabella, but her memory hung over the crowded little bar as palpable as smoke. Henry wondered how these people would react if they learned what he suspected. And then, as the band struck up again, he saw Winston Horatio Nelson.

Saw him, but for a moment did not recognize him. Winnie Nelson, back in his own environment, had shed the somber outer coating of a diplomat as a butterfly sheds its cocoon. He was wearing bell-bottom cotton pants striped in gaudy pink and purple, and over them a loose shirt printed with brilliant tropical fish cavorting in a bright blue sea. He was dancing—and dancing beautifully—with a breathtakingly lovely black girl whom Henry recognized as one of the receptionists from Pirate's Cave.

The second time around the small dance floor, he noticed Henry. Abruptly, he stopped dancing and turned his back on his partner, who was immediately claimed by one of the score of single men hanging round the bar. Nelson made his way over to the Tibbetts.

"Chief Superintendent," he said, with exaggerated mock courtesy and a marked upper-class English accent. "What a pleasant surprise. I had no idea you were on the island." He swayed slightly, and Henry realized that he was more than a little drunk.

"Sir Edward kindly suggested that we should spend a few days' holiday at Pirate's Cave," said Henry. He was surprised that Nelson had not heard of the arrangement. "I don't think you've met my wife. Emmy, darling, this is Mr. Nelson, First Secretary at the Embassy in Washington."

"Hello," said Emmy. "How nice to meet you. I'm just crazy about your shirt—I'd love to take one home. Can you get them here on the island?"

Emmy had spoken perfectly sincerely and spontaneously, but as soon as the words were out, she saw that she had blundered.

"Not at Pirate's Cave, madam," said Nelson. "Not in the kind of shop that *you* would deign to patronize."

Dr. Duncan said, "Winnie..." in a soft, warning voice, but Winnie took no notice.

Suddenly, he began to shout. "Slumming! That's all you're doing here! Slumming! Why can't you stay in Pirate's Cave where you belong, with all the damn Yankees and the fat cats and the bloody Watkinses? Pity Dorabella didn't finish off the whole family while she was about it!"

For once, Henry was glad of the deafening blare of the music, which prevented more than a handful of people from hearing Winnie's outburst. Trying to sound unembarrassed, he said with a smile, "I met Mr. and Mrs. Watkins for the first time today. They're going home tomorrow, and I think they're wise. They don't seem to fit in here very well."

"No goddam whites fit in here!" yelled Nelson. "Why don't you get out, all of you? Pirate's Cave, goddam Navy, the lot! This is our island!"

By now, quite a group of people had gathered around Nelson, most of them encouraging him and nodding their heads in emphatic agreement. Henry noticed with a pang of real alarm that Dr. Duncan had slipped away from the bar and disappeared.

One of the young Americans from the Pirate's Cave staff saved the situation by walking over to Nelson, slapping him on the back, and saying easily, "Come off it, Winnie. Where would your economy be without us? You can shout all you like, but you need us and you know it."

"That's what you think! You wait. You just wait. I'm telling you—"

At that moment, a huge, bearded black man elbowed his way through the crowd, calling, "Nelson! Winnie Nelson!"

Winnie turned toward him. "What's up, Barney?"

Barney jerked his thumb toward the back of the room. "Telephone," he said, laconically. "For you." Then, to the band, who had momentarily ceased operations, "That's enough beer break, boys. Give the folks their money's worth."

The band broke into another ear-splitting number, Barney ambled behind the bar and began serving drinks, and the little group of militants dispersed as Nelson shouldered his way toward the telephone. The dangerous moment had passed. Dr. Duncan appeared, apparently from nowhere, and resumed his seat at the bar.

"Thank you, Barney," he said. "Winnie's a little upset, which is perfectly understandable. Lucky Eddie was in. He'll have him safely up at The Lodge in no time." He turned to the Tibbetts. "Sorry about that. Still, no harm done. Ah, there he goes." Winnie Nelson, expressionless, was making his way quickly out of the crowded bar and into the street. "Now, what are you drinking, you two? Make that three beers, Barney, and have one yourself. Have you got a moke for these good people tomorrow? They plan to drive over to Sugar Mill Bay…"

When Henry and Emmy got back to Pirate's Cave just before midnight, the whole place seemed to be asleep. The band had stopped playing, the bar was dark, and only a few cottages still showed lights. Evidently, the rich and beautiful either went to bed early, or continued their revels in the spicier night spots of the town. Henry and Emmy were glad of the muted gleam of the lanterns to guide them back to their cottage. There was no light on the Belmonts' side of the building. By the light over the doorway, he could see that a piece of paper had been pushed halfway under the door. Henry picked up the paper as he went in.

The message was short. It read: "The Tampica Research and Development Company. Chairman, Francis Fletcher (barman, Pirate's Cave). Only Tampicans may buy stock. List of stockholders impossible to obtain. O.S."

The next morning, Henry and Emmy went snorkeling, as planned. Emmy had had serious doubts about even trying the sport, as she was not a strong swimmer and had always been averse to putting her face under water. However, spurred on by Henry's ecstatic accounts of submarine marvels, she finally struggled into the awkward flippers, adjusted the mask over her eyes and nose and bit firmly on the rubber mouthpiece which, by means of the orange breathing tube, would keep her in contact with the upper air.

Her first two attempts ended in spluttering failure. Panicking, she managed either to open her mouth or to submerge the upper end of the air tube, thus inhaling sea water before shooting to the surface and ripping off her mask, certain of imminent death by drowning. These two setbacks might have turned Emmy against snorkeling for ever—except for one thing. At the second attempt, just before she came to disaster, she had caught a brief glimpse of the magical world under the sea. For a fleeting moment, she had seen yellow, blue and purple fishes swimming nonchalantly among the petrified forests of coral: she knew that she must see that world again.

And so, in the course of the morning, Emmy mastered her flippers and mask, and found to her delight that she could spend many minutes drifting lazily above and around the reef, watching the brilliantly colored fish that were apparently oblivious to the larger and clumsier human swimmers invading their world. She also saw and grew to recognize the dangerous and painful black spines of the sea urchin, nestling in clefts of coral, as well as the lovely but treacherous jelly fish, white and lilac, floating like bridal veils in the clear water, but capable of administering a nasty sting.

Lunchtime came around all too quickly. At half-past two, one of the young Americans on the staff came to the terrace table where the Tibbetts were finishing their coffee, and announced that Barney had delivered their mini-moke to the parking lot, and here were the keys.

The mini-moke is the packhorse of the Caribbean. Lighter and flimsier than the Jeep, these astonishing little cars perform miracles on the unmade roads, taking in their stride near-vertical climbs over boulders and streaming gullies, or hairpin descents on slippery concrete at a forty-five degree angle, with only the skill of the driver and the reliability of the vehicle between the road and the Atlantic breakers hundreds of feet below.

This is all the more remarkable since most of the island mini-mokes are innocent of handbrakes, rear mirrors, direction indicators and other "effeminate" gadgets considered desirable on safer highways. As Henry and Emmy discovered, the first drive in a mini-moke on island roads is a somewhat hairy experience. After that, should you survive, the thing develops into a lifelong love affair.

The moke which Barney had allocated to the Tibbetts was painted bright yellow and had *Tampica Taxi and Traction Company* painted in purple on one side of the chassis. It was open to the elements, with the exception of a sort of hood, like the canopy of a four-poster bed, held in place by four iron poles and made of red and white striped canvas. Like the surrey in the song, it also had a fringe and bobbles, giving the little car the appearance of a miniature traveling circus. Barney had come along to give Henry some basic driving tips on the way back to the garage. Then he set them on the right road for Sugar Mill Bay, and they were on their own.

As Dr. Duncan had said, the road started off smoothly enough, leading first into the town of Tampica Harbour and then snaking up the hillside towards The Lodge. True, some of the hairpin bends were somewhat steep, but the surface was tarred and a low wall gave at least an illusion of security on the seaward side. However, once past the imposing iron gates of the Prime Minister's residence, the picture changed abruptly. The tarred surface gave way to a dusty track, and the road narrowed. As the gradient grew steeper, so did the surface deteriorate, for the autumn rains had turned it into a series of rivulets, each of which had scored its own sinuous path over the uneven surface. Then the stones and boulders began to appear.

Henry clung grimly to the wheel, urging on his game little vehicle, bouncing dizzily from rock to rock, not daring to slow down for fear of never starting again (he was uncomfortably aware of a total absence of handbrake). Double-declutching with a roar into bottom gear, the moke screamed round a tight S-bend to be faced with a rock-strewn climb apparently up the face of a wall. Emmy let out a small squeak of alarm and protest, but there was no turning back. It seemed impossible, but the moke did it. With her last ounce of growling power, she heaved herself over the top, and Henry was rewarded by the blessed sight of a few hundred yards of almost flat track before the dirt road plunged down again on the other side of the mountain. They had reached the summit.

There were no parapets or other protections from the precipice up here, but there was a parking space scooped out of the rock, so that drivers could pull off the road to admire the view. Thankfully, Henry pulled into this space and switched off the engine. He was not surprised to find that his hands were not quite steady. He and Emmy climbed out of the car and walked to the edge of the road.

The view took their breath away. Far, far below them, the dark green wooded mountain gave way to crescent beaches of golden sand, against which the sapphire waters crawled and crested. They could see the town of Tampica Harbour, with its yacht marina and fishing port laid out like a toy on a nursery floor. Higher up the hill, the red roof of The Lodge peeped from among clusters of brilliantly flowering trees—the spectacular deep scarlet of the flame of Barbados, the delicate pink of the so-called white cedar, the bright yellow blossom and fernlike greenery of the peacock tree. They could even make out the steeply raked roof of the Pirate's Cave dining area, and see the tiny figures on the beach.

Below them, out at sea, a great schooner of old-fashioned design plowed majestically through the rippled water, her long bowsprit tapering toward the sky, her complicated rigging and ratlines tracing geometric patterns against the white of her square sails. It took no great feat of imagination to picture her crew not as millionaire holidaymakers, but as pigtailed, straw-hatted seamen sweating at the halyards and swarming up to the yardarms and finding a new dignity and pride in their ancient trade, thanks to the revolutionary attitude of their captain—a small, slight man who in those days still had two arms and two eyes, and was always seasick for the first few days out.

Then Henry and Emmy turned to look ahead of them, to the north of the island. They picked out Sugar Mill Bay at once. The characteristic cone-shaped tower of the mill—now in ruins—stood on a bluff just above the beach. Between it and the water, there was a straggle of buildings painted pink, blue and green; at the ramshackle wooden jetty, several small boats were tied up. The only other structure in sight was a good-sized house, built like a single level rambler, which stood on the far side of the bay in a couple of acres of flowering garden. This, surely, must be the Tibbetts' destination, the home of Miss Lucy Pontefract-Deacon, uncrowned Queen of Tampica.

Meanwhile, between their present dizzy vantage point and Sugar Mill Bay, they could see the thin ribbon of sandy road as it wound downwards at terrifying angles towards the sea. From here, it looked as though the drive up had been child's play compared with the shorter and steeper drive down.

This proved to be quite true, and, given the lack of adequate brakes, extremely hair-raising. However, by down-shifting and praying the engine would not stall, Henry managed to hold the little car under control until at last they reached the settlement of sugar-almond houses at the waterfront.

There was no need to ask the way. A group of barefoot children crowded around the moke, pointing enthusiastically.

"You go Miz Luce? This way, Miz Luce. We ride with you?"

It was not really a question. The children leapt onto the moke and clung to it like a swarm of flies, giggling and yelling and pointing. Henry made his cautious way around the tiny harbor and up the slope to the house.

At the gate, the children dropped off the car, ran to open the gate, and then rushed ahead through the garden towards the house, shouting to "Miz Luce" that she had visitors. Henry was glad that he had not tried to pay a surreptitious visit to Miss Pontefract-Deacon.

Before Henry had finished parking the moke in the graveled drive, the door of the house opened and a woman came out. Henry had been looking forward to this encounter with some curiosity, and was not sure what to expect. One thing that he certainly had not anticipated was to find himself face to face with Prudence Barrington.

"Good heavens," she said abruptly. "Mr. Tibbett."

"The surprise is mutual," Henry assured her. "I'm delighted to see you. Weren't you expecting us?"

"Oh, Lucy said something about somebody coming to tea—but that happens every day. How naughty of her—she should have told us that you were on the island. And you must be Mrs. Tibbett. I really am pleased to meet you, my dear, and I'm very sorry you didn't come to dinner with your husband in Washington. I simply didn't realize he had a wife—not in America, anyway...that's to say..." As usual, Prudence was losing her way in a spate of verbal good will.

Henry said, "Yes, Mrs. Barrington, this is Emmy. Darling, you remember me telling you about Bishop and Mrs. Barrington?"

"Of course," Emmy said warmly. "So you and your husband are staying with Miss Pontefract-Deacon, are you, Mrs. Barrington?"

"Yes, just for a few days. We always come to Lucy when we manage to get back to Tampica. Of course places like Pirate's

Cave are quite out of the question for simple people like us. Where are you staying, Mrs. Tibbett?"

"At Pirate's Cave, of course," said a deep feminine voice. "I am so pleased you could come over, Mr. Tibbett...and Mrs. Tibbett... I am Lucy Pontefract-Deacon."

Miss Pontefract-Deacon was a tall woman, slightly stooped but still agile, despite her snow-white hair and wrinkled, suntanned face. She was standing on her own front door step, with a small black child comfortably straddled over each hip, and four others pulling at her skirts. Instantly, Henry realized why she was called the Queen of Tampica, and why she knew everything that happened on the island.

Henry said, "I'm so pleased to meet you. It was most kind of you to invite us—"

Lucy Pontefract-Deacon cut through these unnecessary niceties. "You are Chief Superintendent Tibbett from Scotland Yard. You are here because of Mavis Ironmonger and Dorabella Hamilton, and I very much want to talk to you. Prudence, dear, please show Mrs. Tibbett the garden and the beach, and collect Matthew on your way back. Tea will be ready at four." Abruptly, she bent her knees and flung out her arms, dislodging her two small passengers, who tumbled to the ground in gales of laughter. "Off you go now, all of you! Come to the kitchen at four and you'll get some cake. The one who finds the most seashells can feed the rabbits."

The children scattered, leaping and giggling: Prudence was already leading Emmy down toward the sea shore. Lucy Pontefract-Deacon said, "Do come in, Mr. Tibbett, and sit down. I think we have quite a lot to talk about."

CHAPTER FIFTEEN

THE HOUSE WAS comfortable and very much lived-in. Miss Pontefract-Deacon led the way through the drawing-room to a terrace overlooking the sea, shaded by white cedars and frangipani. Once Henry was comfortably settled in a canvas chair, she said, "If this was your first drive over the mountain in a moke, I am sure you need a drink. With your permission, I will bring a couple of weak rum punches."

Two minutes later, she was back with the drinks. She sat down, stirred her rum punch with a thin crystal stick, and said, "You were called in, quasi-officially, to assist Sergeant—I'm sorry, Inspector Bartholomew in his investigation of Mavis Ironmonger's death. The result is that Dorrie Hamilton apparently confessed to murdering Mavis and then killed herself. Am I right?"

"Not quite," said Henry. "She confessed as she was dying, after her suicide bid."

"Well, be that as it may, you see that I know quite a lot about you, Mr. Tibbett. I don't imagine you know very much about me."

Henry sipped his drink, and considered. "I know that you are called the Queen of Tampica. I know that you know everything that goes on here, often before it happens. I know that you are loved and trusted."

"That is a great compliment," said Miss Pontefract-Deacon. "I will tell you a little about myself. My father was a clergyman. He came here with my mother in 1884, as vicar of Tampica Harbour. I was born here during the nineties. I grew up here. I have seen…" She hesitated. "…much. When my father retired in 1920, he went back to live in England. My mother had died some years before. However, I decided to stay here. There was nothing heroic about my decision, I can assure you. I stayed because I liked the place and the people, and it was my home. I did not spend my life nursing or teaching or doing good works—although, of course, I helped Alfred and Matthew and Prudence whenever I could. My father was a man of substance, and I have always been comfortably off. I want to make it quite clear that this island has been my benefactor, rather than the other way round."

Henry smiled. "You've made your point," he said. And then added, "And you never married."

"I never married, for reasons which I do not propose to discuss. There are compensations for remaining single, you know, Mr. Tibbett. People come to me and tell me things. That is why I am so well-informed. For some quite unfounded reason, they imagine that their secrets are safe with an old maid who has no family to tattle to."

"And are they, Miss Pontefract-Deacon?"

The old lady smiled, very sweetly. "That all depends," she said. "I am perfectly capable of keeping a secret. I disseminate knowledge in those quarters which I judge to be appropriate." She paused. "I can see that you want information from me. I am assuming that you will favor me with your confidence in return. Please tell me about this wretched business—and about Dorrie Hamilton in particular."

Somewhat to his own surprise, Henry found himself doing

as she asked, without misgivings. He outlined what had taken place at the Embassy reception: Mavis Ironmonger's outburst, removal and subsequent death. He went on to talk about Dr. Duncan's analysis, and the Alcodym.

At once, Miss Pontefract-Deacon said, "That must have come from Dorrie."

"You knew? About her drinking problem?"

"Of course I did."

"But even Dr. Duncan didn't know. She went to another island for treatment!"

"Certainly. I advised her where to go and whom to see. I did not think it advisable to tell Alfred. He is a great gossip, you know."

Henry said, "I see what you mean about keeping secrets, Miss Pontefract-Deacon."

"Please call me Lucy."

"Thank you, Lucy." Henry went on to describe the inquiries which he and Inspector Bartholomew had made, and finally the circumstances of Dorabella's death, and her last words in the hospital.

"It looked so obvious," he said. "Suicide in a fit of remorse. But Mrs. Drayton, who is known to her friends as Bella, was convinced that she heard her name being called from the street just before the accident. The way I see it is this. Dorabella was walking home along Exeter Place to keep her appointment with me. A car came along, driven by somebody she knew. It slowed down, and the driver called her name—Dorabella. That's what Mrs. Drayton heard. Miss Hamilton must have run across the quiet street to talk to the driver—whereupon he accelerated murderously, hit her and drove off at high speed. The doctor assures me that she was so badly concussed, apart from the injuries that killed her, that she certainly wouldn't have remembered any details of the accident when she regained consciousness briefly in hospital. What she tried to say then was what she wanted to tell me at our meeting."

Lucy Pontefract-Deacon nodded seriously. "That would be about the Alcodym, of course," she said. "Dorrie undoubtedly supplied it, and probably put it in the drink, without realizing it was part of a murder plot." She frowned, and said, "I don't understand about the handbag."

"That puzzled me," Henry agreed. "I can't be sure, of course, but the doctors seem to think that Dorabella was flung into the air by the car, not run over. In that case, the bag must have flown off her arm and landed on the roof or bonnet of the car. The murderer had to make a getaway with that embarrassing piece of evidence still with him...or her. The obvious course was to take it back to the Embassy as soon as possible and leave it in Dorabella's office—having carefully wiped it clean. Winston Nelson obligingly found it there and put his prints all over it."

Lucy Pontefract-Deacon considered. "That points very clearly to somebody at the Embassy," she said. "Have you checked on where people were? I mean—who has an alibi?"

"Nobody," said Henry. "Among the possible suspects, that is. Winston Nelson was working late—he was alone in the office section of the Embassy. He could easily have followed Dorabella when she left, and still been back in time to take my phone call. Michael Holder-Watts was on his way home, and it wouldn't have taken him far out of his way to go via Exeter Place. I haven't been able to find out just where his wife was.

"Sir Edward was invited to a cocktail party at the British Embassy, which is some distance from Georgetown. He left about five o'clock—before Miss Hamilton—driving himself in his own car. I haven't been able to check exactly what time he arrived at the British Embassy on Massachusetts Avenue—but the party didn't start until six, so he must have been off on some private errand first. He had ample opportunity to be in Exeter Place at a quarter past five."

"You haven't questioned him about it?" Miss Pontefract-Deacon sounded accusing.

"No," said Henry. "You see, you and Emmy are the *only* people in the world who know that I suspect anything other than suicide. We are supposed to be here on holiday. I particularly don't want to alarm anybody by appearing suspicious."

"I shall have to give this matter some thought," said Miss Pontefract-Deacon. "There are several things that...well, never mind. Thank you for being so frank with me. Now, what did you want to know from me, Mr. Tibbett?"

Henry said, "How much do you know about the Tampica Research and Development Company?"

Lucy gave him a long, hard look. "A certain amount," she said.

"Such as?"

"It is a speculative venture. The stockholders are banking on the breakdown of negotiations between the United States and Tampica over the naval base. The company is busy buying up property around Barracuda Bay. If the U.S. Navy remains in Tampica, the land will be worthless and the speculators will lose. If not, there are fortunes to be made."

"I understand," Henry said, "that only Tampicans may own stock. Do you know the names of the principal investors?"

"I know of one person who has bought a considerable amount."

"And who is that?"

Lucy Pontefract-Deacon smiled, conspiratorially. "Me," she said.

Henry threw back his head and laughed. "I congratulate you on your business acumen, Lucy."

"Thank you."

"And the other stockholders?"

She regarded him, head slightly on one side. "I'm not sure that it would be proper to tell you. Francis Fletcher from Pirate's Cave is the Chairman, and has some shares. Alfred Duncan, I think, has a modest holding. So has Barney. I think that is as far as I should go."

"Sir Edward Ironmonger?" Henry asked.

Lucy leaned forward and patted his hand. "I won't tell you I don't know," she said, "because you wouldn't believe me. I shall simply say that if I did know, I wouldn't tell you." She paused. "Eddie is a delegate at this conference, you know. If he had a financial interest in its outcome, it would be most improper for him not to declare it and disqualify himself. And the same goes for his staff. Ah, I see your charming wife coming back from her walk with Prudence. And Matthew has joined them, after his dip. Shall we have tea?"

She picked up a small silver bell, which tinkled elegantly. A moment later, a goodlooking Tampican boy in a white jacket came out onto the terrace.

"This is Martin, Mr. Tibbett. Martin Fletcher, Francis's brother. I don't know how I'd run this house without him. He's been with me—how long is it now, Martin?"

"Six months, Miss Lucy."

"That's right. Ever since Eddie and Mavis stole Walter Jenkins from me to take him to Washington. Ah, well, I couldn't blame him for going. Sugar Mill Bay isn't the liveliest place in the world, is it now, Martin?"

Martin grinned broadly, but said nothing. Lucy went on, "Oh, it's all very well for you, my lad. You've got at least two girls here and heaven knows how many in Tampica Harbour." Martin's grin stretched even wider, until it threatened to break his face in two. "Well, be that as it may, we're ready for tea, if you please. There will be five of us. And I've told the Bailey children to come to the kitchen for some cake."

"O.K., Miss Lucy," said Martin cheerfully, and disappeared into the house just as Emmy and the Barringtons came climbing up the stone steps from the beach.

"You see, Lucy?" Prudence called out. "Success! Dead on time! We actually met Matthew on his way up from the beach at exactly five to four. Show Mr. Tibbett your new watch, Matthew."

A little sheepishly, Matthew Barrington held out his left

wrist to display a handsome watch in a stainless steel case. "Good to see you again, Tibbett," he said. "Yes, this is my new toy. Waterproof, shows the date, everything. Prudence gave it to me for my birthday last week. I lost my old one—can't think how..."

"The old one was a disgrace," said Prudence. "I'm delighted that you lost it. And you really like the new one, don't you, dear?"

"I'm getting used to it," the Bishop admitted, "but I'm not sure that I enjoy knowing the right time after all these years. Well, I suppose we all have to make our little sacrifices in the cause of progress. Now, if you'll excuse me, I'll go and put on some more seemly clothes for tea."

As soon as Matthew had disappeared into the house, Prudence leaned forward and said conspiratorially, "Matthew didn't lose his old watch at all! I stole it!"

"Whatever for?" asked Emmy, laughing.

"It was driving me mad, never being able to rely on Matthew being on time for anything. I tried to get it repaired, but the man said it must have been running slow for years, and there was nothing he could do. So I just let Matthew go on thinking he'd lost it, and bought him the new one. You must promise never to tell. It's a great secret."

"It won't remain one for long, Prudence," remarked Lucy Pontefract-Deacon, "if you persist in telling all and sundry whenever Matthew isn't here. If you want a secret kept, keep it yourself."

The glass door from the house opened and Martin appeared, wheeling a trolley-full of delicacies—cucumber and watercress sandwiches; brown bread and butter sliced thinly, with Gentlemen's Relish; homemade shortbread; chocolate and walnut sponge cakes topped with cream; crisp brandy snaps and lady fingers. The centerpiece was an enormous silver teapot, decorated with an extravagance of Victorian frills, twirls and grace notes.

"Tea," said Martin, unnecessarily, "is served."

The drive back to Tampica Harbour was less hair-raising than the trip over, due to the fact that the reassurance of familiarity had already begun to assert itself, and there was not the feeling that every bend in the road might reveal a new horror. However, Henry's concentration was all on his driving, and not until the moke reached the tarmac surface at The Lodge did conversation become a practical possibility.

Emmy said, "What a marvelous old lady. I'm so glad we made the effort and drove over. What did you and she talk about all that time?"

"This and that. The island. The case. How did you get on with Mrs. Barrington?"

"Oh, she's very sweet and so is the Bishop—but she does tend to ramble on. She was telling me in tremendous detail all about the night Lady Ironmonger was killed and how they heard about it on the television news. It seems they almost missed it, thanks to the Bishop's old watch, which was obviously a family joke. Now, tell me what you found out."

"I'm getting more and more interested," said Henry, "in the Tampica Research and Development Company. It's perfectly clear that the stockholders are vitally concerned that the naval base talks should break down and the Americans leave. It's also clear from what Belmont said that Ironmonger is the strong man. If he should drop out of the picture, the United States would make a deal with Drake-Frobisher, and the navy would stay. Do you see what I'm getting at?"

"I see," said Emmy, "that it would be interesting to know who holds the stock."

"Lucy Pontefract-Deacon is a big stockholder," Henry said. "She told me so. Dr. Duncan has some shares, too—and so do many of the islanders. That's all perfectly proper; they can take a gamble if they want to. What would be extremely improper would be if Ironmonger or any of his staff owned shares. They know that, so if any of them are concerned in this, their stock will be held by a nominee. I think we should have a word with Francis Fletcher."

They were in the town of Tampica Harbour by now, threading their way along narrow streets to reach the water-front before taking the road to Pirate's Cave. Henry said, "It's extraordinary how helpful it can be to go right through the case with a complete outsider, as I did this afternoon. It clarifies things in one's mind."

"And answers questions?"

"No, I wouldn't say that. It poses questions—things I should have asked myself sooner."

"Such as?"

"Well, for a start, why was Mr. Finkelstein being intro-duced to Lady Ironmonger?"

"That's easy. Because he was a guest at the reception and she hadn't met him before."

"Exactly. And then—"

Henry got no further. As he stopped at a red traffic light, a squeal of recognition from the pavement revealed Mr. and Mrs. Watkins, laden with paper bags from various souvenir shops. "Yoo-hoo! Mr. Tibbett! You going back to Pirate's Cave? Mind if we hop in the back?"

They scrambled in just as the lights changed. "I feel quite exhausted," said Pauline Watkins. "We were just doing some last-minute shopping—little gifts for people back home, you know. We're off this evening, you see." She simpered. "The Prime Minister's yacht sails for Antigua tonight, and Sir Samuel has kindly suggested we travel on her, to catch the plane to London in the morning. So much more restful than getting the early flight from here tomorrow."

"Pity you couldn't find that picture postcard of the boat to take home," Hubert remarked.

"Never mind, I shall take a nice snap of her in Antigua tomorrow. The ladies at the bridge club will be most interested. After all, it's not every day one travels in the Prime Minister's yacht." Pauline preened herself. Henry thought—poor Mavis... poor Dorabella... He turned the moke in through the gate of Pirate's Cave.

"This is where we get off," trilled Pauline. "Thanks ever so much, Mr. Tibbett. Come and see us if you're ever in Penge..."

Henry parked the moke, and he and Emmy walked through the scented twilight toward their cottage.

"What were you going to say, Henry? Before the Watkinses caught us?"

"I...I forget..."

George and Magnolia Belmont were having a drink on their verandah and cordially invited the Tibbetts to join them. George looked glum when Henry inquired about the progress of the talks.

"We're meeting again Monday," the Senator said, "but if you ask me, there's no way. Ironmonger won't give an inch, and if I'm to be frank with you, there's a couple of East Coast liberals on our team who aren't giving us the support we need. You may have noticed that Otis Schipmaker turned up on the island yesterday. I don't need to tell you what that means."

"Some people," declared Magnolia, "are just not patriotic. Some people don't even deserve to *have* a navy. When I think that Otis's brother's wife's sister is married to a fine young naval officer—well, some people don't have any family feeling any more, either. Did you *see* Ginny Schipmaker on the beach this morning?" she added, addressing Emmy.

"I'm afraid not. I was trying to learn to snorkel."

"Well...I can only say that some people can wear bikinis and others shouldn't even try...let me freshen your glass, Henry..."

Later, in the bar, Henry and Emmy saw the Schipmakers deep in conversation with a man whom they recognized as one of the "East Coast intellectuals." Schipmaker smiled and Ginny waved graciously, but it was clear that both were very much otherwise engaged and had no time for purely social conversation. Henry and Emmy found themselves bar stools, ordered drinks, and then took advantage of a lull in business to have a word with Francis Fletcher.

Henry started the ball rolling. "We met your young brother today, Francis."

Francis grinned. "Which one? There's a whole heap of us."

"Martin. Out at Sugar Mill Bay."

"Oh, him. Sure. Got a good job. Ain't nobody knows how to run a house like Miss Lucy. Martin's learning his trade the right way."

Henry said, "I gather that you and Miss Lucy are both interested in the Tampica Research and Development Company."

Francis grinned again. "Sure are."

"Of course, Miss Lucy's just a stockholder, but she tells us you are Chairman of the Board."

"Sure am."

"That must be quite a job."

Francis's grin was immovable. "Not so bad. Nothing much doing as yet. Could be big things one day, for sure."

"You have some shares yourself?"

"Two rum punches, Francis!" called a suntanned man in a bright orange shirt from the other end of the bar.

"Yes, sir, Mr. Robertson. Right away, sir." And Francis was gone.

The bar was filling up with pre-dinner drinkers, and the chance for conversation had passed. As he signed his chit, Henry said, "What time do you finish here, Francis?"

"Ten...ten-fifteen...all depends how long people sit up. There's no dance tonight, so we're liable to close early."

"We thought we might drop in to Barney's Bar later on," Henry said. "I've got to hand back the moke. Perhaps we might see you there. We'd like to buy you a drink."

Francis Fletcher looked at Henry, bright-eyed and still smiling. "Might just see you there," he said.

Barney's Bar was noisy and crowded and more relaxed and cheerful than it had been the night before. Henry and Emmy sought out Barney and returned the keys to the moke. In return, Barney invited them to have a drink. Nobody mentioned the incident of the previous evening, and everybody seemed to be going out of the way to be friendly. It was not long after ten o'clock that Henry saw Francis Fletcher coming into the bar. He looked around, spotted the Tibbetts, and made his way between the gyrating dancers to where they sat.

"Hi, there," he said. His grin was as wide as ever. He sat down, accepted a beer, greeted friends as they danced past, and—in the short interval between deafening band sessions—asked Henry and Emmy how they had enjoyed their snorkeling, and offered to show them some of the best reefs on outlying beaches.

Then the band struck up again, and Fletcher leaned toward Henry. In the same good-humored tone, and with the same smile, he said quietly, "I don't know who you are or what you want, but I'm here to warn you, man. Keep your nose out of the Research and Development Company. That's Tampican business, man, for Tampicans only, and any goddam foreigner who meddles in there is going to get hurt. You won't be warned again, and you better take it seriously." As the cacophony of the band died down, he stood up, still smiling. His hand went to his coat pocket, and Henry could see his fist clenching through the thin fabric, as though it was grasping something small and heavy. "Well, good to see you folks. Remember what I said, now. I really mean it." And he strolled out of the bar.

Henry said to Emmy, "Finish up your drink. We'll leave, too."

There was no sign of Francis Fletcher when the Tibbetts emerged from Barney's Bar into the tropical night. They walked silently between the hedges of oleander, glimmering palely in the moonlight, through the gates of Pirate's Cave and across smooth lawns to their cottage. Once inside, Henry closed the windows and the door leading to the verandah. When he was satisfied that they could not be overheard, he said, "I'm sorry you were let in for that, darling. But it's interesting, isn't it?"

Emmy shivered. "I thought it was frightening," she said.

"Not really," Henry assured her. "Fletcher is trying to pull a bogey-man scare on us, but actually he's the one who is frightened. This is a not-too-intelligent reaction by a man who knows he's on the wrong side of the law, and is scared of being found out. It's just about proof positive that Fletcher is the front man for people who have a financial interest in the company, even though they know they have no right to—which must mean politicians and diplomats."

Emmy said, "I can hardly believe that Sir Edward..."

"He's the hard-liner, remember. He's doing his best to ensure that the talks break down. The Prime Minister himself appears to be ready to compromise—which either means that he's not financially concerned, or else that he's being very clever and using Ironmonger as a front. And then there are the others at the Embassy—Nelson and Holder-Watts."

"They can't affect the outcome of the conference," Emmy objected. "Holder-Watts isn't even here, and Nelson is only a member of Sir Edward's staff."

"Nevertheless, if they do hold stock secretly, it's vitally important to them that Ironmonger should continue to take his hard line, whether or not he's in a conspiracy with them." Henry paced up and down the room, rubbing the back of his neck with his hand. Then he said, "This is beginning to make a sensible pattern for the first time. Somebody...maybe several people...have a vital financial interest in keeping Ironmonger in office. Somebody realized that his career would never survive a really serious scandal in Washington—that it would certainly wreck his chances of becoming prime minister in the near future, which is what the Research and Development people are really after. That could provide a very good reason for disposing of Mavis Ironmonger."

Emmy said, "But Henry, she *did* create a scandal just before she died! The person who fed her Alcodym…"

"…certainly didn't intend her to start singing bawdy and insulting songs to a distinguished diplomat," said Henry. "The idea was that she should pass out quietly, in order to stage a supposed suicide. Sir Edward would have behaved with great dignity, and received much sympathy. And his road to the premiership would have been wide, wide open."

"Poor Mavis," said Emmy. She paused. "I never met her, but I can't help thinking of her as Mavis, and in a funny way I can't help liking her. She may have been immoral, but she doesn't seem to have done anybody any harm—and yet they all hated her. Mrs. Holder-Watts and Dorabella were jealous of her. Nelson and Michael Holder-Watts thought she was ruining her husband's career. Even Sir Edward himself…I mean, it's just possible, isn't it?…and now that this Development Company has come into the picture…"

Henry said, "It's interesting, what you've just said. There were three different and distinct motives for doing away with Lady Ironmonger. Personal dislike, political ambition and money. It's just occurred to me that there's one person who had all those motives. Eleanor Holder-Watts."

CHAPTER SIXTEEN

THE NEXT MORNING, Henry and Emmy went snorkeling again. This time, they reserved one of the Pirate's Cave fleet of small motor boats, and were ferried out to a crescent of sandy beach on a tiny, uninhabited island called Little Goat. The boatman waved them good-bye, promising to return at mid-day—and they found themselves living the legendary daydream of being alone on a tropical island of their own.

They swam and sunbathed naked, and—with the help of flippers and mask—explored a living coral reef as freely and naturally as the brilliant fish who made it their home. Bright blue angel-fish with mouths curved upward in perpetual smiles; black and white striped zebra fish; pale yellow fishes, almost transparent, with long, drifting tails and fins, floating like ghosts among the forests of lacy coral… Twelve o'clock came round with indecent speed, sending Emmy grabbing for a beach towel as the chugging of the engine from around the point signaled the return of the motor boat.

After lunch, Henry telephoned to The Lodge and asked if it was possible to speak to Mr. Winston Nelson. After a long period of silence, the operator returned to ask Henry's name and business. Henry gave his name, said the matter was personal, and waited again. He was on the point of hanging up, when a deep voice at the other end of the line said, "Ironmonger."

"Sir Edward! Tibbett here. I'm afraid there has been a mistake. I wanted to talk to Mr. Nelson."

"No, there has been no mistake." Ironmonger sounded tired. "I hope you are enjoying your holiday."

"Very much indeed. Tampica is a beautiful island."

"And will become even more so in the future, I trust." Sir Edward's voice had a wry edge to it. "However, I understand that you had an unpleasant experience at Barney's Bar the other evening. I'd like to apologize, on Mr. Nelson's behalf, to you and your wife."

"You're very kind, Sir Edward, but it really isn't necessary. I'm afraid we may have behaved tactlessly. I must explain that we were invited to the bar by Dr. Duncan—"

"You don't have to explain, my dear fellow. I know exactly what happened, and I'm very sorry about it." A little pause. "And now you want to speak to Nelson. May I ask why?"

"Just a small point. Concerning the reception at the Tampican Embassy. Inspector Bartholomew and I are preparing our report," said Henry mendaciously.

"I see. Well, I'm afraid you can't talk to him. I sent him back to Washington yesterday."

"You did?"

"Immediately following the incident at Barney's Bar. I sent a car to bring him back here, and I told him to be on the first plane in the morning. I do not intend to tolerate such behavior among my staff. In any case, his real work here was to arrange things before the conference opened; he will be more useful in Washington. However, perhaps I can help you. What was it you wanted to know?"

Henry hesitated, then said, "It's a small point, Sir Edward, but I wondered why Mr. Finkelstein was being introduced to Lady Ironmonger so late in the evening. Surely he must have passed along the receiving line and shaken hands like everybody else? Or did he arrive so late that the line had broken up?"

At once, Ironmonger said, "No, no. Just the reverse. He arrived too early."

"Too early?"

"Yes. Let me explain. For some reason, our reception was a popular event—and parking in Georgetown is not easy. Quite a few guests arrived well before six o'clock. I was ready to receive them, with Dorabella and Holder-Watts and Nelson, but my wife...well, you know what women are like. She took rather a long time to dress, and she didn't come down to join the receiving line until nearly a quarter past six—by which time Mr. Finkelstein and quite a lot of others had already shaken hands and moved on. I can't imagine why you should think it important, but that's what happened, so your mystery is easily solved."

"Yes," said Henry. "Yes, thank you, Sir Edward. I had it all the wrong way around. I thought he must have been late."

Monday started for the Tibbetts with an unenergetic game of tennis, after which they went for a long walk on Goat Hill. They arrived back for lunch, to find a message that Miss Pontefract-Deacon had been calling Mr. Tibbett. Would he be kind enough to go down to the Tampica Harbour Yacht Marina the following day and call her up on the Children's Hour?

Henry was baffled. "What on earth is the Children's Hour? And why wait until tomorrow? Why can't I call her today?"

The young American at the desk explained. There were no telephone lines to Sugar Mill Bay. However, Miss Pontefract-Deacon was equipped with a two-way radio, which could be tuned to the frequency used by shipping. Private messages and conversations—which must be kept brief—might be exchanged between half-past eleven and half-past twelve each morning, a period which was locally dubbed the Children's Hour. And now, if Mr. and Mrs. Tibbett would care to avail themselves of the cold buffet...?

After lunch and a siesta, Henry and Emmy went down to the beach at about half-past three, and were surprised to find both George and Magnolia Belmont sunning themselves under an artificial palm tree.

"Hi, there," Magnolia called. "We wondered where y'all were this afternoon. Come and join us."

"As soon as we've had a dip, we'd love to," Emmy said. She dropped her beach bag and towel onto the sand, and splashed her way into the crystalline water. A few minutes later, much refreshed, she and Henry were lying on towels spread on the warm sand, letting the sun dry the salt water off their skin.

Henry said, "We didn't expect to see you so early, Senator. Is the meeting over for today?"

George Belmont grunted. "Haven't you heard?"

"Heard what?"

"The communiqué hasn't been officially issued yet, but I thought everyone at Pirate's Cave knew."

"Not everyone," Emmy assured him. "We've been out most of the day. What's happened?"

"Deadlock. That's what happened. Talks called off, with no prospect of agreement in sight. We're making pious noises about going home to consult our government, but the fact of the matter is that Ironmonger has won. We can't possibly agree to his terms, and he won't let Drake-Frobisher budge an inch. So the navy might just as well start packing its bags—which is exactly what these people want."

"And we have to go home tomorrow, instead of spending all week here," said Magnolia, with a pout.

"Now, look, honey," the Senator protested, "I told you—you stay here just as long as you want. But I have to go back."

"It's no fun here on my own," said Magnolia. Then, to Emmy, "How long are you folks staying? If you were going to be here…"

Emmy rolled over, propped herself on her elbows, and looked inquiringly at Henry. He said, "I think we'll be leaving very soon, Mrs. Belmont. Tomorrow or the day after."

"But y'all just got here! And all the way from England!"

"Oh," said Henry, "this is just one stop on quite an extended tour. We go to the States next."

"Well, imagine! If you come to Washington, you surely must come and see us, mustn't they, George?" The Senator grunted again. "Do you reckon to be around the District of Columbia any time, Mr. Tibbett?"

"It's possible," said Henry. Then, to Senator Belmont, "Tell me, sir—this is a purely hypothetical question—but what effect would it have on these talks of yours if it came to light that certain political figures in Tampica had a financial interest in the development company you mentioned yesterday?"

"They wouldn't be allowed to hold stock," said the Senator flatly.

"Not in their own names. But there's such a thing as a nominee—"

The Senator, who had been lying on his back with his eyes closed, now opened them. "I can't say what it would do to the talks," he said, "but it sure would be one big scandal. Say, do you have information on this? I couldn't even find out the name of the company, let alone the stockholders. As far as I'm concerned, it's just a bunch of rumors."

"Well," said Henry, "it might be worth making a few more inquiries—before the next round of talks."

The steel band played again that evening. Henry and Emmy, leaving the dance floor, saw Otis and Virginia Schipmaker sitting alone at a secluded table in the shadows at the edge of the terrace overlooking the sea. Henry led Emmy over and said, "Hi. Nice to see you. Mind if we join you for a while?"

"Of course not. Come and sit down. What are you drinking?"

Drinks were ordered and served, and conversation turned to the day's activities—Virginia enthusing over the beauty of Tampica, and her husband confessing that he preferred St. John's. "We'll be moving on there tomorrow for a few days," he added. "You've heard about the breakdown of the talks? No sense in staying on here. Everybody will be back in Washington by tomorrow afternoon."

"By the way," Henry said, "many thanks for your note. I gather that the information you gave me is pretty hard to come by."

Otis Schipmaker looked a little uncomfortable. "I just happened to hear the name of the company," he said. "I can't imagine why there should be any mystery about it."

Ginny Schipmaker leaned back in her chair and sent a twinkling glance in Henry's direction. "I'll tell you a secret," she said.

Otis said, "Ginny—" but his wife went on as if she had not heard him. "You remember when you mentioned the company the other evening, and Otis pretended to know nothing about it?"

"I remember."

"Well, afterwards I reminded him that he had talked to me about a Research and Development Company. He wasn't sure if it was the one you meant, but I said it must be, and that he should tell you. Now, have I earned a dance?"

"Mrs. Schipmaker," said Henry, "you certainly have."

Much later, in their cottage, Emmy said, "How odd that Otis Schipmaker knew about the development company all along. I wonder how he found out?"

"Haven't you figured that out yet?" Henry asked.

"No, I haven't. He hasn't been to Tampica for years, and he only met the Ironmongers for the first time at the reception…"

"Of course," said Henry. "I forgot that you didn't know. It seems that Otis Schipmaker had a somewhat tempestuous love affair with Mavis Ironmonger here in Tampica, before he met Ginny. I heard about it from his brother, who's married to the Barringtons' daughter. Virginia knows nothing about it to this day—which is why she was so keen to come here and he wasn't, and why she's quite relaxed and he's like a cat on hot bricks."

Emmy said, "Do you think they met in Washington recently—Mavis and Otis, I mean?"

"I'd be surprised if they didn't," said Henry. "Mavis was an open and uninhibited girl, and she didn't know many people in Washington. She may not have known that Otis was married. Anyhow, it would be the most natural thing in the world for her to contact him. It must have given him a nasty shock—with his political ambitions, a scandal was the last thing he wanted."

"And yet you think he went to see her?"

"Probably to tell her about Ginny and ask her to keep her mouth shut. Which I am sure she did, as far as her affair with Otis was concerned. But when it came to the Research and Development Company…"

"You mean, Otis heard about it from her?"

"Where else?" said Henry.

The Harbour Master's office at the Tampica Yacht Marina was spruce and ship-shape, its prosaic filing cabinets and desks enlivened by walls covered with charts; a couple of model sailing vessels; tattered burgees from epic voyages, framed and mounted—and, of course, the radio receiver/transmitter which muttered away to itself in a corner, as curt but important messages passed between ships and shore bases.

At eleven-thirty precisely, the Harbour Master turned up the volume, threw a switch, picked up the hand microphone, and said, "Sugar Mill Bay? Sugar Mill Bay? Tampica Marina here. Are you receiving me?"

A moment later, Lucy Pontefract-Deacon's impeccable English voice floated over the crackling circuit. "Sugar Mill

Bay to Tampica Marina. Receiving you loud and clear. Is Mr. Tibbett there? Over."

The Harbour Master handed Henry the microphone. "All yours," he said.

"Miss Pontefract-Deacon..." Henry began, tentatively.

"Please address me as Sugar Mill Bay. I have been thinking over our conversation, and the matter of timing. I am worried about Prudence Barrington. Over."

"I know what you mean, Sugar Mill Bay. Over."

"Then do not discuss it over the air. What action are you taking, Tampica Marina? Over."

"I am going back to Washington. So long as Prudence is with you—"

"She is not, Tampica Marina. She and Matthew flew back to Washington yesterday. Over."

"Did you speak to her before she left, Sugar Mill Bay? Over."

"I fear not. The significance of the situation only dawned on me later. Over."

"Does she still have—?"

"Yes, she does. What is your comment, Tampica Marina?"

"I'll get back there and do what I can. And God help her, Sugar Mill Bay. Over."

"Amen, Tampica Marina. Over and out."

❀ ❀ ❀

Henry's next move was a visit to police headquarters in Tampica Harbour, where he found Inspector Bartholomew in the inevitable green-and-cream office, engaged in preparing the report which would declare officially that Dorabella Hamilton had murdered Mavis Ironmonger by administering Alcodym and vodka to make her insensible, and then shooting her; and that subsequently Dorabella had committed suicide by throwing herself under the wheels of a car in Exeter Place N.W., Washington, D.C. She had made a deathbed confession (see attached affidavit by Doctor Miles). The case was closed.

Bartholomew looked up as Henry came in, and smiled. "Chief Superintendent! I had no idea you were in Tampica. This is a great pleasure. Do sit down. What can I do for you?"

Henry sat down. "You can tell me what you know of the Tampica Research and Development Company, Inspector."

"The what?"

"Tampica Research and Development Company."

Bartholomew looked bewildered. "I've never heard of it," he said. "I suppose it's another foreign company planning to build a hotel, like the Pirate's Cave people. Is that it?"

"Never mind," said Henry. "You've answered my question. How's the report going?"

"Very nearly finished. I'll be happy to get it out of the way."

"In that case," said Henry, "I'm sorry to disappoint you, but my visit may not be much of a pleasure after all. You see, you're going to have to tear up that report and start again."

"Tear it up? Why?"

"Because it's inaccurate. I'm going back to Washington tomorrow, and I think you should come with me."

Bartholomew threw his hands toward the ceiling in a gesture of mock despair. "I don't understand! What is all this about?"

Henry hesitated a moment, and then said, "Look, Inspector, I'm in a hellishly difficult position. Officially, the case is closed and I'm here on holiday. However, I'm absolutely certain now that we made a mistake. Our reasoning was wrong, and the real murderer is still free. What's more, I think another life may be in danger."

Henry noticed, with respect, that Bartholomew did not break into a spate of questions. Instead, he said quietly, "I presume that you've discussed all this with Sir Edward. It's surely up to him to decide whether or not I should go back to Washington."

"That's just the difficulty," said Henry. "I haven't told anybody, except you. I dare not."

For the first time, Inspector Bartholomew looked really shocked.

"You are not implying that Sir Edward—"

"What I'm implying," said Henry, "is that the situation is so delicate that I dare not confide in anybody who was personally involved in Lady Ironmonger's death. And that goes for her husband."

Bartholomew said, flatly, "I can't go back to Washington unless I'm ordered to do so."

"Aren't you perhaps due for some leave?"

Bartholomew raised his eyebrows. "Yes, as a matter of fact, I am. But if you think I can afford a trip to Washington… and in any case, what would my wife say? We were planning to spend a week with her mother on St. Mark's."

"Don't you think your wife might enjoy Washington, Inspector?"

"Please talk sense, Chief Superintendent. Of course she would love it, but who is to pay? The air fare alone…"

Henry reached into his pocket and pulled out an envelope. He said, "Do you have transport? A mini-moke or something?"

"I have a Jeep."

"Then I suggest that you drive over to Sugar Mill Bay at once. Give this letter to Miss Lucy and see what happens. Call me at Pirate's Cave when you get back."

Immediately after lunch, Henry went to the reception desk at Pirate's Cave, and asked if reservations back to Washington could be made for Emmy and himself for the following morning. The dusky beauty who had been Winston Nelson's dancing partner was on duty, and she wrinkled her exquisite nose in a rueful smile.

"You'll be lucky, Mr. Tibbett. There's a real exodus, now that the conference has broken up. I can tell you right away, you won't get first-class seats from Antigua. It's all filled up with diplomats and delegates—why, I've even had to book Mr. and Mrs. Schipmaker in economy class."

Henry said, "I don't care where we sit, just so long as we get that plane."

"I'll ring through to Antigua right away," promised the girl, and she swayed beguilingly over to the other desk. A few minutes later she was back with the news that Mr. and Mrs. Tibbett were booked on the last two seats on the morning flight. No more reservations could be accepted.

Half-an-hour later, Bartholomew called. Henry decided not to take the call from the reception desk, but asked the Inspector to hold while he made his way to the privacy of his own cottage. Nevertheless, he was aware that the receptionist could listen in if she wanted to, and he hoped that his Tampican colleague would be discreet.

"Chief Superintendent? Bartholomew here. I hear that you are going back to Washington tomorrow."

"That's right."

"Perhaps you could give me your telephone number there. You see, I have a week's leave coming up, and my wife and I intend to spend it in Washington."

"This is very good news," said Henry, meaning it. "Where are you staying?"

"That is not yet decided. We will find a small hotel. I had hoped to travel on the same aircraft as you, but unfortunately it is fully booked. However, we've been lucky enough to get seats on a stand-by plane. We arrive in Dulles at two o'clock."

Henry gave Bartholomew Margaret Colville's address and telephone number, and asked him to call as soon as he got to Washington. Then he said, "I'm so glad you're able to make this trip."

"Thanks to the generosity of a very great lady." Bartholomew hesitated a moment. "She...she has given me some tips on what to look out for in Washington. I'm sure it will enhance our stay."

Henry rang off feeling happier about the future. Lucy Pontefract-Deacon had summed up the situation and dealt with it in a masterly fashion. What was more, she was able to dish out money for air fares and accommodation without undue strain. She would, of course, be reimbursed later.

"It's all very well to give Margaret's number," Emmy remarked, emerging from the shower, "but she doesn't even know we're coming back. Supposing she can't put us up?"

"Good Lord, I'd forgotten. We'd better telephone her."

Fortunately, Margaret was delighted, if baffled. "What's the matter with you? Aren't you enjoying yourselves? I can tell you, I wouldn't pass up a free vacation at Pirate's Cave. What's it all in aid of, Emmy?"

Emmy said, "Oh, well—Henry has to get back to London in a hurry, but we couldn't resist making the trip via Washington."

"Ah, well, Tampica's loss is my gain. See you tomorrow..."

Emmy rang off, and turned to Henry. "And now," she said, "you might explain just what it *is* all in aid of."

Henry said, "I have been very stupid. The answer has been under my nose the whole time, and I never saw it—not until I spoke to Lucy Pontefract-Deacon. She was much quicker than I was. But even if I'd worked it all out in Washington, I couldn't have done anything about it. I had no proof and no motive, and I couldn't have made it stick. Now, when I get back, I can lay hands on proof and motive—but the trouble is that in the meanwhile Prudence Barrington is in great danger."

"Mrs. Barrington? Why on earth—?"

"Because she's a serious threat to a desperate person."

Emmy laughed. "Oh, come off it, Henry. Prudence wouldn't threaten anyone."

"That's just the dangerous part. She doesn't know she's a threat—which means that she'll walk into any trap that's set for her. Especially if it's set by a friend."

"Then shouldn't you warn her?"

Henry hesitated. "It's difficult to know what to say over the telephone," he said, "but you're perfectly right. I should at least try. I suppose it'll take forever to find her telephone number..."

As a matter of fact, it took a surprisingly short time, but the exercise proved fruitless. Prudence, according to Matthew, had gone off to spend a couple of days with Jean and Homer on their boat, which they kept on the lower Potomac. No, there was absolutely no way of contacting her this evening. However, she would be home in the morning, and if Mr. Tibbett would call then…

"Well, I suppose at least she's safe in the middle of the river," said Henry to Emmy. "Anyhow, there's nothing more we can do."

CHAPTER SEVENTEEN

TAMPICA'S TINY AIRSTRIP was alive with activity on Wednesday morning. Every available light plane had been mustered to ferry the illustrious parting guests, and every few minutes a little aircraft buzzed down the dusty runway and soared into the sky like a humming bee.

Henry and Emmy shared their little cabin with George and Magnolia Belmont, and the co-pilot's seat was occupied by one of the conference secretaries. As they gained height and circled the island before setting course for St. Mark's, Emmy looked down nostalgically at the now-familiar landmarks—Pirate's Cave Hotel, Barracuda Bay, The Lodge, Tampica Harbour's waterfront, and the dirt road snaking over the hills to Sugar Mill Bay.

"We must try to come back someday, somehow," she said to Henry. "Not to Pirate's Cave, of course—that would be out of the question—but there must be cheaper hotels..."

"Pretty soon there'll be more cheap hotel accommodation on Tampica than you can shake a stick at," grunted

Senator Belmont. "Once the navy goes, and Barracuda Bay is developed."

"It's a *shame*," Magnolia said. "It'll just ruin this cute little island. Imagine the sort of people who'll be able to afford to come!"

Emmy nudged Henry, who remarked, "People like us. I agree. A disaster."

Fortunately, the whirring engine prevented Magnolia from hearing. She went on, "And cruise liners! Have you *seen* them? Why, I declare, George and I were in St. Thomas one time…well, I just won't even *try* to tell y'all what it was like…"

The blue, crystalline water lapped quietly on the golden sand. The coconut palms stretched their long green fingers towards the sun. From her terrace, Lucy Pontefract-Deacon waved a good-luck salute to each tiny plane as it circled, even though she had no idea which one contained the Tibbetts, and she doubted if she could be seen from the air anyway. When the last one had headed out to sea, she rang the silver bell for Martin Fletcher, and ordered a glass of iced tea. Tampica was back to normal again.

At Antigua, the Belmonts were ushered away to a VIP lounge, and the Tibbetts only just glimpsed them as they boarded the aircraft ahead of the throng and were installed in their first-class seats. Even earlier, Sir Edward Ironmonger—who had, of course, arrived in Antigua aboard the Prime Minister's yacht—was escorted with great ceremony to the plane. Nevertheless, Henry reflected, once airborne this class distinction boiled down to a curtain hanging between the small first-class section and the rest of the fuselage, slightly wider seats and free drinks. In idle moments, he had sometimes tried to calculate how many drinks an economy-class passenger would have to buy before his outlay approached the cost of a first-class ticket.

The flight was smooth and uneventful. Henry saw Otis and Virginia sitting some rows further up the aircraft, but there was no chance to talk to them, or to discover why they had changed their minds about going to St. John's. Probably no more than Ginny's political acumen triumphing over Otis's naturally sybaritic tastes. He wondered how much Otis really wanted to be a senator, and how much his wife and her family were getting behind him and pushing.

At Dulles Airport, the senators and diplomats left the plane first, passed through a special Customs section and were whisked off in waiting limousines. Henry and Emmy, along with other ordinary mortals, waited patiently for their baggage to appear on the conveyor belt, claimed it, and subjected themselves to the routines of Customs and Immigration. Margaret was waiting with the Volkswagen, and before long they were on the Parkway. Then Key Bridge came into sight, together with the Watergate, the Kennedy Center and the tall spires of Georgetown University.

"I've only spent a few days here," Emmy said, "and yet I feel as if I were coming home."

Margaret grinned. "Georgetown has that effect on people," she said. Then amended herself. "Some people, I should say. Others just don't see the point—why live in a cramped little townhouse, when for the same money you could have a split-level rambler and a swimming pool in the suburbs? I never try to give an answer to that argument. There isn't one."

The Volkswagen trundled over Key Bridge, turned right into the busy commercialism of M Street, and then left up 33rd Street—up the hill and into Georgetown.

Henry and Emmy had been away for less than a week, but the whole neighborhood was transformed. In an annual miracle, between one day and the next the blossom had come out. Pink and white dogwood trees had erupted into seas of leafless blooms; the red, purple, golden and white azaleas had opened their buds in an explosion of color; even the sycamores and plane trees lining the streets had burst into an extravagance of greenery, and wisteria hung in pale mauve swathes against red-brick and white-painted houses. It is this effect of instant spring which more than anything reminds a visitor to Washington that he is in the South.

Inside the little blue frame house, Margaret said, "I am trying not to be nosy—well, not *too* nosy—but really, Emmy, you'll have to think up a better story than hurrying back to London via Washington. Talk about going to Birmingham by way of Beachy Head...so, what's up?"

Emmy looked at Henry, raising her eyebrows, passing the question. He said, "You'll know soon enough, Margaret, but there's no time to waste now. I must call Mrs. Barrington at once. Do you have a Maryland directory?"

Margaret shrugged. "Yes, but it won't do you any good."

"What do you mean?"

Margaret glanced at her watch. "It's quarter past one. Mrs. Barrington won't be home."

"How do you know? I didn't think you even knew the Barringtons?"

"I've never met the Bishop, but Mrs. Barrington and I belong to the same women's club—the Chevy Chase Episcopal Ladies'—and at this moment she's taking a group of them on the Georgetown Garden Tour. I was supposed to go myself, but I called it off to meet you at Dulles."

"What's the Georgetown Garden Tour?" Emmy asked.

"Just what it says. Every year at this time, when the gardens are looking their best, nine or ten of them are opened to the public for charity, just for two days. You pay five dollars and have a marvelous time peeking at other people's gardens—and some of their houses, too, because you have to walk through some of them to get to the gardens."

"These would be the huge estates you were telling us about, I suppose," Emmy said.

"No, not all of them. They generally have two or three big show-place gardens on the tour, but there are also little ones—some no bigger than ours. It's fascinating to see what some people have been able to do with just a tiny plot of land."

Henry said, "I suppose it's common knowledge that Prudence Barrington will be on the tour today?"

Margaret laughed. "She's what they call here a garden nut. She hasn't missed a tour since she's been here."

"Do you have a list of the gardens that are open today?" Henry asked.

"Yes, on my ticket. Come into the drawing-room, and we'll take a look."

Moments later, Henry was sitting beside Margaret on the sofa, studying the list of addresses on the back of the card. He said, "What exactly happens? Does everybody assemble at a certain time—?"

"Oh, no. The gardens are open from half-past eleven to half-past five, and you can visit them at any time, in any order."

"So anybody could be in any garden at any time?"

"Well...yes. But the gardens are listed in topographical order, as it were. To do the tour with the minimum of walking, you start either at the beginning or the end, and visit the addresses in order. Our group planned to start at the top of the list and work down."

"The top being—?"

"Dumbarton Oaks. That's the most famous house in Georgetown...where the Dumbarton Oaks Conference was held. The gardens are world-famous. It all belongs to Harvard University now, but the previous owners spent years landscaping the gardens, all the way down from Dumbarton Rock to Rock Creek. You simply must see them."

"Some other time. What time did Mrs. Barrington's group plan to meet, do you know?"

"Yes. Dumbarton Oaks, main gateway, twelve noon— having eaten an early snack to keep up their strength. They plan to take the other gardens in turn, ending up at the Georgetown Children's Home—that's what it's all in aid of— for a supper tea at half-past four."

Henry glanced at his watch. "Then we haven't much time. Tell me about the other gardens."

Margaret adjusted her reading glasses. "I haven't really studied the program," she said. "Let's see. 3320 Dent Place—

oh, I know the people who live there. It's a beautiful garden, quite small. And then a house on 34th Street…I only know it from outside, but the garden can't be very big…P Street…32nd Street…those must be small, too…ah, here's a big one— Maycroft House, on Exeter Place. That's one of the biggest estates that's still privately owned—it runs to about four acres. Actually, it belongs to old Schipmaker—Otis's father—and Ginny took me there once. It's beautiful. They even have a waterfall and a maze and all sorts of things." Her eye ran down the other addresses. "All these must be little ones. I expect there are just the two…oh!" She stopped, in obvious surprise.

"What is it?" Henry asked.

"The very last on the list. You'll never guess."

"Then tell me."

"3119 Oxford Gardens. By gracious permission of His Excellency the Tampican Ambassador. *That* should be a big attraction. I wonder why Sir Edward ever agreed to include it."

"I doubt if he even knew about it," said Henry. He was immensely intrigued. "You see, if everything had gone according to plan, the Ambassador and his senior staff would still be in Tampica for the naval base talks. As it is, the conference broke up and everybody is back—which may well have put a spanner into somebody's works. The Embassy is out—so my money is on Maycroft House."

"For what?"

"For murder—or attempted murder, if we can get there soon enough. What time do you reckon the Barrington group will get to Maycroft?"

Margaret considered. "They'll spend at least an hour at Dumbarton Oaks—probably more. And since half of them won't have been punctual anyhow, my guess is that they're leaving the Oaks about now. It'll take them ten minutes or so to walk to Dent Place…give them a quarter of an hour there…five minutes' walk to 34th Street…ten minutes to see that garden… half an hour for the other small gardens nearby…ten minutes' walk to Exeter Place—longer if they want to window-shop in

Wisconsin Avenue on the way—I'd say they'll get to Maycroft at about a quarter to three, something over an hour from now."

"Then we're not too late," Henry said. "In fact, I can make a couple of phone calls. Can you find me the number of the M Street Police Station?"

A minute later. "Officer Stanton? Tibbett here...yes, I'm back in Washington for a few days...look, can you tell me how I can contact Franklin D. Martin?... Yes, I do mean him... You don't have him in custody at the moment?... Pity...well, if you could possibly get me a phone number on him...yes, I'll hold on...ah, thank you very much." Henry scribbled on the phone-side pad. "Yes, it is urgent...no, I wouldn't say all Englishmen are crazy, Officer—just most of us...thanks a lot...by the way, if I do contact him, he may pay you a visit later on...no, you don't have to talk to him, he'll simply be dropping in an envelope for you..."

Henry was lucky. Franklin D. Martin was at home—actually, he was painting placards which he intended to parade outside selected supermarkets, urging the public to "Boycott Beetroot," for a reason which was not entirely clear. He sounded surprised at Henry's questions, but answered them without hesitation.

"Yeah, man, sure I remember...yeah, just before we got busted, man...oh, yeah, before that...sure I'm sure...write it down and take it to M Street...Officer Stanton...hey, man, you think I'm about to do the fuzz's work for them?..."

"Look at it this way," said Henry. "Officer Stanton would be very grateful..."

"Yeah, man, sure. Yeah, that's neat. Know something? Don't ask me why, but I kinda dig you..."

"It's mutual," said Henry. "Thanks a lot, Franklin." He rang off, and turned to Emmy. "Come on, then. We're off on the garden tour."

"I'll come with you," said Margaret at once.

"I'm so sorry, Margaret," Henry said, "but I must ask you to stay here. Inspector Bartholomew should be calling about half-past two from the airport. Please tell him to go straight to the Tampican Embassy as soon as he possibly can, and not to be surprised by anything he finds there. Tell him I'll be along as soon as I can. By the way, how do we get tickets for this thing?"

"You can buy them at the gate of any of the gardens. But one of you had better use mine—pity to waste it."

"I'm really sorry, Margaret—but this is serious and can be dangerous. Please stay here—you can go on the tour tomorrow."

"It's not the same gardens," said Margaret wistfully. "I may not get to see the Tampican Embassy."

"That may be very lucky for you," said Henry.

It came as no surprise to realize that Maycroft House was the vast establishment referred to laconically by Belinda Drayton as "3018, over the way." Exeter Place was full of garden enthusiasts, mostly feminine, mostly middle-aged. Some were in couples or threesomes, but others wore little identity tags and roamed in herds of fifteen or twenty, shepherded by a harassed leader who was continually demanding to know if everybody was there.

This surging crowd had a common goal—the big wrought-iron gateway which led into the grounds of Maycroft House. The gates stood open, and immediately inside them was a trestle table at which sat two elegantly dressed ladies, each wearing a silk emblem, like a small pennant, on which the word "Hostess" was woven in gold on a white background. On the table were piles of tickets, a brochure outlining the history of Maycroft and the geography of its garden, and several cups of coffee.

Emmy produced Margaret's ticket. One of the hostesses (blue-rinsed hair and a floral hat) scored through the name "Maycroft House" with a firm pencil, and remarked, "So you've come to us first. A good choice—I'm sure you will enjoy us." Henry, meanwhile, was buying his ticket from the other hostess—a slim, gray-haired woman in a Chanel suit.

"I was wondering," he said, "if the Chevy Chase Episcopal Ladies have arrived here yet?"

"I don't think so. I'm not sure. We have a lot of groups, you know. Caroline, have the Chevy Chase Episcopal Ladies been here?"

"Prudence Barrington's party?" The behatted lady beamed at Henry. "Yes, indeed. They got here just a few minutes ago. Mary is new to this job, or she'd know Mrs. Barrington. Such delightful enthusiasm. I hope you'll buy the map of the garden. Just one dollar, all proceeds to the Day Care Center. Thank you so much."

Henry said, "How do we get out of here?"

"I beg your pardon?"

"I mean—everybody seems to be coming in by this gate, but nobody's going out. I suppose there's an exit somewhere."

"Right. If you follow the plan of the garden, you'll see that it goes downhill in a series of terraces until you reach the maze. Beyond the maze, there's an exit into the alley, which runs between 31st and 30th Streets. Don't get lost now!" The hostess gave Henry a brief smile of dismissal. Behind him, the Horticultural Society of Southern Alexandria was assembling in chattering impatience, tickets held high. Henry and Emmy moved away from the table and into the gardens of Maycroft House.

It has been mentioned before that Georgetown is built on a hill, which slopes down to the River Potomac in the south, and more steeply into Rock Creek on the east. Consequently, all Georgetown gardens present interesting problems in landscaping, for there is always a sharp slope to consider. The obvious answer is terracing—which means that every garden is in fact a series of smaller gardens on different levels, giving plenty of scope for diversity, privacy and a sense of enhanced space. In a garden the size of Maycroft's, four acres dropping steeply towards the river had been made to appear like a never-ending series of enclosed and secluded enchantments.

At the back of the big red-brick house, a paved terrace opened onto a clipped lawn, bordered by a hedge of boxwood carved into traditional topiary shapes of pyramids, globes and peacocks. Apart from a drift of pink-and-white dogwood blossom glimpsed above this hedge, nothing more could be seen from the terraces; but a flight of steps led down through a cutting in the hedge to reveal, on a lower level, a big goldfish pool in which two rearing stone dolphins spat eternally at each other, and eternally missed. The pool was surrounded by a rose garden, and at its eastern end an archway festooned with rambler roses led to a tennis court, with a small pavilion and a fountain in the shape of a mer-horse straddled by an impudent Cupid. Each of these gardens was complete, separate and secluded. Looking at the sketch plan, Henry saw that there were no less than three succeeding levels, each lower than the last. Below the tennis court came the swimming pool, the azalea garden and the Dutch formal garden; next, the orchard, grotto and waterfall; and finally, under the shade of huge magnolia trees where few flowers would bloom, the curiosity of the boxwood maze.

They caught up with the Chevy Chase Episcopal Ladies in the azalea garden. There were about a dozen of them, ranging from young-middle-age to sprightly senile, all neatly labeled, sensibly shod, and simmering with enthusiasm. Several of them had cornered a woman wearing a Hostess tag, and were plying her with horticultural questions which she was patently unable to answer (she was a second cousin of Mrs. Schipmaker's, a staunch New Yorker who had needed coaching to be able to say, "These are the azaleas"). Prudence Barrington, in a khaki-colored linen suit and a big straw hat, was acting as sheepdog.

"Come along now! Are we all here? Where's Mrs. Merriwether...? Ah, there you are, dear...yes, aren't they pretty... Come now, Mrs. Merriwether, you mustn't flatter me...well, mine may be larger, but these have more interesting colors... Now, ladies, please!" Prudence clapped her hands and raised her voice. "We are moving on to the orchard...just follow me...oh, fancy, Mr. Tibbett and Emmy... I thought you were in Tampica...are you enjoying yourselves?... This way, ladies... down the steps...forgive me if I don't go very fast...touch of arthritis...yes, Mrs. Merriwether, I have tried it, but you can't believe everything you see on television...come along, now, everybody..."

Prudence maneuvered her flock through a trellis archway festooned with delicate-flowered clematis, and down a winding flight of stone steps towards the sea of blossom that was the orchard.

Henry said to Emmy, urgently, "Join the party. Keep your eye on Prudence and make sure she stays with the others. I'm going on to the maze."

Before Emmy could answer, Henry was off. He had noticed another opening in the boxwood hedge, another flight of steps down, which was considerably less populated than the route which Prudence had taken. He vanished, like a rabbit down its burrow, as Emmy hurried to catch up with the Episcopal Ladies.

The cherry blossom was past its best, but the apple and almond trees were bursting into fat pink and white buds, and the burgeoning dogwoods, interspersed with the fruit trees, made a breathtaking sight. The ladies exclaimed with delight, and showed a disposition to linger in the welcome shade— for the temperature was in the eighties. The neat phalanx dispersed, and Emmy went over to Prudence Barrington, who was explaining the finer points of fruit-tree pruning to an interested group.

"May I join your party, Mrs. Barrington?"

Prudence looked surprised. "Of course, dear—but where's your good husband?"

"He...he had to leave. He suggested I might finish the tour with you."

"Well, of course, we'll be delighted." Prudence clapped her hands. "Ladies, this is Mrs. Tibbett, who is joining our group."

"I'm afraid I haven't got a badge," said Emmy, "but I can tell you by yours. We...we all keep together, don't we?" Emmy was doing her best.

"Nobody is *compelled* to keep together," said Prudence, "but as some of our members don't know Georgetown well, I think it's best if we remain a single party. In a place as big as this, a newcomer can easily get lost. And since, fortunately, I know it well…"

"Especially in the maze," said Emmy, with what was intended to be a light laugh, but came out more like an hysterical giggle.

"The maze is no problem," said Prudence. "The way through it is clearly marked. Now, as I was saying, in the spring you should never attempt to…" She was off into a spate of technicalities.

Prudence allowed her group ten minutes of relaxation under the shadow of the trees, and then summoned them to the grotto. This, on the same level as the orchard, was a triumph of man's ability to imitate nature. A small granite cliff had been built, over which gushed a waterfall—apparently natural, but actually pumped electrically. The water fell in a rainbow-glinting cascade into a miniature lake, whence it descended in a series of terraced pools, becoming progressively tamer until at the lowest level water lilies floated and goldfish swam about their business. Finally, the water was sucked underground and pumped to the top of the cliff to begin its descent all over again.

The whole thing was liberally scattered with stonework—pineapples and griffins, nymphs and satyrs, and a delightful pair of harpies—the heads of elegantly coiffed eighteenth-century beauties set on crouching animal bodies with fierce claws and swishing tails.

Prudence was not impressed by the harpies. "You will see," she admonished her Ladies, "that they are an inferior copy of the pair we saw in the orangery at Dumbarton Oaks. Now, if you have all seen enough, we can move on to the maze. Are we all here…? Mrs. Merriwether, please, we are ready to move on…eight, nine, ten…that seems to be everybody…if you would be kind enough to bring up the rear, Mrs. Tibbett…?"

Emmy did as she was asked. In such a compact group, and with the maze clearly signposted, it seemed unlikely that Prudence would come to any harm. If an ambush had been planned, Emmy thought, it would surely be at the Tampican Embassy. She waited until the main body of the group had disappeared through the boxwood archway and down the steps, scooped up a couple of Episcopal Ladies who had become fascinated by a rather lewd satyr, and propelled them down to the level of the maze. Where she stopped dead, in surprise and alarm.

Not that the scene was alarming. The entrance to the maze was clearly marked by a large sign, and policed by a bevy of hostesses. A bright red cord at waist level disappeared between the hedges, and a plethora of signs warned visitors *Follow the red cord. DO NOT take any side turning, or you may lose yourself.* None of this was surprising. What alarmed Emmy was that there was no sign of Prudence. A woman whom she recognized as one of the group—an imposing figure in a magenta trouser suit—was assembling the Episcopal Ladies at the maze entrance. Emmy caught the tail end of her remarks.

"...as efficient a guide as Mrs. Barrington, but I shall do my best. The maze seems to be the one place where it is impossible to get lost—but please keep to the official route, and all stay together. Then we will assemble at the rear entrance, and go on to..."

Emmy pulled the sleeve of the woman standing next to her. "Where's Mrs. Barrington?"

"Oh, didn't you know? She told us earlier that she'd be leaving us here—she has an important appointment. She's hoping to rejoin us, either at the Tampican Embassy or at the Children's Home for tea, but she said she couldn't be sure. Ah, we seem to be moving off. I've not been in a maze before. It's rather exciting, isn't it?"

Emmy hesitated in an agony of indecision. Henry had specifically told her to make sure Prudence remained with the group—but Prudence had had other ideas. There seemed little point in wandering around the maze now—the important thing was to trail Prudence. Henry had said he was going to the maze: where was he? Then Emmy realized another fact. The maze, dark and mysterious under the overshadowing magnolia trees, occupied the whole width of the garden. There was no way of getting to the back gate except through the intricate network of boxwood lanes.

So Prudence had not evaded the maze. She had merely gone ahead on her own to keep her appointment, leaving a deputy to shepherd the slow-moving group. If Emmy wanted to follow Prudence, the red cord through the labyrinth was the only guide. Emmy made up her mind, and plunged into the maze, plowing through the mass of Episcopal Ladies blocking the narrow alleys.

"Excuse me...in rather a hurry...so sorry...if you don't mind..."

Once clear of the Chevy Chase Ladies, Emmy found the going easier, although still impeded by strolling visitors. She was thankful for the red cord, because she soon lost all sense of direction, and numerous alleys were opening up on either side, apparently promising to lead much more quickly and directly to the bottom of the garden.

In fact, hurrying as she did, Emmy quite soon reached the center of the maze—a circular clearing embellished by a small fountain and stone benches for relaxation. The red cord led her out on the other side, and before long she rounded a corner to find herself at the exit, facing the back gate. She reckoned she could not be more than a few seconds behind Prudence now, for the older woman had been walking with a slight limp, presumably due to her arthritis. The back gate—a simple wooden affair—was open, and unattended by hostesses. Emmy ran through it.

She found herself in a concrete-paved alley, not wide enough for motor traffic, and bordered on either side by high walls. The back gate of Maycroft House was about midway along the alley, which stretched for half a block in either direction. At each end, Emmy could glimpse the passing traffic on the busy north-south streets. The only other gateway giving on to the alley belonged to the vast mansion to the south of Maycroft House. It was secured by a rusty but very stout padlock, which had obviously not been opened in years. And the alley was completely deserted.

Emmy stood still, baffled. She had really been expecting to catch up with Prudence in the maze, given her greater rate of speed. It was simply not possible that Mrs. Barrington could have been so far ahead of her as to have traveled the length of the alley and reached the street by now. She could not have been picked up by car.

There was only one answer. Prudence was still in the maze. But she certainly had not taken the officially marked route. She must have tried to take a short cut, and by now was probably lost. And neatly isolated from her group and everybody else. Well, there was nothing for it but to try to find her. And where on earth was Henry? Miserably, Emmy went back through the gate and into the maze again.

This time, she was going against the stream, and also against a barrage of well-meant information that she was going the wrong way.

"Sorry...have to go back...yes, I do know, thank you... forgotten something...yes, you're very kind, but I do know..."

A side alley turned off to the left, and momentarily Emmy had the short, grassy corridor to herself. She dodged under the red cord and into the unknown.

As the notice had predicted, within a very few minutes she was hopelessly lost. The path turned sharply right, then left, doubled back on itself and ended in a T-junction. Emmy turned left, and soon found herself at a dead end. She retraced her steps—but somehow the path from which she had come seemed to have disappeared. The voices of the visitors were almost inaudible now—she seemed to be getting farther and farther from the official path, and was by now quite incapable of telling in which direction she was going.

Then, suddenly, she heard footsteps. Somebody else was wandering in the forbidden part of the maze. Henry? Prudence...? Or...? She dared not call out. She quickly turned up a side alley and round a bend, and then peered cautiously back to see who was coming. She was too late. The running figure was past the end of the alley before she could identify it. All she could see was that it was a tall person, wearing a beige raincoat. Definitely not Prudence, definitely not Henry.

All at once, the ludicrous side of the situation occurred to Emmy, and she nearly laughed out loud. The whole area of the maze could not have been much more than an acre, and much of it was occupied by Episcopal Ladies and other visitors, strolling and enjoying themselves. And yet, in this confined space at the bottom of somebody's garden, were four people—herself, Henry, Mrs. Barrington and the unknown—stalking and seeking each other, and so far, apparently, failing to make contact.

"Oh, God, for a helicopter," Emmy said aloud, and set out to try to follow the running figure.

A moment later, she froze in her tracks. A voice was coming from the other side of the dense boxwood hedge. It was Prudence Barrington's voice, and it was saying, "What on earth are you doing here, Mr. Tibbett?"

CHAPTER EIGHTEEN

HENRY HAD REACHED the maze well ahead of Prudence Barrington's party, and entered it along with a small group of unlabeled visitors. As soon as the coast was clear, he had left the main route and escaped into a side alley, from which he could—at the price of considerable discomfort, for the hedges were intentionally bristly and impenetrable—watch the passing tourists on the red-corded path without being seen.

He had been exasperated but not really surprised to see Prudence coming into the maze alone, ahead of her flock, and hurrying as much as her stiff leg would allow. Emerging onto the official route once more, and keeping at a safe distance, he had tailed his quarry.

It was obvious that Prudence knew the maze intimately. She did not hesitate for a moment, but made her way confidently down the main alley for some time, until she reached a point where a path led off to the right. Here she dawdled, letting the party of South Alexandria Horticulturists get ahead of her. Henry dodged out of sight. When he looked again, a moment later, Prudence had disappeared. She could only have taken the right-hand pathway. It was clear that Mrs. Barrington had a rendezvous somewhere in the maze, and that she was on her way to keep it.

Henry glanced at his watch. Twenty-past-three. The appointment was probably for three-thirty. Prudence would be early—or perhaps her watch was wrong. Anyhow, it gave him a breathing space, a small gift of time in which to find her in this madhouse of a maze. Hoping that Prudence's friend was not also early for the appointment, Henry began his search.

Like Emmy, he soon discovered that the maze was far from simple, but had been specifically designed to confuse the sense of direction. By the time Henry reached the alley which Prudence had taken there was, of course, no sign of her. Round every corner was a baffling choice of paths. Henry was lost.

At one point, he found himself divided by only one hedge from the official route and its chattering voices, and among them he heard Emmy's. "So sorry…forgotten something…"

"You're going the wrong way, you know!" broke in a high-pitched female voice.

"Yes, I know…must go back…"

Poor Emmy. Prudence must have given her the slip, and now she, too, was involved in the merry-go-round. Nothing to be done about it. Henry pressed on, and soon the voices grew faint, and the oppressive silence of the maze blotted out all sound. By now, Henry's only hope was that, like boats drifting in a fog, he and Prudence must inevitably collide. True, Prudence was not drifting, but… He came to a T-junction. Right or left? What the hell does it matter? He turned right, followed a zig-zag path, rounded a corner—and there, in a small dead end clearing, was Prudence Barrington. She was sitting on the grass at the foot of a small bronze statue of goat-footed Pan, which leered wickedly from its stone pedestal. She had removed her shoes, and was wiggling her naked toes in patent satisfaction under the thin spray of a little fountain. She looked up, saw Henry, and said accusingly, "What on earth are you doing here, Mr. Tibbett?"

"Looking for you," said Henry.

"For me? What a bizarre idea. In any case, your wife told me you had abandoned the tour."

"I abandoned it to find you, Mrs. Barrington. Unfortunately, you obviously know this maze and I don't. I got lost trying to follow you."

Prudence Barrington smiled. "I don't suppose anybody outside the family and staff knows this garden as well as I do," she said. "You see, Eunice—Mrs. Schipmaker—knows of my interest in flowers and…but we are wasting time. I'm so sorry, Mr. Tibbett, but I must ask you to leave. I have an appointment at half-past three."

Henry said, "Mrs. Barrington, please, you must listen to me—"

Prudence sailed serenely on. "Did you know that Eddie Ironmonger was back from Tampica? The talks seem to have broken down—such a pity, but Matthew says it's all part of Eddie's policy. I'm afraid politics are above my head, but I do know that the base gave my girls a chance to meet such nice young men. However, that's beside the point. What I'm getting at, Mr. Tibbett, is that I had a phone call from the Embassy this morning—Eddie wants to talk to me urgently. I said I couldn't abandon my ladies—at least not until I'd got them this far—so we came up with the bright idea of the maze. I explained very carefully how he could find the Pan statue, and there couldn't be a more secluded spot for a chat. I don't know what Eddie wants to see me about, but it's obviously confidential and he'll be here any minute, so if you don't mind…"

Henry said, rudely, "Shut up, for God's sake!"

Prudence looked at him, openmouthed, but she shut up.

There was a full minute of silence. Then, panting slightly from his exertions, Winston Horatio Nelson came around the hedge and into the little clearing.

He said, "Mrs. Barrington..." and then, seeing Henry, "Tibbett! What in hell—?"

"I was expecting you, Mr. Nelson," said Henry.

"Well, I certainly wasn't," said Prudence. "Where's Eddie?"

"Sir Edward knows nothing about this," Henry said. "It was Nelson you spoke to on the telephone, wasn't it?"

"Well—yes. He's Eddie's right-hand man, after all, and now that Dorabella—"

"Mrs. Barrington," said Henry, "do you still have your husband's old watch—the one that he thinks he's lost, and that the watchmaker said must have been running slow for—"

"Why, yes. Certainly I do."

Nelson's hand went to the pocket of his raincoat, and Henry caught a glint of steel. He said, "No, Mr. Nelson. You can't get away with it. Mrs. Barrington, perhaps. No alarm would have been raised until she failed to come home this evening. Even then it would have taken time to find her here. You, of course, will have arranged an unbreakable alibi back at the Embassy. You might have brought it off—but now you can't. There are two of us—no, I'm sorry, there are three of us. My wife is at this moment on her way to the Embassy to fetch Inspector Bartholomew."

"Bartholomew?"

"I brought him back to Washington. I thought you would rather face trial in Tampica than in the United States."

Prudence was looking from one man to the other in utter amazement. She said, "I don't understand any of this—"

Henry said, "Think back to the evening of the Tampican reception, Mrs. Barrington. You and your husband lingered in the garden, forgetting the time, and then suddenly you thought you would be late for your appointment with Nelson."

"That's right. Matthew's watch said five past seven, so we hurried in—"

"And found that, in fact, you were dead on time, according to the clock in the library. It was just striking seven, I believe."

"Yes. Matthew's watch was wrong—but there's nothing unusual about that."

"Ah—but that would have meant that his watch was fast. Later that evening, you wanted to watch television news, and you almost missed it, although he assured you that it was only just starting. In fact, his watch was slow—had been for years. Mrs. Barrington, it was after quarter-past seven when you and your husband got to the library."

"But...the clock..."

"Which normally keeps perfect time, had been set back by fifteen minutes. Later in the evening it was keeping perfect time again. Somebody had moved the hands back—and then on again. Hadn't he, Mr. Nelson?"

Winnie said, "This is a perfect rigmarole. Who would go around altering clocks?"

"It was a mistake to produce that knife," said Henry. "Please don't do it again. You went around altering that particular clock so that you could leave the reception room just before seven, give yourself a quarter of an hour to see Mavis Ironmonger collapse and be bundled up to her room, go up after her and shoot her. And still appear to leave the Embassy just after seven."

Prudence stood up. She had replaced her shoes, and she looked like the bastion of Empire. She put her arm round Nelson's shoulder and said, "Don't you worry, Winnie. This man is obviously mad, and nobody will listen to him. We all know that we left the Embassy at seven, or just after—you and me and Matthew. We'll support you, Winnie. You've nothing to worry about."

Winnie looked down at the small, determined figure, smiled and said, "Thank you, Mrs. Barrington. This Englishman is some sort of a crazy guy. He can never in a million years prove something from an old broken watch. What an idea!"

"Mrs. Barrington," said Henry, "you must listen to me. This man came here this afternoon to kill you—just as he killed Mavis Ironmonger and Dorabella Hamilton. You must believe me."

Again, Prudence looked from one to the other. Her arm tightened round Winnie's shoulder. She said, "Well, I still have that old watch, whatever it proves or doesn't prove. But you're certainly not going to use it against Winnie."

"I don't need to," Henry said. "You see, I have an independent witness."

Nelson shouted, "That's not possible!"

"Oh yes, it is. Do you remember the demonstration outside the Embassy that evening?"

"I remember," said Prudence, "that we had to step over some people on the pavement..."

"Well, I have the testimony of their leader, Franklin D. Martin, who will swear that Mr. Finkelstein left the Tampican Embassy *before* Mr. Nelson and his party."

Prudence had never looked so imperial. "Franklin D. Martin? Are you going to take the word of a well-known troublemaker and drug addict against that of a fine young diplomat? Shame on you, Mr. Tibbett."

Henry said, "It's not a question of taking his word. Mr. Finkelstein arrived at the Embassy too early to shake hands with Lady Ironmonger, which was why he was being formally introduced later on. When he got to Oxford Gardens, the demonstrators hadn't even arrived. Yet Martin saw Finkelstein, and described him and the car he was driving. He could only have seen him leaving, not arriving. And he is quite definite that your party was the last to come out of the Embassy before the police arrived and arrested him."

"But Mr. Tibbett, it's all so senseless!" Prudence exclaimed. "Why on earth should Winnie do such terrible things? Now Dorabella—I don't say it's easy to understand, but I can believe that she might have killed Mavis. I know she hated her—and Alfred says the Alcodym was hers. You're not disputing that, I hope?"

"No, no. It was hers. You got it from her, didn't you, Nelson? Of course, she didn't know how it was to be used. I suppose you told her that Sir Edward wanted to give it to his wife, to make sure she didn't drink on the evening of the reception. In fact, you must have asked her to administer the normal dose—she would have done anything if she thought it was for Sir Edward. That's what she meant when she said, 'I did it' just before she died. Of course, she didn't know that you had taken pills from the bottle and put a double dose in Lady Ironmonger's drink, together with the vodka.

"All you had to do then was leave the reception and await developments. You turned the clock back, and waited in the hall—you knew Mavis Ironmonger would collapse in a matter of minutes. You had taken the gun earlier in the day. The rest was easy. I don't know when you set the clock right again— probably while Mrs. Barrington was getting her coat."

Prudence said, "That's all very well. You haven't explained why."

"Ah," said Henry, "now we get to the heart of the matter. Mr. Nelson is deeply involved in an enterprise known as the Tampica Research and Development Company."

This seemed to galvanize Nelson. "That's a lie!" he shouted. "I don't own a goddam share!"

"Not in your own name. But you should have chosen a more reliable nominee than Fletcher. When he realized murder was involved—"

Suddenly, Nelson's control seemed to snap. "I'll kill him!" he yelled. "I'll kill that no good son-of-a-bitch if he said that! It's Michael that's up to his neck in that racket, not me! Okay, I killed her—I killed her for Tampica! I killed her for Eddie, for his own good! You say I'm in that Development company, by God I'll kill you—" There was a flash of steel as he whipped the knife out of his pocket and lunged at Henry.

"Get out, Mrs. Barrington!" Henry shouted. He managed to grab the wrist that held the knife, but he knew he could not fend Nelson off for long. All sense of reality and even self-preservation had deserted Winston Nelson. All he wanted was the wild catharsis of violence and revenge.

"Run!" Henry shouted again.

Prudence Barrington did not run. Instead, she walked calmly up to the two struggling men, and laid her hand on Nelson's arm.

"Now, Winnie, dear," she said, "be a good boy and give me that knife. It's very dangerous, you know, and your mother would be upset if anybody got hurt."

Nelson was grunting and struggling, and Henry felt his own grip growing weaker. Sharply, Prudence said, "I shan't tell you again, Winnie. Give me that knife. Then you can go home."

It was the word "home" that did it. Nelson quite suddenly collapsed onto the ground, his whole body heaving with great sobs. Words were just distinguishable. "I did it for Tampica, Miz Barrington...not for money...no money...poor Dorrie... for Tampica..."

"That's right, Winnie," said Prudence. "I believe you."

Winnie continued to sob, his face buried in the soft grass. Slowly he held out his right hand, offering the knife to Prudence. She took it.

"Thank you, dear," she said.

Then there was the sound of running feet, and Emmy arrived with Inspector Bartholomew and a member of the house staff who had led them through the maze to the Pan statue.

Henry rubbed his wrist. He said, "He's unarmed and he won't be any trouble. I suggest you take him back to the Embassy and make the arrest there. Then you can fly him back to Tampica on the night plane."

Inspector Bartholomew reached down a vast hand, took Nelson by the shoulders and pulled him to his feet. "C'mon, man," he said, gently. "C'mon Winnie. Come take a walk."

CHAPTER NINETEEN

MUCH LATER THAT evening, Henry, Emmy and Prudence Barrington were sitting in Sir Edward Ironmonger's study at the Tampican Embassy. Winston Nelson, all the fight gone out of him, had made a full confession to the murders of both Lady Ironmonger and Dorabella Hamilton, and was already on his way back to Tampica, stoutly escorted by Inspector Bartholomew. Sir Edward Ironmonger, naturally shocked and deeply upset, had demanded a full explanation of the case from Henry before making a public statement.

Henry had outlined Nelson's plot, and his achievement of a lost quarter-of-an-hour. Sir Edward said, "He couldn't have known that Bishop and Mrs. Barrington would go into the garden just then."

"No, he couldn't—but it wouldn't have mattered if they hadn't. The one thing he could rely on was that they would not be likely to keep the appointment on time—or even to have more than a hazy idea of what the right time was. The Bishop's watch was notorious. Once he had left the reception and altered the library clock, he didn't have to worry. If the Barringtons had, in fact, been punctual, they would have inferred from the library clock that they were early, and just waited for Nelson. And of course he was able to time Lady Ironmonger's collapse very accurately, by slipping her the doctored drink at the right moment.

"You'll see from his confession that I was right about Dorabella—he convinced her that the request for the Alcodym came from you, Sir Edward, and he had her add a normal dose to some plain tomato juice in the kitchen. That way, he reckoned he would implicate her, so that she wouldn't dare to tell on him, if things got difficult.

"It was Dorabella who put the bottle of Alcodym into Lady Ironmonger's bathroom cupboard when she went in to get the talcum powder—she was trying to protect you, Sir Edward, thinking that if Alcodym were to be traced, the bottle would prove that Lady Ironmonger was taking it, voluntarily.

"Nelson realized that was a blunder. He didn't want Alcodym to come into the picture at all. He had a good try at removing the bottle when he went up with the undertaker—but Sir Edward foiled it by coming up and ordering him out of the room. So the next day he ordered Dorabella to remove it—he dared not do it himself. Unfortunately for Nelson, she didn't get a chance to do so until after Dr. Duncan had stuck his inquisitive nose into the cupboard and seen the bottle. If he hadn't, he wouldn't have dreamed of looking for it during the autopsy—and even if you had suspected murder, you'd never have been able to prove it."

"I may be very silly," Prudence said, "but I still don't see just how you worked out that Matthew's old watch could be dangerous to me."

Henry smiled. "The credit should go to your friend Lucy Pontefract-Deacon," he said. "She was quicker than I was. That is, we both came to the same conclusion at the same time, but I had had far longer to think it over. After I had discussed the case with her, and we both had had time to get it sorted out in our minds, we both realized that on the evening of the reception your husband's watch—while undisputedly wrong—had contrived first of all to be fast, and then slow. Lucy also remembered that while you were on the island you had told many people—including Nelson—that according to the watchmaker that watch had been running slow for years."

"That's right. When he came to tea. I never thought—"

"Of course you didn't. But he has been scared stiff that somebody, somehow would find out about the time discrepancy—the lost quarter-of-an-hour. He was a desperate man by then. He had killed Dorabella because he overheard a telephone conversation in which I mentioned Alcodym to her and she promised to meet me and make a clean breast of things. That would have included the fact that it was actually Nelson and not Sir Edward who had asked her to doctor Lady Ironmonger's drink. Up to the end, she must have believed that you were guilty, Sir Edward—but she was going to tell me that you knew nothing about it, and take all the blame herself. That accounts for what she said in the hospital. Poor Dorabella."

Softly, Sir Edward echoed, "Poor Dorrie. If only she'd spoken to me about it, outright..."

Henry said, "Both Dorabella and Nelson were cases of misguided loyalty, in different ways. I must admit that at first I was sure Nelson was involved in the Research and Development Company—but there's no doubt that he wasn't. He acted purely out of a misdirected sense of patriotism." Henry sighed. "Well, a financial scandal in Tampica is no affair of mine, but I'm afraid, Sir Edward, that when you investigate it, you'll find that Holder-Watts is pretty deeply implicated— and possibly his wife, too. I suspect it may have been the main reason why he took Tampican nationality."

Sir Edward said, "You are probably right. I was puzzled that he chose to do so. I was very glad to have him on my staff because of his experience—in spite of the fact that, as you probably know, I have never liked him. I'm afraid this is going to be a messy business—but, as you say, it's nothing to do with you, Tibbett. Well, that all seems quite clear. It only remains for me to thank you."

"Not me," said Henry. "The people to thank are Miss Pontefract-Deacon, and Mrs. Barrington, and my wife..."

"Me?" said Emmy, greatly surprised.

"Yes. You did splendidly this afternoon, getting hold of Inspector Bartholomew so quickly."

"Incidentally," Emmy said, "how on earth did you know I was there?"

"By the grace of God," said Henry, "I heard you calling on the Almighty for a helicopter from the other side of the hedge. I reckoned that if I could hear you, you could hear Mrs. Barrington and me, and that you'd stay to listen and then take the hint."

"I thought I'd never find my way back to the main path," Emmy said. "In fact, in the end, when I found myself just on the other side of the hedge, I broke all the rules and a lot of boxwood by simply scrambling through. I expect the owners will be furious."

"Don't worry, my dear," said Prudence. "Eunice and I are...sort of sisters-in-law. By marriage. That is to say, she's my daughter's mother-in-law, so that makes us...oh dear, I never did understand the Table of Kindred and Affinity..."

"And as for you, Mrs. Barrington," added Henry, "you certainly saved my life. You were extremely brave."

"Brave? Nonsense. I've known Winnie since he was a little boy." She took a tiny white handkerchief out of her bag and quickly wiped away a tear.

"And right up to the last moment, you believed in his innocence," Henry said.

Prudence looked at him sideways. "You think so?"

"Well, didn't you?"

Prudence said, "Winnie has always been an impetuous and somewhat unstable person. He is also one of the finest knife-throwers in Tampica. You were simply making him angry and upset—and dangerous. You said I saved your life. My dear man, I was saving my own. I'm a sort of mother figure to him, and if I had turned on him and started accusing him at that moment, the knife would have been out and you'd never have saved me." She sighed. "Poor Winnie. It's a good thing that I know him so well…"

EPILOGUE

F ROM *THE WASHINGTON Post, June 16th*

Today the United States lost one of its oldest naval bases. At the conclusion of talks on the island of Tampica, it was announced that no agreement could be reached, and consequently the Navy is making plans to withdraw from its station on Barracuda Bay.

Sir Edward Ironmonger, newly elected Prime Minister of Tampica, told reporters that government plans were already in hand to develop the area as a tourist resort and a harbor for cruise liners. He confirmed that a group of private speculators had endeavored to exploit the situation by buying up land in the area, but said that the company had been nationalized.

It will be remembered that British-born Michael Holder-Watts, Counsellor at the Tampican Embassy in Washington under Sir Edward, resigned last month, following allegations that he had been involved in improper property deals in Tampica.

From *The Washington Post, The New York Times, The Boston Herald*, etc., etc.,

December 1st.

(Advertisement)

Come to sunny Tampica for Christmas! Don't miss the Grand Opening of the luxurious Barracuda Bay Hotel! Fun and sun at YOUR prices! Lowest rates in the Caribbean! Book now!